CW00894239

Mark of ~~the De~~

Inspector Jim Carruthers Book 3
By
Tana Collins

Dear Fi
Enjoy the read!
Best wishes

Tana Collix.

www.bloodhoundbooks.com

Print ISBN 978-1-912604-18-0

Also By Tana Collins

Inspector Jim Carruthers Series
Robbing The Dead (Book 1)
Care To Die (Book 2)

Praise for Tana Collins

"I'm already a fan of this series and as Collins as a debut writer and am anxious for the next book to be released." **Amy Sullivan - Novelgossip**

"I have to say how much I love this authors style of writing. She's certainly one I'll be following." **Sue Ward - Sue And Her Books**

"I read this story in one and I hadn't a clue where it was going to go but it mixed history with modern day and came up with a belter." **Susan Hampson - Books From Dusk Till Dawn**

"This is a very enjoyable book, made so by the depth of the characters." **Misfits Farm - Goodreads**

"An author to keep an eye on and a series that will be one to watch in the future." **Gemma Myers - Between The Pages Book Club**

"A very good emotional read. I liked the story and the characters." **Susan Angela Wallace - Goodreads**

"Altogether a first class read and a worthy 5 stars." **Alfred Noble - Goodreads**

"This story is about past evils ,so dark ..a story of murder ,buried history and an innocent caught in the crossfire..An Excellent read..." **Livia Sbarbaro - Goodreads**

"The story is exciting and convincing: it won't disappoint, it certainly didn't disappoint me." **Owen Mullen - Author**

"I would highly recommend this well-written book. The pace is fast and the characters believable." **Nicki Southwell - Goodreads**

This book is dedicated to Miller Brown.
Loved and missed by so many.

One

Joe peered over the edge of the cliff. Her body lay in a crumpled heap at the foot of the rocks; pink skirt bunched up around milk-white thighs, one sandal still on her foot, the other gone. The man squinted in the warm sun, tasting rancid sweat on his top lip. He wiped it away with the back of his hand then he dug deep into the large pocket of his wax jacket until he found the bulky object he was searching for.

Overhead, gulls of huge wingspan screamed as they dive-bombed the rocks, their movement accentuating the stillness of the girl's body. Only her skirt rippled in the wind. Despite the heat of the day the man was being buffeted by the strong north-easterly wind. It whistled around his head, making his eyes water and nose run. He steadied himself as he looked through the binoculars, taking in the sweep of the beach for any other sign of human life, but the silver sands were empty, cut off by the rocky outcrops and dangerously crumbling cliffs. He trained the binoculars once more on the body, adjusting the lens for a clearer view.

The woman was lying on her front, head turned to the side. He could now see the deep gashes in her legs and arms, the sand discoloured where the blood from a head wound had bled out. His eyes widened in horror and revulsion. There was a gull pecking at her face and in that instant he knew she was beyond help. He opened his mouth, sucking in salty damp air. His shout was swallowed by the cries of the birds.

The man stumbled back from the cliff face and turned to where he had last seen his colleague. Derek – Deek – was spreading the fresh meat above some rocks. He straightened up, putting a penknife back into his pocket.

'Havenae seen a sign of them. No' like those fucking seagulls. Christ, they're aggressive. One of them nearly took ma heid off. What's up with you? You look like you've seen a ghost.'

Joe's breaths came out in sobs. He wiped his wet nose with the back of his hand. 'Worse than that. A dead body. On the beach. We need to ring the police.'

'What you on about?' said Deek. 'Are you mental? And get caught? We could get a prison sentence for this. And what would the boss say? By the time he'd finished with you, you'd end up wishing you had gone to fucking prison.'

'But…'

'Look.' Deek grabbed Joe's arm and shook him. 'Just show me where the body is. Then we'll tell the boss. He'll ken what to do. But I tell you one thing for nothing. He willnae want the cops sniffing round, so keep your mouth shut.'

* * *

DI Jim Carruthers sipped his lukewarm coffee and sighed in frustration. Placing his glasses further up onto his greying head he searched his desk for the latest report on the recent spate of art thefts. Pushing away other paperwork, he managed to knock over two nearly empty polystyrene cups. A trickle of liquid spilled onto the report he had been searching for and in attempting to blot it with his right hand he only succeeded in smearing it right across the page. He swore. The heat and the broken air conditioning were making him cranky.

'Don't forget the brief in five minutes,' DS Andrea Fletcher, with her elfin face and short dark hair, said as she entered his office. He looked up, thinking her new bob suited her.

He smiled at her. 'I hadn't forgotten.' He stood, gathering his notes as she left.

The briefing started when they'd taken their seats. Dougie Harris, as ever, was the last to arrive. Carruthers cleared his throat as soon as the middle-aged detective sergeant squashed his bulky frame into a chair, slapping a copy of the *Racing Post* onto the table in front of him.

'What do we know of the latest break-in?' Carruthers made eye contact with DS Gayle Watson as he said this.

Her large brown eyes were serious in her heart-shaped face. 'Similar MO to the last two,' she said.

Carruthers frowned.

'They don't seem to have touched anything except the works of art.' She consulted her notebook. 'Got away with a Jack Vettriano.'

'I seem to know that name,' said Carruthers.

'Local boy,' said Watson. 'Comes from Methil. You'll know him from *The Singing Butler*.'

Carruthers frowned. He couldn't recall.

'Elegant couple in evening attire dancing on the beach under umbrellas?' prompted Watson.

Carruthers nodded. He could now visualise the painting. 'Do we know what the stolen painting was worth?'

Watson flicked the page of her notebook over. 'Last valued three years ago at £200,000.'

Harris whistled. 'These people mean business. You could buy a fucking racehorse for that.' He idly glanced at the horse-racing paper in front of him.

Fletcher snorted. 'A Vettriano's worth a lot more than a racehorse.'

'Any leads?' asked Carruthers, ignoring Harris and Fletcher's petty squabbling, which he was used to.

'None, at least not yet,' said Watson. 'No unexplained fingerprints. Thief must have been wearing gloves.'

Carruthers looked over at her. 'Did anyone see or hear anything?'

Watson turned the sheet of her notebook over. 'Burglar alarm went off. Burglars made a lot of noise by shouting. They woke up the owners who were in the upstairs bedroom. Where they stayed, too scared to come down–'

'Which was the purpose of all the shouting,' said Carruthers. 'To keep them upstairs. Who are the owners?'

Watson riffled back over her notes. 'Couple called McMullan. In their sixties. Live out near Cupar.'

'Did the neighbours see or hear anything?' asked Carruthers.

Watson shook her head. 'Nearest are half a mile away.'

Carruthers stroked the bristles on his chin. He needed a shave. He could also smell the sweat on him over the heat of the room. He strode over to the incident board. 'So burglars target yet another isolated location. The fact their victims are at home doesn't deter them. Nor, it seems, does the fact they set off the burglar alarm.'

'Apparently they were in and out within a few minutes,' said Watson. 'And did the robbery in the dark.'

'Which suggests an intimate knowledge of where everything was in that house,' said Fletcher. 'The likelihood being that they'd been in the house before.'

'Or seen photographs,' said Watson.

'What are your thoughts?' asked Fletcher.

'Same feelings I had after the first two robberies,' said Carruthers. 'These are no amateurs. They have all the hallmarks of a professional gang of art thieves.'

'Three robberies within a few weeks. They're targeting the area,' said Fletcher. 'To pull this off and leave no leads must have taken a huge amount of research. And manpower. Not to mention luck.'

'You're looking at a highly organised bunch of crooks,' said Carruthers. 'And unfortunately, they've landed on our patch.'

Fletcher scrutinised the incident board that had three red pins in the map of Fife. 'There's got to be a common element that links all these robberies,' she said. 'They're so well planned. The question we need to focus on is whether the person or persons behind the robberies are known to their victims in any way.'

The door opened and Detective Constable Willie Brown put his balding head round. 'Jim, we've just had a call. Burning vehicle in a field five miles from Cupar.'

Carruthers stood and grabbed his notebook. 'Doubt it's joyriders.' He was thinking back to the abandoned burning cars that had been found after the first two robberies. Turning to

Brown's retreating back he said, 'Any reports of stolen cars come in yet?'

Brown swivelled round. 'No. Things have been as quiet as the grave.'

'Owners are probably away,' said Fletcher, leaping up. 'Let's get forensics down there.'

Carruthers nodded. 'I've got Superintendent Bingham breathing down my neck. This latest victim is a friend of his. We need results. At some point their luck has to run out. Let's pray it's sooner rather than later.'

Harris sniffed. 'A little redistribution of wealth doesnae bother me,' he said, standing up, burying his *Racing Post* under his right arm. 'That lot's got too much money.'

'Whatever your personal view of our class system, a crime's a crime,' said Carruthers. 'And with the value of what's being stolen, this one's big. We're lucky nobody's been hurt or worse.' Carruthers grabbed his coat. 'C'mon, Andie, we'll head to the scene and then pay the McMullans another visit.'

* * *

The fire brigade had put the blaze out, and left the burned wreckage dripping wet. The SOCOs were already busy on the scene. As he parked his car, Jim noticed one SOCO slip in the wet and glower at the firefighters as they were packing up their gear.

Carruthers and Fletcher stepped out of the car. The air was still acrid in the aftermath: burnt oil and upholstery fumes that would take time to dissipate. It caught Carruthers by the throat, making him cough. It was a warm summer's day in August and the heat trickled over Carruthers' shoulder blades and down his back. Within minutes his white shirt was stuck uncomfortably to his skin. The thought of going back to an office with broken air con was not a pleasant one. He surveyed the burnt-out wreckage, taking in the vast expanse of scorched earth where the barley had also caught fire.

He strode towards one of the SOCOs. The man looked up from his painstaking search of the ground. 'It's a tinderbox over there. Surprised the whole field didn't go up.'

Carruthers rubbed his hand across his damp brow. 'We've had an unusual spell of weather.'

'That's global warming for you,' said the SOCO.

Carruthers frowned. He didn't think global warming worked like that, but kept his mouth shut. He said instead, 'Farmer won't be happy. Anything turn up yet, Ian?'

The SOCO grinned. 'Not yet. Be patient.'

Carruthers grimaced. 'A commodity in short supply, I'm afraid.' He noticed that the SOCO had beads of sweat on his forehead, too.

'We'll give you a call when we find something,' said the SOCO.

'Must be hell, dressed like that, in this heat,' said Carruthers, grateful he wasn't wearing the latex gloves and what looked like boiler suits. He kept as far back as he could.

'You get used to it.'

'In Scotland? Give me a break.'

The SOCO grinned.

Carruthers addressed his next comment to Fletcher. 'These robbers are making us look like fools.'

She pulled her notebook out.

'A four-by-four,' said Carruthers. 'Just like the others.' He spotted a ruddy-faced man in mustard-yellow cords briskly walking towards them, a sheepdog at his feet. 'C'mon,' he said, 'let's leave the SOCOs to their jobs and go interview the farmer.'

Walking towards the man, Carruthers flipped open his ID before the farmer had a chance to speak. The dog barked excitedly at Carruthers' heels.

'Rambo, quiet,' the man shouted. The dog obediently sat by his owner's feet.

'DI Jim Carruthers and this is DS Andrea Fletcher,' said Carruthers. 'Do you own this land?'

'Aye. What the hell's been going on? Looks like I've lost half my field. I've been away to Dundee to pick up some supplies.'

Some of the fencing's down.' He nodded over to the blackened vehicle. 'Is it joyriders again?'

'Have you had problems with joyriders before?' asked Fletcher.

'Not me. Friends of mine. Couple of years back.'

'Where was this?' asked Fletcher.

'Gargunnock, just outside Stirling.' He shook his head, looking through narrowed eyes at the blackened charred remains of part of his barley field. 'I'll have to get hold of my insurers.'

'We don't think it was joyriders, Mr…?'

'Adamson. Charlie Adamson.'

Adamson frowned at Carruthers for a second then looked to the burnt-out vehicle, his face pale. 'You don't mean someone was…'

'No, no, nothing like that,' Carruthers assured quickly. He noticed the dog was starting to wander off. 'We need to ask you a few questions, though. We believe this vehicle may have been used in a recent robbery. It's likely been stolen for the job. Have you seen anything suspicious, recently? Anybody hanging around? Strangers you haven't recognised?'

Adamson shook his head. 'No, nobody. You're talking about those art thefts, aren't you? I've read about them in the paper.'

'The gang haven't been caught yet. We believe they are still in the area,' said Fletcher.

'Look, if you've finished with me, I really need to contact my insurers,' said Adamson. He whistled and Rambo ran back, breathless, tongue lolling from side to side.

Carruthers gave Adamson his card. 'If you think of anything you want to add…' he said.

The man was already striding off.

Carruthers touched Fletcher's arm. 'Let's get over to the McMullans. You drive and I'll call some of my old colleagues at the National Crime Agency. They might be able to give us an idea about who this bunch might be.'

* * *

Carruthers turned to Mr McMullan, a portly man in his late sixties whose bulbous red nose and vein-lined face told of someone who undoubtedly liked his drink. He reminded Carruthers of a cockerel in his roost. 'Can you go over a few details again?' he asked the man.

He and Fletcher had been ushered into the kitchen where they were sitting at a heavy oak table opposite an original Aga. Mr and Mrs McMullan sat opposite them, their chairs angled away from each other, indicating that they'd had some sort of argument.

'Have you had any tradesmen in the house in the last few months?' Fletcher addressed her question to Mrs McMullan.

Carruthers studied the grey-haired woman. If her husband was the rooster, then, with her beady nervous eyes darting between the two of them, she was the hen.

'We've already answered that,' said Mr McMullan. 'Why are you repeating the same questions? Why aren't you out doing your job, catching whoever's responsible?'

Carruthers was well used to this question. He also understood how the McMullans would be feeling – upset, vulnerable, violated and, no doubt, poorer. The Vettriano hadn't been fully insured, according to Watson. The McMullans simply hadn't wanted to pay the premiums. He kept his thoughts to himself. 'It's surprising what else people remember after the first interview. Well?' he asked.

Mr McMullan sighed.

'Can you think of anyone?'

'No, except we had a leaky roof so we called someone in about that. We've already given the details. But they never saw the Vettriano, didn't need to come in the house at all.'

'Well,' said Mrs McMullan, 'I did make him a cup of tea so he came into the kitchen. But he didn't come through the main hall,' she added quickly. 'He used the tradesmen's entrance.'

'Am I right in thinking the tradesmen's entrance leads straight into the kitchen?' said Carruthers, surprised that he hadn't been asked to use the tradesmen's entrance too.

'Yes, it's through that door, there,' said Mr McMullan.

'So other than the kitchen he didn't come into the house at all?' said Carruthers.

'Oh dear,' said Mrs McMullan.

'What now?' asked Mr McMullan who, Carruthers was realising, wasn't the most patient of men.

'I've just remembered he asked to use the toilet.'

'Oh for God's sake, woman,' said Mr McMullan.

Mrs McMullan fiddled with her wedding ring as she said, 'I think I may have forgotten to mention that in the previous interview.'

'Where's the nearest bathroom?' asked Fletcher, standing up and disappearing to the door. She poked her head round the corridor.

'Out of the kitchen, two doors down, on the left.'

'So at that point he was unaccompanied in the house?' asked Carruthers.

'Yes,' said Mrs McMullan, 'but he was only gone a few minutes.'

'But in those few minutes he could have done a recce of a couple of the downstairs rooms, including the living room where the Vettriano was hanging,' said Fletcher. 'Have you ever used that company before?'

'No,' said Mrs McMullan.

'We'll need the name of the firm before we leave, and some contact details,' said Fletcher.

Mrs McMullan nodded.

Carruthers turned to Mr McMullan. 'Who knew you owned a Vettriano?'

Mr McMullan shrugged. He picked up a wooden pipe that was lying on a sideboard. Opening a drawer, he extracted a packet of tobacco and started pulling the strands out. Maddeningly, he took what Carruthers felt was an age to respond.

'Our friends, but we've already given you the names. Anyone who's been here for a dinner party. Some of the people I know at the golf club.'

'Why would you have told them?' asked Carruthers.

Mr McMullan looked up. 'You don't seriously think anyone at the golf club's responsible, do you, man?'

'Why not?' asked Carruthers.

'Because they're all vetted. Anyway, as I'm sure you know Jack Vettriano's a local boy. Some of my friends at the club know him personally. He's come up in conversation occasionally.'

Carruthers wondered if McMullan had seized the opportunity to brag about the fact he had an original Vettriano. Perhaps that had been his downfall.

'You know much about Vettriano's work?' asked Carruthers.

'Most of his paintings are in the hands of private collectors. He has some very famous fans,' said Mrs McMullan. 'Hollywood actor Jack Nicholson, composer Tim Rice and actor Robbie Coltrane have all got paintings by him.'

Owning an original would put the McMullans in good company, then, thought Carruthers. But once more kept his own counsel. He had a particular dislike of golf and golfers and knew of more than one career criminal who had membership of an exclusive golf club. In his experience, some of the wealthiest people made the most ruthless of criminals.

'Which golf club do you belong to?' asked Carruthers.

'It's very exclusive membership,' said Mr McMullan. 'You'll be barking up the wrong tree.'

Carruthers' eyes narrowed. Exclusive membership. He knew what that meant. No black people or women. And if it had been based down south, no doubt stuffed full of UKIP voters. He wondered if he was being unfair. He knew he could be judgemental. It was something he was trying to change. Old habits died hard, though. 'The name of the golf club?' asked Carruthers.

'What the hell's that got to do with anything?' asked Mr McMullan, laying his pipe down on the side.

'Mr McMullan, I can chase the criminals you want caught or I can waste time chasing down your background, which would you rather?' said Carruthers. But then he thought, *Go easy on them. They're bound to be feeling rattled.*

'I'm a member of Carrockhall. Your superior's Superintendent Bingham, isn't he?' asked McMullan. 'I've met him a few times at clubhouse functions.'

Carruthers groaned inwardly. Hairs had prickled as soon as McMullan said Carrockhall. Carruthers knew Bingham was a keen golfer and not his greatest fan. All he needed now was to fall foul of the golfing buddy paradigm. *Great.*

'Can we see the rest of the house, please?' said Carruthers.

Mr and Mrs McMullan stood up.

'This won't just be a random burglary,' said Carruthers as they were led by Mr McMullan out of the kitchen through the hall. 'Whoever's responsible will have carefully targeted you. They will at some point have gained entry to the house, possibly taken photos of your works of art and gone away and done their research. This is the third property to have been targeted in the last few weeks.'

'Yes, and what are you actually doing about it?' asked Mr McMullan.

Carruthers sighed. Looking up and ignoring the question he said, 'Have you got any other valuable paintings?'

'Why do you ask? Looks like they got what they wanted. None of the others are as valuable,' said Mr McMullan. He directed them into a large airy living room which led through glass doors to a smaller conservatory. This smaller room was a mess. Carruthers surveyed the scene. In the middle of the ripped carpet still lay the stone bird bath that had been hurled through the glass conservatory doors allowing the thieves entry.

Carruthers stepped back into the living room and looked around him. His eyes settled on the dirty bare wall where the frame of the Vettriano had been. There were two smaller paintings on the walls. Rural scenes. Both looked like originals. Even the gilt-edged frames looked original. 'My advice to you would be to get your other paintings fully insured. And don't talk about them at the golf club,' he added. 'You never know who's listening.'

'Oh yes, I suppose you've got a point, man,' said Mr McMullan. 'There's always staff around.'

Walking away out of the room Carruthers stopped for a moment and turned round. 'I wasn't thinking about the staff. It's the club members I'd be worried about.'

* * *

No sooner had they returned to the station than Detective Constable Brown walked towards Carruthers waving a slip of paper.

'Four-by-four's been reported stolen outside Cupar. Owners were on holiday. Just back lunchtime today.'

'Pretty shitty homecoming,' said Carruthers, taking the slip of paper out of Brown's outstretched hand. 'That could be our burnt-out vehicle. Round the team up, will you.' Carruthers looked at his watch. 'We'll start the brief at four.' He calculated he just had time to get himself a coffee and make a phone call to the boys at the National Crime Agency.

Carruthers rolled up his shirtsleeves before he began the brief. He wished he'd bought a fresh shirt to work with him. His collar felt grubby and the acrid smell from the fire still clung to his clothes.

'OK, listen up,' he said. 'Four-by-four's been reported stolen just outside Cupar. What's the betting it's the same vehicle? And before you ask, there's nothing back from the SOCOs yet.' There was a collective groan. Carruthers put his hands up for silence. 'It's not, however, all bad news. I've spoken to pals at the National Crime Agency and this has all the hallmarks of a gang currently operating out of the South East of England. MO's virtually identical. Targeting elderly people in isolated spots for their valuable works of art. Stealing a different vehicle for each job then abandoning and torching it.'

'Shite, that's all we need,' said Harris, 'more English folk in Scotland.' He yelped as a paper dart thrown expertly by Fletcher hit him squarely on the nose.

'Anyway, like I mentioned,' said Carruthers, 'if it is them, the boys at the NCA have talked me through a probable modus operandi.'

'Which is?' said Fletcher.

'Stealing art to order. Most likely shipped off to a buyer in the US via the Republic of Ireland.'

'Ireland?' asked Harris.

'Apparently Ireland is the gateway for stolen art between Britain and North America.' Carruthers rubbed a sooty smudge he spotted on his shirt. It got worse.

'Do you seriously think a gang from the South East of England would be operating north of the border?' said Fletcher.

'We can't rule it out,' said Carruthers. 'What we do know at this stage is that this will be a huge operation, no doubt involving some seriously wealthy and influential people.' He cast his eye over to Harris. 'Not the redistribution of wealth from rich to poor that you imagined, sergeant.'

Harris shrugged.

'And let's not forget,' continued Carruthers, 'that although my friends at the NCA have told me this particular gang are not interested in hurting people, which is good news, if indeed it is the same gang, we've been lucky that so far there's been no physical harm done to the victims. Let's not underestimate how ruthless criminals like this can be. Art theft is often used to fund other criminal activities. Gangs often have links to money laundering, guns and drugs and, according to the NCA, are becoming increasingly violent.'

'Did your pals down at the NCA tell you anything else?' asked Harris, repairing the bent nose of Fletcher's paper plane.

'The annual theft of art and antiques in the UK is estimated to be worth £300 million,' said Carruthers. 'More costly than vehicle crime and second only to drug dealing in terms of criminal proceeds.'

Harris put down the paper plane and looked up at Carruthers.

'To answer your question, as a matter of fact they did,' said Carruthers. 'Told us to check out the local flying schools and private airfields.'

Harris frowned but the dawn of recognition lighted on Fletcher's face.

'They could be taking aerial photographs of the homes they're going to rob, although you could get that information from Google Earth,' she said. 'Anyway, either way, they'd be looking for the most isolated spots. Places furthest away from police stations. Roads leading in, roads out, that kind of thing. Where best to ditch the vehicle. In fact they've probably got a map of Fife marked with potential locations. If we're smart, we might even be able to predict the next robbery.'

'The NCA are going to send details of this gang,' said Carruthers. 'They know who they are, just don't have enough evidence to arrest them. The gang members live in Kent. But, like I said, let's not assume it's the same gang just because the modus operandi is similar, could be a copycat. The geography is against the Kent gang doing this. They've never been known to travel this far north before. And there is one other thing. This gang from Kent have been stealing works by lesser-known artists. They haven't stolen any big-name stuff.'

The brief continued for another hour, at the end of which Carruthers' stomach growled, reminding him he'd not stopped for lunch. He thought of the sausage roll he'd picked up on the way to work but hadn't yet eaten.

'How likely do you think it is to be this gang from down south?' asked Fletcher, as other members of CID filed out of the room, leaving just the two of them.

'Well,' said Carruthers, 'there's a couple of things bothering me. I said in the brief the MO was almost the same. But I also said the group down south go for lesser-known artists.'

'So?' said Fletcher. 'Perhaps they got lucky up here.'

'Let's take this to the coffee machine,' said Carruthers, leading the way.

A few minutes later he was blowing on his coffee, back against the coffee machine in the hall. Fletcher sipped hers.

'One of the boys at the NCA said something interesting,' said Carruthers. 'He said the true art to a heist isn't the stealing, it's the selling.'

'Meaning?'

'Meaning criminals who steal high-value artworks tend to be better thieves than businessmen.'

'What does that mean?'

'It means the better known the artist, the less likely the thief will be able to sell the picture on. According to this guy at the NCA, the rate of recovery of a masterpiece is ninety per cent, whereas for a lesser-known work it's a paltry ten per cent, so it makes sense for the professional art thief to target works by lesser-known artists. Apparently these works are less likely to be registered on international databases and don't make headlines when they go missing.' He took a sip of coffee, stared into the cup thoughtfully.

'I have to admit I know very little about art theft,' said Fletcher. 'I've never worked on a case like this before. I always thought the criminal would have high-end artworks stolen to order to furnish his or someone else's ostentatious home.'

Carruthers laughed. 'That's a popular misconception the public hold, I'm sure. I blame Ian Fleming for that.'

'What's Ian Fleming got to do with it?'

'Have you never read *Dr No*? He bragged to Bond he'd stolen a Goya to order. In fact the storyline of the stolen artwork was based on a real life theft from the National Gallery the year before.' Carruthers enjoyed a good Bond book, much preferring them to the films. 'Apparently the public loves the idea of the super-villain stealing priceless works of art to order. But what the guy at the NCA said is that in reality no international criminal would really want the attention a missing masterpiece invites.' Having said that Carruthers had a vague memory of a heist in Paris some years back. Hadn't it involved stealing a Picasso and Matisse to order for dishonest collectors? It clearly did happen, but must be rare.

'How do you know that stuff about James Bond and the missing Goya?'

'I went to an Ian Fleming exhibition in London a few years ago,' said Carruthers. He remembered the occasion well.

He'd taken his then wife. They'd rowed. He couldn't even remember what the row had been about now. Something small, no doubt. Stupid. He put all images of his ex-wife out of his mind. 'I'm just wondering if it's a different gang. Not a gang of professional art thieves at all but ordinary criminals involved in other types of criminal activity, like drugs or guns. Then one day they realise what big money's involved in art theft. They decide to give it a go. They've heard about the gang down south and decide to copy their tactics.' He looked up at Fletcher. 'Sorry, just thinking things through.' They walked back to his office. Somewhere in the distance he heard a phone ringing.

Carruthers sat down behind his desk and gestured for Fletcher to pull up a chair. Fletcher put her coffee down on his desk, took the proffered chair. Smoothed her black skirt down before sitting. 'Surely they'd already be on our radar. I don't know any gangs that would fit that description in Fife, do you?' said Fletcher. 'Or elsewhere in Scotland. Nothing on the database. And we've registered the stolen artworks on the stolen property index in case they turn up in other parts of the country.'

Carruthers continued, 'There's just one other problem with this theory and that is that the art heist usually involves stealing from public galleries, not private collections. Anyway, like I said, the NCA are sending us details of the Kent gang. At least it's a start but I think it would be dangerous to just assume it's them.'

'I'll say one thing,' said Fletcher, 'if they're not pros they're certainly doing a good impression of professional art thieves. So far, they've left no clues, there've been no descriptions of the perpetrators. It's been a textbook heist.'

Except it isn't, thought Carruthers. After Fletcher had left his office he looked at the congealed remains of the sausage roll and pushed it away. Still hungry, he headed to the canteen, picked up a limp looking ham sandwich and another black coffee and went back to his office. He was three bites in and thinking that it tasted every bit as bad as it looked and that he should have just finished off the cold sausage roll when Fletcher put her head round the door again.

'What is it?' he asked. He noticed she had her handbag on her right shoulder and her lightweight jacket over her left arm.

'We've just received an anonymous phone call. Woman's body's been found on Kinsale beach over at a secluded part of Pinetum Park Forest.'

Taking another bite of his sandwich, Carruthers stood up, dumping the remains in the bin. 'You'd better fill me in as we go,' he said, with his mouth full. He sighed, thinking of yet another evening lost to the job. 'Hope you didn't have plans tonight?'

Fletcher raised her eyebrows. 'Not anymore.'

Two

The waves were about thirty metres away from the edge of the cliffs and the tide was coming in fast. Despite the blue sky the wind was gusting from the north, making it feel much colder than the balmy twenty-one degrees. Although Carruthers felt his eyes smart, the cool air was a welcome relief from the heat of the office.

He was standing on a clifftop with the first uniformed PC on the scene, a short woman, blonde hair in a bun, who was pointing down the beach. Carruthers followed the line of her hand through the heather and wild rose. His heart jumped when he saw the woman's body lying on the sand. There was something in its awkward position that told him she was already dead.

'Christ,' he said, 'how far away are the SOCOs? We're going to lose any evidence.' He inhaled the salty sea air, tasting it in the back of his throat.

'That's if she fell from the cliffs,' said Fletcher, coming up behind him, fishing out her iPhone and putting it on camera mode. 'If she's come in with the tide then evidence will be lost already. The current's fast here.' She started to take photos with her phone. 'You'd be surprised at the quality,' she said, when Carruthers looked at her questioningly. 'And it's better than nothing.'

'We need to get down there,' he said, looking for a path between the rocks. His foot slipped, and some pebbles and rocks fell away from the cliffs.

Fletcher pulled him back. 'Watch it, Jim,' she said. 'More to the point, how's Mackie going to get down there with his back?' She was referring to John Mackie, the police pathologist, who wasn't exactly in the first flush of youth.

'Look, I'm going to see if I can find a safe way down,' said Carruthers. 'You and…' he looked up at the police officer who was standing as far away from the edge of the cliff as she could.

'PC Brenda Rix, sir.'

'Right, Andie stay here with PC Rix and wait for the SOCOs.'

'OK,' said Fletcher, 'but for God's sake be careful. I don't want to be having to deal with two dead bodies.'

He left her shielding her eyes, scanning the beach, and made his way further up the cliff line. He thought he heard her call him at one point but the noise was lost in the raucous sound of the screeching gulls and the buffeting wind. When he turned to look at her she was standing with her back to him peering out to sea. *It must have been the gulls*. He carried on, peering down the craggy rocks for a path to the beach.

Suddenly he saw something ahead of him further up the cliffs. An incongruous black object. He made his way towards it, screwing up his eyes in the brilliant sunshine. As he grew closer he recognised it. A pair of binoculars lying on a tuft of grass. He itched to produce a plastic bag from his pocket and carefully bag them but he knew this must be the work of the SOCOs who would need to document in situ. He searched around the vicinity for anything else and discovered a cigarette butt. It looked recent. It would need to go the same way as the binoculars. If they were lucky it might give them some DNA. The question was, how had the binoculars got there?

He straightened up and gazed down at the beach. From this vantage point he had the perfect view of the woman's body. He thought of the binoculars. Were they hers? Had she been out looking for seals or bottle-nosed dolphins? Perhaps she put the binoculars down to get a closer look at something, got too close to the cliff edge and taken a tumble? This nature reserve was well known for its flowers and butterflies. It wouldn't be the first time the police had been called to such a scene.

Or were the binoculars used by the person or persons who had reported the body? Carruthers felt uneasy. Couldn't pinpoint why.

Something about this wasn't right. He once again stared out towards the sea and the lifeless body further inshore. Suddenly his eye caught movement on the beach. Five figures were running towards the woman. He saw two of the figures were Fletcher and Rix. He felt a moment's irritation with her for disobeying him. He saw an older man with them with his trademark black bag – Dr Mackie. And the two figures in spacesuits were SOCOs. They'd found a way down to the beach. He retraced his steps to where he'd last seen Fletcher. Finding a steep path in between two lines of tall, pink rosebay willowherb, he half stumbled half slid, ripping his shirt on some gorse on the way. He felt a sharp burning pain in his arm. He realised he'd been cut, warm blood seeping through the ripped shirt. He cursed. It was one of his best work shirts. He ran towards the group through the sand and long marram grass.

'What took you so long?' Fletcher walked towards him grinning. 'She's definitely dead. You OK? What have you done to your arm?'

'Just a scratch. And did I not give you instructions to stay where you were?'

'Sorry. I saw the SOCOs had arrived. And you'd disappeared. Mackie doesn't think she's been dead for long,' said Fletcher.

As with any suspicious death Carruthers knew this was now a crime scene, and as he knelt by the body, as close as he could without incurring Mackie's legendary wrath, he started taking in the details of the woman.

When he examined her face, the part not obscured by sand, he felt sick to his stomach. He swallowed the bile back down. Birds had already been pecking out her left eye and much of her face was missing. He noticed with surprise her eyebrows were so blonde they were almost white. He forced himself to take an emotional step back and look at her dispassionately. She had sustained some sort of head wound. There'd been a lot of blood and from the angle of the neck Carruthers could tell it was broken. Although she was lying on her front, head angled to the side, covered in a film of sand, he could tell she had been an attractive girl.

There was a hideous wound in the back of her left leg and lesions and cuts all over her body.

'How soon will you be able to do the post-mortem?' he asked.

'First thing tomorrow morning,' said Mackie.

'No sooner?' asked Carruthers.

Mackie glanced at his watch. 'It's gone seven now.'

Carruthers was surprised. He hadn't realised it was that late. He now knew he wouldn't get home before ten.

When Carruthers had finished telling both Fletcher and the SOCO team about the binoculars and cigarette butt, Fletcher said, 'It's worth conducting a more thorough examination of the cliff, then.'

'We need to get a team in before it gets too dark,' he said.

'Why don't we make a start now?' she said. He agreed. They started their search. After thirty minutes Fletcher shouted for Carruthers to come over.

'Is there a raptor's nest nearby?' she said.

'Why do you ask?'

She pointed. High on a rocky promontory was a slab of what looked like raw meat. 'There's been trouble in this area before with land owners poisoning birds of prey, hasn't there?'

Carruthers swore. 'Before my time.' He had only been at the station a year and a half, having moved up from London. He'd started his career in Scotland but an opportunity had come up to work in London and he'd taken it. He'd been happy in London until his wife had left him and moved back to Fife. That had been a bad time in his life. He'd misread the signals. Thought he could win her back and moved to Fife to be closer to her. *Love can make a fool out of all of us,* he thought. He dragged his mind back to the case.

'It needs to be bagged and sent for analysis.' He wondered if sea eagles had been the target. He'd read a recent article about them. What had he done with the magazine? Perhaps he'd already chucked it into the recycling. He resolved to ask his friend, Gill, who worked at SASA, the Scottish Agricultural Science Agency, over in Edinburgh.

He pulled his mobile out of his pocket. 'Get a team over ASAP.'
'What do I tell them?'

'Tell them we've got a suspicious death and have discovered evidence of illegal poisoning of birds of prey.'

Three hours later Carruthers let himself into his cottage in Anstruther with a weary sigh. He was desperate for a shower and change of clothes. He was also hungry. Not surprising, given that he'd skipped breakfast and his lunch lay in the bin at work. He went straight to the kitchen, started rummaging around his cupboards. He'd forgotten to do a food shop. There was a tin of tuna, a couple of cans of coke and a bag of pasta. Screwing up his face he walked to the bedroom, stripped off his shirt and, after smelling it and examining the rip, threw it into the bin. He looked at his arm. There was an angry red weal.

Taking a quick shower he pulled on a T-shirt and blue jeans, grabbed his house keys and wallet. Would have headed to his favourite pub, the Dreel Tavern, to treat himself to a pie and pint but it had shut the January of that year and in any case he would have missed last orders. The Dreel was currently under scaffolding. It had gone the same way as a number of other pubs and restaurants in the area although he'd heard that the Royal had reopened. He missed the Dreel. He headed instead to the Waterfront Bar down by the harbour where he was friendly with Georgina behind the bar. She'd been known to cook him something this late before.

As he speared a piece of meat from his pie, his thoughts drifted back to the day's unexpected events. The last moments on this earth of the blonde girl on the beach. Where had she come from? Was it an accident, suicide or foul play? Who made the anonymous call? And how was it all connected to the discovery of the binoculars and slab of meat on the clifftop?

They hadn't yet found any evidence of poisoning but he knew that if birds of prey were being poisoned the perpetrators would be disposing of the bodies in an attempt to get rid of the evidence. After a second pint he headed home, squeezing past a family of holidaymakers who had stopped on one of the many narrow street corners to admire Buckie House, the famous Victorian house covered in shells. He fell asleep that night dreaming not of the dead girl but of works of art being washed up on the beach to the background noise of a ringing phone.

* * *

Dr Mackie took the sheet off the young girl. The pathologist stank of cigarette smoke; Carruthers couldn't blame him. Even though he was an ex-smoker he was tempted to ask Mackie for one of his fags and save it for later. Carruthers swallowed hard, trying to put the unwelcome smells of disinfectant and decaying flesh out of his mind. He looked at the almost boyish figure. She looked so vulnerable lying there, if a person could look vulnerable when dead.

'She looks about twenty,' Carruthers said.

'I think she's a bit older. I would estimate between twenty-five and twenty-eight.'

Carruthers was surprised.

'Eastern European, is my guess.' Mackie was leaning over her, glasses on the end of his nose.

Carruthers frowned. 'What makes you say that?'

'A hunch.'

Carruthers raised his eyebrows. He'd learned to take note of Mackie's hunches. He was often spot on.

'How long dead?' said Carruthers.

'Can't say with any accuracy until I've done all the tests but several hours at least.'

Carruthers knew better than to push him.

'Various puncture wounds,' the pathologist continued.

'She's been knifed?'

'No, no. Not that sort of puncture wound.' Pushing his glasses back onto the bridge of his nose, Mackie probed a wound in her thigh with his gloved hand. 'More consistent with being caught on rocks.'

'Where she fell?' asked Carruthers. 'Or would these be rocks in the water?'

'There's no evidence she's been in the water yet,' said Mackie. 'But I'll know more when I examine the lungs. I know what you're asking. Did she fall to her death from the cliffs? That's what you want to know, isn't it?'

Carruthers nodded.

Mackie made eye contact with him. 'Don't quote me on this. I'm not even a third of the way through the PM but if pushed I would say early indications are that she died at the scene by falling from the cliffs.' He examined her blonde hairline. 'Broke her neck. No gunshot or stab wounds. She has a severe head injury, which most likely occurred on impact when she hit the ground. You'll notice there was significant amount of blood at the scene.'

'Could she have sustained the head injury before she fell?' asked Carruthers, trying to avert his eyes from the mass of congealed blood and bone splinters in the head.

'It's possible.' Carruthers watched Mackie patting his breast pocket. Absentmindedly looking for his cigarettes. Carruthers would take the smell of cigarette smoke over the smell of a corpse any day.

'Force of habit, I'm afraid.' The pathologist carried on. 'The injury is to the frontal lobe which means if it was inflicted by someone else she would have had to be facing her attacker. She could have staggered backwards and fallen, hitting her body on the rocks which would account for the gashes in her thigh. This is interesting,' he said. He was staring at the girl's left ankle. 'Tattoo. Not one I've seen before.'

Carruthers moved closer and peered at the tattoo. It was of an open eye shielded by an eyebrow and what looked like a tear drop underneath. There was also a strange curved line coming out of the bottom left of the eye. 'Can we get a photograph? It might help with the identification. I'll then get it circulated.' Carruthers looked at his watch. It was a few minutes after eleven. 'We've got a team brief at noon. If you get any results, I'll be on my mobile.'

'Right you are,' said Mackie.

Carruthers turned to go. He heard Mackie calling him back.

'If you want a ciggie, they're on my desk.' Carruthers raised his hand in acknowledgment. He was tempted, but this time he managed to bypass them.

* * *

The team brief started on time. There was a lot to get through. Carruthers shuffled his notes whilst gazing round the room.

Gayle Watson was fanning herself with a file. It was suffocatingly hot. Carruthers could smell cigarette smoke mingled with sweat. He wondered if Harris had just had a crafty fag outside.

'We'll start with the girl on the beach.' He recounted the findings of the post-mortem. 'Likelihood is that she's fallen from the cliffs. However, I left Mackie mid-PM so final results are not yet in.'

'Suicide?' asked Harris, cramming his face with a doughnut.

'It's possible,' said Carruthers. 'Or accident. We're not ruling anything out. However, if it was an accident, where were her personal possessions? We found no handbag, rucksack, keys or phone.'

'Definitely suicide, then,' said Harris, cheeks bulging. 'Why would you take yer gear with you if you were gonna top yersel.'

'Taken by the person who made the anonymous call?' asked Watson.

'Possible. My gut feeling says not,' said Carruthers.

'Nah, reckon it's a suicide,' said Harris.

'They'd have to be one callous bastard to steal her things,' said Fletcher.

Harris shrugged. 'There's a lot of desperate people out there. Maybe they were taken by an immigrant. Can't move for Poles and Lithuanians nowadays.'

Carruthers caught Fletcher throwing Harris a filthy look. Harris was well known for his view on immigrants and Fletcher for her dislike of Harris. Carruthers wondered, in light of Britain's shock decision to leave the EU, how many Eastern Europeans would still be here after Article 50 was triggered.

'We can't rule out foul play,' said Carruthers, wondering idly if Harris had bothered to vote in the EU Referendum. It wasn't a discussion he was prepared to have. He remembered all the bad feeling the Scottish Referendum had caused, having heard stories of members of even the same family being on opposing sides. The station had been no different. He glanced over at their latest recruit. No-nonsense Gayle Watson was a strong advocate of Scottish Independence. He looked back at the photo of the dead girl on the incident board, shuddering as he remembered the details of the post-mortem. He also remembered Mackie's surprising speculation that the girl might have been Eastern European.

Frowning, he looked at Harris reaching for a second doughnut with his pudgy hand. Wondered if the girl could be an immigrant. Or asylum seeker. There was a big trade to be made from trafficking illegals into the UK. He dragged his thoughts away from the worsening situation at Calais and the increasingly desperate refugees. But the dead girl hadn't looked Middle Eastern.

'We also have reason to believe there may be activity of bird poisoning in the area,' Carruthers continued. 'The meat we found has been sent for analysis. But we did get lucky. Found a set of binoculars on the top of the cliff, also sent off for examination. Maybe we'll get even luckier and find some fingerprints or DNA. I've called in a favour so we should get the results back pretty quickly.'

'Could they be the girl's?' asked Harris.

'What would she be doing with binoculars and no other personal possessions?' said Fletcher. 'If she was using the binos to look at the wildlife you might expect her to have, say, a rucksack? Butterfly or bird book? House keys? Mobile?'

Carruthers shuffled his papers again. 'It's possible the two activities are linked, but not necessarily. The binoculars user may have seen the body on the beach and been our anonymous caller. The binoculars user and the poisoner might not even be the same person or persons. At this stage we really can't be sure of anything.'

'What if she was a bird watcher who ran into the poisoners?' said Watson. 'Could they have killed her and taken all her possessions to prevent identification or to make it look like a suicide? Maybe they got careless and left the binoculars behind?'

'It's certainly a theory,' said Carruthers. 'Apart from it being a nature reserve I understand it's an area of Special Scientific Interest.' He looked over at Fletcher who nodded.

'Attracts a lot of wildlife enthusiasts,' she said. 'It has the pearl-bordered fritillary for starters.'

'What's that when it's at home?' asked Harris.

'A butterfly. It's pretty rare in the UK but it's making a comeback in Scotland.'

Carruthers smiled. He knew Fletcher liked her butterflies. He'd seen the Butterfly Conservation magazines in her flat.

'We've traced the anonymous call. Came from a phone box over at Windygates.'

Carruthers gazed around the room. 'Right. Jobs. I want Gayle to chase up the artist's impression of the girl. I know the poor lassie only had half a face but we should be able to work on the half we do have to get a decent likeness. Also get an interview set up with the media.'

Gayle Watson nodded. 'Will do, boss.'

'The only distinguishing feature of the girl that we have is this tattoo.' Carruthers gave copies of the tattoo photo to Fletcher. She handed them out to the team. 'Make sure that gets to the press as well,' he told Watson.

'Anyone familiar with this tattoo?' he asked. His question was greeted with silence. 'OK, well, ask around. It may be recognised as the art of a particular tattooist. Has it been done locally? Does the tat itself have a meaning? There's some interesting tattoos out there. Let's see if we can find a home for this one.' He looked at the tattoo of the eye once more.

'Does it have to have a meaning?' asked Fletcher. 'It might have none whatsoever. Might just be a tattoo.'

'Maybe,' said Carruthers.

'Yer no going to suggest bringing in a tattoo expert, are you?' This from Harris who, snorting, was wiping away a smear of strawberry jam that had inadvertently squirted all over his sheet of paper.

Carruthers caught Fletcher's eye. 'That's not a bad idea. Can you get me a list of local tattoo artists, Andie?'

'You graduates are all the same,' Harris continued. 'Last year you brought in that psychologist. That was a pure waste of time.'

Carruthers thought back to the big case that had absorbed the team the winter before. The psychologist had been helpful in giving them the heads-up on the potential effects of abuse on a child. Of course, that depth of knowledge and lateral thinking had been lost on Harris. It had been a difficult case. A difficult case with a surprising ending. He hoped none of these cases were going to be as complex.

'Moving on to other crimes, no less important,' said Carruthers. 'Let's turn our minds to the art thefts. Andie, I want you to do some research on local airfields close to the robbery. Get a list of all those who've taken planes up. It's possible that the robbers took aerial photographs when planning who to target. I'd also like you to work with Dougie, pulling any information we have on local bird poisoners.'

'Is there any news on when this friggin' air con's going to get fixed?' said Harris. He sniffed one of his armpits. 'I smell rank.'

'I shouldn't worry,' said Fletcher. 'This is Scotland. If we have sun for more than two consecutive days you Scots call it a heatwave. The weather will break soon enough.'

Carruthers concluded the brief and they filed out. Fletcher fell into step with him.

'Jim, if you can spare me for an hour or two I'd like to visit Ink It,' said Fletcher, referring to Castletown's only tattoo parlour. 'They may recognise the tattoo on our victim's ankle.'

'OK, happy for you to do that,' said Carruthers. 'I was going to go myself but I should probably wait for the final PM results.'

* * *

'I've never seen a design like this before,' said the tattooist.

As he spoke Fletcher was trying not to stare at the skull pinned through the fleshy part of the man's nose, or his long black greasy hair. Ink It was on the other side of Castletown, down a steep flight of stone steps into a basement shop. It had a good rep. The back of her legs complained just taking the few steep steps. She realised she hadn't had any proper exercise for months. She'd been so fit before her pregnancy but after her miscarriage and Mark walking out on her she'd found it hard to get motivated. She would also have to do something about the extra weight she was now carrying.

The tattoo artist was scrutinising the photograph, holding it inches from his face. Fletcher wondered if he was short-sighted. She listened as he started to talk again. 'It's on the girl's ankle, though. That can be meaningful.'

'Can it?' said Fletcher, feeling a bit more hopeful. And also ignorant, knowing next to nothing about tattoos. Getting a tattoo had never appealed to her. She looked around her at the photographs on the walls of men and women sporting them. Then back at the tattoo artist in front of her. His face was mercifully free of body art but his skinny arms were covered in a variety of saltires and Celtic designs.

The long-haired man nodded his head rigorously so that the skull dangling between his nostrils moved alarmingly. 'The ankle is a delicate part of the body. Very sexy in women.'

He glanced down towards Fletcher's ankles. She was glad she was wearing trousers.

He reluctantly looked up at her face again. 'It's very popular with women to get a tattoo on the ankle,' he said. 'Usually feminine designs. You know, butterflies, flowers, that sort of thing. Oh yes, it's a popular patch of the human canvas,' he said knowingly. 'Do you have any tattoos?'

'No.'

'Interested in getting one?'

He smiled and Fletcher recoiled in horror at the blackened state of his teeth.

'No.'

'Pity.' He resumed his study of the photograph. 'She's got a lovely ankle. I wonder what the rest of the body's like?' he said.

'The girl's dead,' said Fletcher, a bit more harshly than she intended.

'Of course. Wasn't thinking. Sorry.'

'Possibly murdered,' she said unnecessarily. 'So you don't know where she would have got this tattoo?'

'There's literally thousands of tattoos.'

'But you've never seen a tattoo like this?'

The man shook his head. Took a closer look. 'An eye with what looks like a tear drop. Interesting tat. Haven't seen this particular design before, mind. It doesn't shout the style of any artist I'm aware of. Course it could be something the canvas designed herself.'

'Do most tattoos that you give have a meaning?' asked Fletcher. She wasn't really enjoying her visit to the tattoo parlour, finding the man rather sleazy, but at least being underground it was cooler here, something to be grateful for.

'Well of course, ignore the tattoos people get when they're pissed. Sometimes the tattoo does have a meaning or the reason behind getting the tattoo might have meaning.'

'Such as?' said Fletcher.

'A rite of passage, a life-changing event, the passing of a loved one. All of those events have meanings, even if the specific tattoo doesn't.'

Fletcher remembered the tattoo of a bluebird on the body of one of her first murder victims in Fife. The man had been a Cardiff City fan. A bluebird had been the football team's emblem. She stared at the photograph of the tattoo on the girl's ankle. But she also remembered watching a recent documentary on a man who was obsessed with tattoos. None of his had had meaning. He'd got them all when drunk and had since regretted half of them.

The man ran his hands through his long greasy hair. 'I find the teardrop interesting. I know a bit about teardrop tattoos.

Saw a documentary about it. To do with prison gang culture in the States.'

'What did you learn?'

'Gangs use tattoos as a way of showing loyalty. So for example, the closed teardrop is a heavily symbolic prison gang tattoo.'

'Ever done any of those?' asked Fletcher.

'Nah,' the man said. 'Course not. It's American. But, like I said, it's a highly symbolic tattoo though. Can have several meanings.'

Her curiosity growing, she said, 'Like what?'

The man shrugged. 'Can signify the number of years spent in prison or the number of times the person was raped whilst incarcerated.'

Fletcher went cold. Different world. She knew there were beatings and rapes in British prisons but American prisons were another thing entirely if the documentaries were anything to go by. And that was the prison system in a supposed first world country.

The man was clearly just starting to warm up. 'Or the tear might signify the loss of a loved one or fellow gang member or the fact the wearer has killed someone.' He stared at the photocopy Fletcher had given him. 'An eye with a tear. Perhaps she's been in prison. And not a British prison.' Fletcher wondered just how much of this was relevant to their investigation.

'Want me to keep this and ask a few people?' said the man. 'Maybe someone's seen it before.'

'Be my guest.' Fletcher thanked him and turned to go. She had just opened the door when she had a thought. Could the tattoo be connected to a crime after all? Weren't prostitutes being run by gangs in Eastern Europe tattooed as a mark of ownership?

Still standing in the doorway she chewed her top lip whilst she thought about this piece of information. Brought back the Eastern European connection. Perhaps it hadn't been a waste of time after all.

'You sure you don't want a tattoo?'

Fletcher turned round to see the tattoo artist was looking at her curiously. No doubt wondering why she was still there.

'No thanks.' Fletcher turned away as the man smiled, deciding she didn't need to see his blackened teeth again.

Feeling a glimmer of hope for a possible lead, Fletcher left the subterranean premises and walked once more back into the brilliant sunshine.

* * *

Just as Carruthers returned to his desk with another black coffee his mobile rang. Bringing it out of his breast pocket he saw the caller ID – Dr Mackie. Eager to learn the findings of the post-mortem, he answered.

'Jim, I've finished the PM.'

'What have we got?'

'First thing is she didn't drown. No water present in the lungs. In fact, she hasn't been in the water at all. Toxicology, of course, won't be back for a while. However, she had recently had sex and from the bruising between her legs it may not have been consensual.'

'She'd been raped?' asked Carruthers, feeling his insides curdling.

'It's a possibility. Also her dental work's most likely Northern or Eastern European,' said Mackie. 'What I mean by that is that she has some of the best dental work I've ever seen. And she's had a lot done, for her age. There's been a lot of decay in her mouth.' He turned to Carruthers as he spoke. 'My guess is she's eaten too many sweeties. Did you know countries like Norway, Finland and Estonia lead the world in chocolate consumption?'

Carruthers didn't. 'Why's that?'

'Thought to be something to do with seasonal affective disorder. Along with depression and lethargy some folk get a disproportionate craving for sweets.' Carruthers digested all this. 'Also she's very blonde. Looks Nordic.'

'Anything else?'

'I'm afraid so. She was pregnant. About eight weeks.'

As soon as he finished the call, Carruthers' mobile rang again. This time it was Fletcher.

'Anything useful from the tattoo artist?'

'I drew a blank with the design, Jim. He hadn't seen it before. He did say some interesting things about the tear drop, though. It can be a sign of gang or prison culture in places like the States.'

Carruthers felt his insides twist with disappointment. He couldn't see how that piece of information would be useful to their investigation. 'That it?'

'Thought of something as I was leaving. Eastern European criminals are now branding their prostitutes with tattoos, aren't they? Mark of ownership. Might be worth keeping in mind.'

Carruthers perked up. 'Yeah, that's true. There might be something in it. Mackie's got back with the rest of the PM results. He thinks the victim's dental work was Northern or Eastern European. He had a hunch about her nationality. Thought she looks Nordic.'

'So it's possible our victim is Eastern European or from one of the Baltic states,' said Fletcher. 'Perhaps a prostitute.'

'Let's keep an open mind. Whether she was a prostitute, at this moment in time that's pure speculation. However, there are some disturbing findings.' Wondering how Fletcher would take the news that the victim had been pregnant and possibly raped, he filled her in on the rest of Mackie's call.

Three

'Boss?'

Carruthers swung round to see Fletcher. He'd been heading in the direction of the coffee machine. He needed another caffeine fix after doing paperwork for the last three hours.

'You've had a phone call,' Fletcher continued. 'Your mother. Something about your brother. Can you give her a call?'

Carruthers' heart leapt in his mouth. His brother had had a serious heart attack some months earlier. Alan had had to have a bypass. It had been a difficult time. He hoped the call wasn't bad news, as guilt for not keeping in better contact pricked him. He looked at his watch. Midday. His mother would have left for her gym session by now.

Carruthers caught Fletcher staring at him with a concerned look. 'Jim, I don't think it's anything to worry about. Your mother sounded fine.'

Carruthers allowed himself to expel a relieved breath he hadn't realised he was holding. He instantly felt better. 'Thanks, Andie.'

'He's OK, isn't he? Your brother?'

'As far as I know.' He thought of Alan's long road to recovery and of the impact it had had, particularly on Alan and their mother.

'As far as you know?' queried Fletcher. 'I thought you were going to try to keep better contact with him.'

The guilt returned. Carruthers dropped his head a fraction and struggled to make his thoughts unreadable to his efficient but nosey DS. When Alan had first had his heart attack, Carruthers had kept his distance from his older brother. He'd felt impotent and not a little guilty that it had been the fitter, healthier sibling who'd suffered such a devastating heart attack completely out of the blue. Carruthers knew that his staying away in the early days had upset his family.

He turned his attention to Fletcher. 'Are you OK? How are *you* getting on?'

She nodded her head. 'I'm fine. You shouldn't worry about me, you know. Making me see a counsellor after I lost Lara really helped. And I'm tougher than I look. I'm not going to fall apart because a dead girl was pregnant, as sad as it is. Anyway, if we can talk shop for a moment, I've got Dougie checking up on flying schools. I'm pulling the information on any known local bird poisoners. I'll have it later today. Oh, I nearly forgot to tell you. Superintendent Bingham wants to see you. And don't think I didn't notice you changing the subject when we were talking about your brother. It's what you do best when you feel uncomfortable. Change the subject, I mean.'

Carruthers knew his DS was right. When he found a personal subject difficult to deal with he either changed the subject or made a joke of things. He wondered if she was doing the same thing now. He didn't know Andie had named her bump.

Bingham can wait, he thought. He called his mother back. Managed to get her on her mobile. Andie was right. His mother was fine, and just wanting to know if he was able to do a family meal that weekend with his brother. They weren't close, him and his brother. He'd hoped that might change after Alan's heart attack but it hadn't. Most communication between him and his brother still went through their mother. Carruthers wondered if this was normal. It bothered his mother more than it bothered him. Since his brother's heart attack and with his father dead, his mother had become worryingly needy and over-protective, on the phone at the slightest thing. He'd had to have a word with her about it in the end. He'd felt guilty for doing so, but she had backed off. Chasing the moment of regret away, he walked towards the coffee machine again. Moments later, with his hands wrapped round a scalding cup of steaming black liquid, he walked down the corridor to Bingham's office.

Carruthers rapped twice on the door, opened it and popped his head round. He caught a whiff of what smelled like stale cigarette smoke. Bingham was on the phone. He waved Carruthers to take a seat in the low-back chair opposite his mahogany desk. Carruthers came in but remained standing. It was a game they played. Carruthers refused to take a seat in Bingham's office. He disliked being inferior in height to Bingham and hated that particular chair. It always reminded him of the day he had been seated in it when he'd been demoted back to DI. He had not sat in it since.

Bingham finished his phone call. Looked Carruthers up and down with a furrowed forehead. Rubbed his hand over his balding head and said, 'Have you got those forecasts you were doing for me?'

Carruthers' heart sank. Another dressing-down was on its way. 'Not yet.'

'Look, this really isn't good enough, Carruthers. I asked for them a week last Tuesday. What have you been doing?'

Carruthers opened his mouth to speak but before he'd had a chance Bingham waved at him dismissively. 'I've heard. Consorting with tattoo artists, apparently. That is not your job. You're a bloody DI.'

Carruthers could feel the corners of his mouth turning down. How had Bingham found out they'd seen a tattoo artist? Most likely candidate was Harris, based on his reaction in the brief. But then Harris wasn't known to be a station grass.

'The forecasts'll get done,' said Carruthers. 'Anyway, it was Andie who saw the tattoo artist.'

'So when are you going to get them done? Bloody Christmas, the rate you're going.'

'I'll do them tonight,' said Carruthers. He spent the next few moments wondering whatever possessed him to lie so blatantly. It seemed to satisfy Bingham, though.

'See you do. I want them on my desk tomorrow morning. Now, give me a quick update on the art theft case.'

Carruthers felt heat suffuse his face. 'Don't you want to know about the body on the beach first? After all, we haven't ruled out foul play. I would have thought a suspicious death takes precedence over theft.'

Carruthers enjoyed seeing Bingham turn red and watched, fascinated, as the man's hands bunched into fists. The veins looked like they might pop at any minute. One thing could be said about their relationship; they certainly knew how to press each other's buttons.

Bingham looked at his watch and sighed. 'Body on the beach?' He looked confused for a moment. 'Most likely suicide or accident. Go on then. Fill me in. But be quick about it. I need to know what progress you've made on the art thefts. People to report back to. That kind of thing.'

Most likely your golf cronies, thought Carruthers, despising Bingham for being the social climber that he was.

* * *

Carruthers almost collided with Gayle Watson as he left Bingham's office. She adjusted her tie.

'You're wearing a particularly dapper shirt today, Ms Watson,' he said.

This seemed to please Gayle Watson. Her infectious smile lit up her face giving prominence to her dimples. 'Thank you very much.' She put on a fake upper-crust English accent. 'One does what one can.'

'Did you want to see me?' he asked. He wondered where she bought her shirts. Rumour had it that she got them from Hawes and Curtis, in George Street, Edinburgh. They looked expensive and she was always so well turned out. He often wondered what older cops like Willie Brown and Dougie Harris made of the new intake of police officers. Both Fletcher and Watson were two strong no-nonsense women.

'Aye, just to let you know,' said Watson, 'I've set the interview up with the media. That's later this afternoon. We've also pulled the information on the bird poisoners. I gave Andie and Dougie a hand with that.'

'What's that?' asked Carruthers, eyeing a bunch of scrolled papers in her hand.

'Photocopies of the artist's impression of the girl.'

'Good,' he said. 'Are you free at the moment?' She nodded. 'I'd like you and Dougie to go door-to-door round that local beauty spot by Pinetum Park Forest. See if anyone knows the dead girl. Find out if she was known locally.'

Gayle Watson saluted. Her dimples creased. Carruthers turned to walk away. Watson called him back.

'Jim, Andie's just put a cheese and onion toastie on your desk for you. Just in case you forget to eat.'

'Tell her thanks, will you?' He couldn't help but smile at Fletcher's thoughtfulness. She'd make someone a great wife one day.

He returned to his desk. He picked up his toastie and bit into it, enjoying the hot tangy taste. His phone rang. He picked it up with the hand that was not currently wrapped round the hot cheese sandwich.

'Afternoon, Gill. What have you found for me? Had the meat been poisoned?' As he asked the question he could picture the vivacious, curly blonde-haired scientist over in the West Edinburgh purpose-built lab that housed the Scottish Agricultural Science Agency.

''Fraid so, Jim. I can't tell you what the poison was, but it's fast-acting and highly toxic.'

Carruthers grimaced. It was a closely guarded secret what poisons were used by these criminals. It was not information anyone wanted in the public domain. It was less of a secret that Dr Gillian McLaren had a level of paranoia about her phone line being bugged that was bordering on the obsessive, something better suited to MI5. She was, however, well aware of this and it had become a standing joke between the two of them. This time nobody was laughing.

As he listened to Gill, one of his favourite people, he wolfed down the rest of his sandwich, gasping as he burnt his tongue on a molten glob of cheese. Absentmindedly he picked up the photograph of the dead girl's tattoo. Turned it upside down. Gazed at it then turned it the right way up again.

'So they're at it again, the bastards.' As he said this, he picked up the wrapping of the toastie with his free hand, scrunched it up savagely and threw it into the waste bin.

'Where did you say this meat had been found?' said Gill.

Carruthers pinpointed the area, telling her about his climb up the cliffs. 'I didn't see any dead birds,' admitted Carruthers.

'Well, the meat was certainly fresh,' said Gill. 'Not long since deposited. What took you out there?'

Carruthers told her about the body of the girl on the beach.

'It's not really what you need, is it?' said Gill. 'Investigating one crime and you come across a second. Still, you've almost certainly saved the lives of some of the UK's most endangered raptors. Meat on that cliff face like that – it was rabbit, by the way. It could have been sea eagles they were after. It may sound surprising to find them on the east coast but they've been reintroduced into the area. In fact, one came to a grisly end not that long ago in Fife. Got caught up in one of the wind turbines.'

Poor bird, thought Carruthers. *What a way to go.* He brought his mind back to people rather than birds.

'Well, we don't know two crimes have been committed yet. Body on the beach is still a suspicious death. May have been an accident or suicide, although…'

'Although what?'

'Sorry,' said Carruthers. 'Just thinking aloud. She had no personal belongings with her so less likely to be an accident. Unless the anonymous caller also stole her possessions before he legged it.' Carruthers knew Gill liked to hear about current police cases. He always threw her a few titbits. Just as much as he could without getting himself into trouble. She'd been helpful on more than one occasion in the past, too.

'It sounds interesting.' There was a pause. 'You free for a drink anytime soon?' she asked.

Carruthers couldn't help but smile. He enjoyed her company. Had started going out a bit more socially again. After his wife had left him he'd turned into a bit of a hermit until he'd started dating Jodie, the pathology assistant. It had ended in disaster. He was grateful Jodie was currently on holiday. Gill was single, too, but they were just friends. He'd made a firm commitment to himself that the odd fling might be OK but nothing serious. And of course, as everyone knew, having a fling with a friend was asking for trouble.

'Full workload just now,' he found himself saying. 'Apart from the body on the beach and the bird poisoners, we have a series of high-end art thefts to deal with.'

'Oh yes, think I heard about them. Jeezo. Well, once it quietens down give me a call and don't eat too many pot noodles in the meantime.'

Carruthers laughed. The police eating nothing but pot noodles when working on a big case was a running joke between them.

'If I can be of any more help, you know where to find me,' she continued. 'Always happy to help the boys in blue.'

'I will do. And I'm not a boy in blue anymore. Plain clothes. CID.'

He heard her laughing. 'Pity. I like a man in uniform. Seriously, I mean it. I'm just the other end of the phone.'

'Thanks, Gill.' Carruthers glanced at his watch. 'Right, had better go. Heading up a brief in five.'

* * *

Last to enter the brief was Harris, who plonked a buff file down in front of the seated Carruthers. 'Details of the bird poisoners we've caught in the last four years,' Harris said.

Carruthers nodded his thanks. He was eager to read the material. Only Harris, Bingham and Brown had been at the station long enough to remember any previous cases. He, Fletcher and Watson were all pretty new. He glanced around the room as the staff were taking their seats.

Watson had been drafted in to take Fletcher's place when she had been off after her miscarriage. He looked over at Fletcher chatting to Watson. It hadn't been an easy ride when Fletcher returned. She admitted she'd lost her confidence having been off for so long and had initially considered Gayle Watson a threat. Carruthers had been worried about Fletcher but now she'd finally gone for the counselling he'd requested, he could see it was helping. As for Watson, she'd settled in so well she'd stayed. Fletcher and Watson had called a truce and a tentative friendship had developed. Looking at them now, he'd suggest the tentative stage was over.

He cleared his throat and started the brief. 'Right, folks, listen up. First, dead girl on the beach.' He stood up and went over to the incident board, pointing to the photos of the girl's body on the beach.

'No luck identifying our dead girl yet, although from her dental work Mackie suggests she's possibly Eastern European.' Carruthers paused before continuing. 'Aged mid- to late-twenties. And pregnant. She'd also recently had sex and it may not have been consensual. Nothing from the door-to-door. Am I right?' He looked over at Watson.

''Fraid not, boss.'

'OK,' said Carruthers. 'I want us to extend the search over a wider area. One other thing. We've got the results of the fingerprinting on the binos back. Clean. No prints.' There were groans. 'OK,' said Carruthers, 'can you get the binoculars back if the lab's finished with them, Gayle? I might just have a use for them.'

'Sure, boss,' said Watson.

'There'll also be a piece on the local Fife news tonight at nine so we'll see what that brings in. The bird poisoning's ongoing. Dougie, can you give me a summary of the information you've just handed me?'

'Aye, Keith Mulholland and Jon Simpson, gamekeeper and ghillie on the Logan Estate, twenty miles north of Pinetum Park Forest both caught poisoning birds of prey in 2012.'

'What happened to them?' asked Carruthers.

Harris shrugged. 'Suspended sentences and a fine. As far as I know they're still both working on the estate.'

'It's twenty miles away,' said Carruthers. 'We could interview them but let's first see if there could be somewhere more local.'

Carruthers pored over a map of East Scotland. 'What's the nearest estate to where the poisoned meat was found?'

'The Ardgarren Estate. It's a couple of miles down the road from Pinetum Park Forest. Owned by a man called Barry Cuthbert. He's a local bigwig.'

'Meaning?' asked Carruthers, disliking him already.

'New money. And lots of it.'

'What sort of estate does he run?'

'I think it's a grouse shooting estate,' said Harris. The overweight detective sergeant made a sound like a snort. He clearly didn't think much of grouse shooting estates.

'This Cuthbert, ever been in trouble with the police?' Carruthers was busy processing the information. Grouse shooting estates were some of the biggest threats to birds of prey. It was definitely worth checking out this estate.

'Not to my knowledge,' said Harris.

'Run a check on him, will you?' said Carruthers. 'Just to be on the safe side. In any case, I think we should pay Mr Cuthbert a visit.'

'We should be handing this over to the Wildlife Crime Unit,' said Fletcher.

'It's not just a wildlife crime we're investigating, though, is it?' said Carruthers. 'That slab of poisoned meat was found in the vicinity of a suspicious death.' Fletcher raised her eyebrows. 'I think we'll keep this to ourselves, for now.'

'They need to know, Jim. We can't sit on this.'

'And we will hand it over. Just as soon as we've interviewed Cuthbert. Have you never heard of killing two birds with one stone?'

Harris groaned. 'Very apt,' said Fletcher.

'Now, we also need to focus on the art thefts,' Carruthers rubbed his brow. He was starting to get a headache. There still hadn't been any sign of the company to fix the air conditioning. Everyone was complaining. The heat was making him feel tired. He was sure there were health and safety rules on it but this was a police station and they just had to get on with it. 'Right. Thefts. So far there's been three of them. These villains have got away with a Constable, a Sisley and now a Vettriano. Total value estimated to be just under four million. We need to find out if there's any common denominators to these robberies. I want us to pool together on this one. What do they all have in common?'

'Well, Constable was an English landscape artist, Sisley an impressionist landscape painter who kept his British citizenship although he lived most of his life in France, and Vettriano is a local Fife boy who is popular for painting people,' said Fletcher. 'The only common denominator I can see is that they're all British.'

'OK, that's a start,' said Carruthers before turning to Harris. 'Dougie, I want you to cross reference the latest robbery at the McMullans' with the previous robberies. These are all wealthy people. Did they use the same caterers, cleaners, roofers? The McMullans used a firm of roofers who had access to the house. I want you to check them out. What did these people have in common? Did they mix in the same circles? Have the same hobbies? Maybe they all belong to the same bridge club? There must be something. And this gang must be stopped before someone gets killed.' He held his hands up. 'I know we've already done this with the first two but I want us to go over it again. Perhaps this recent robbery will throw fresh light on the other two. We may have missed something.'

He retrieved a cream file that had been lying under his paperwork. Opening it he distributed photographs amongst the staff. 'The National Crime Agency have sent over these photographs of the gang wanted in the South East area for the series of art thefts down south. So far they've targeted private individuals in London, Kent and Sussex. As we know from the previous brief the MO is virtually identical in the sense of targeting isolated homes, committing the robberies in the dead of night, usually with the owners at home and using stolen vehicles, which are later abandoned. However, and I want to stress this, they've never operated north of the border before. And they don't usually target big named artists. Just too difficult to shift, even on the black market. So my thinking is to keep our eyes and ears open, memorise their ugly mugs. However, don't assume this is a cut and dried case and we just have to catch these criminals. It may be a completely different gang.' He gazed around the room. 'OK, let's go.'

As the room cleared Carruthers remained standing. He frowned as he stared at the photographs in front of him. Something did not add up. Hadn't he said in a previous brief that the gang were a sophisticated bunch of art thieves? If they had been they would have targeted the works of lesser-known artists. So what did this mean? Either they weren't professional art thieves or they weren't following the usual script.

Four

Carruthers grabbed the bagged binoculars he'd put in his desk drawer, grateful the SOCOs had now finished with them. Unfortunately they'd yielded nothing useful and neither had the cigarette butt. He stood up, pulling his lightweight jacket from behind his chair, picked up a set of keys for one of the station cars and walked to the car park, Fletcher at his heel. 'I'll drive,' he said.

He took a right out of the station car park on the outskirts of the popular university and seaside resort of Castletown and started driving towards Barry Cuthbert's estate. They hugged the ancient city walls of the town passing a large student halls of residence and wild flower-lined verges. It was late afternoon and they were just starting to hit the local rush hour traffic. 'Do you reckon this hot spell's going to continue?' asked Fletcher.

'I hope not,' said Carruthers. 'It's too hot for me.'

Fletcher laughed. 'Wimp. Any idea when the station's air con's going to be fixed?'

'Your guess is as good as mine.'

They drove away from the town and the rush hour traffic and ended up on the emptier back roads in the East Neuk of Fife. Carruthers stared out of his car window, gazing at the tumbledown old stone walls, rolling fields and occasional farm. He noticed bits of fluff blowing across the road. *Must be dandelion clocks and thistles gone to seed,* he thought. A little bit later they drove into what looked like smoke drifting over from a field. He glanced to his left as he drove, to see that it was dust from a working combine harvester. This life was vastly different from the metropolitan bustle of London. He had worried when he first moved up that he would miss the capital with its noise, buzz and fancy restaurants, but he found he was enjoying taking life at a slower pace. And he loved being so much closer to nature and the sea.

Twenty minutes later they buzzed at the security gates of Cuthbert's estate, and Carruthers looked beyond at the opulent mansion.

'How the other half live, eh?' said Fletcher.

'Indeed,' said Carruthers, wondering how Barry Cuthbert had made his money. He clutched the bagged binoculars in his hand. A tinny voice came through the speaker. Carruthers moved closer and said, 'Detective Inspector Jim Carruthers and DS Andrea Fletcher to see Barry Cuthbert.' The heavy gates juddered as Fletcher and Carruthers drove through.

As the car rolled along the sweeping drive Carruthers saw two men coming out of the building. The older man was wearing tweeds and carrying a shotgun. The younger man was wearing jeans and a T-shirt.

'Do you want to interview those two first?' said Fletcher. 'They look like gamekeepers.'

'They'll keep.'

They were shown into the hall by the middle-aged and rather dour housekeeper and escorted to the living area. Carruthers couldn't fail to be impressed by its opulence. The room smacked of money. He thought he recognised a Queen Anne chair in the corner by the red velvet curtains. However, his eye was drawn to the works of art on the wall. One in particular. A magnificent oil seascape hung over the mantelpiece depicting ships engaged in battle. The picture looked pretty old. Carruthers saw a spiral of smoke rise from a leather chair in the centre of the room. Barry Cuthbert was sitting in it, smoking a cigar. He rose when he saw his guests.

'To what do I owe this honour?' he asked in a broad Cockney drawl.

As he shook the man's hand, Carruthers checked Barry Cuthbert out carefully. He didn't like what he saw. Somewhere between forty and fifty years old, Barry Cuthbert had highlighted blond hair, hands covered in signet rings and a perma-tan that looked anything but natural. He reminded Carruthers of an independent financial adviser he'd once met. He also looked completely out of place on a Scottish countryside estate.

'Good afternoon, Mr Cuthbert. We're currently investigating the death of a young woman on Kinsale beach by Pinetum Park Forest.'

Barry Cuthbert raised his eyebrows but shook his head. 'Know nuffin' 'bout it. First I've 'erd of it and I know most of what goes on round here.'

'I saw two of your gamekeepers outside,' said Carruthers. 'Do they ever go over there?'

'No. Why would they? It ain't part of my estate.'

'We're also investigating a case of attempted bird poisoning up by the cliffs, behind where the body was discovered,' said Fletcher. 'What sort of estate is this?' Is this a shooting estate?'

'Yes,' said Cuthbert.

'Grouse shooting?'

'That's right.'

Keeping one eye on Cuthbert, Carruthers moved around the room, glancing at the various pieces of art and furniture. 'So it would be true to say you might have motive for poisoning birds of prey to protect the birds your clients pay good money to shoot?'

Eyes narrowing, Cuthbert said, 'Poisoning birds of prey's against the law. I don't engage in illegal activities, inspector.'

Carruthers smiled. 'Glad to hear it.'

'What about your ghillies and gamekeepers? How well supervised are they?' asked Fletcher.

Cuthbert shook his head once more. 'I make sure they know the law but I'm not their keeper. No pun intended.'

Carruthers noticed Cuthbert undressing Fletcher with his eyes as he spoke. His dislike of the man increased.

Carruthers spoke carefully. 'You do know that those who employ gamekeepers have a strict duty to know what is being done in their name and on their property. The law has changed up in Scotland, Mr Cuthbert. A landowner is now as accountable as his gamekeeper. Bird of prey persecution is illegal under wildlife conservation laws.'

'All very interesting, inspector, but I'm not your man. I'll keep my ears pinned, though. I would have thought a man of your standing would have more important things to do than harass local landowners about the killing of birds of prey.'

'Killing birds of prey's a serious matter, Mr Cuthbert, but then so's the suspicious death of a young woman.' He handed Barry Cuthbert the artist's impression of the woman. Cuthbert took it and looked at it. 'She may be Eastern European.'

Cuthbert shook his head and tried to give the artist's impression back to Carruthers. 'Pretty girl. Don't know her. Sorry.'

Carruthers kept his hands resolutely down by his side. 'Keep it and show your staff, Mr Cuthbert. We believe the people who laid the poisoned meat close to where the body was found may have seen something that will further this investigation. It's possible the anonymous call about the girl's body could have come from one of the illegal poisoners. If it did, they could have come from a local sporting estate. Your estate, Mr Cuthbert, is the closest.'

Cuthbert's eyes narrowed.

Carruthers brought his card out of his pocket and gave it to Cuthbert. 'If you hear of anything or have any information, call me. Oh, just one thing. We'd like to interview your gamekeepers. We could start with the two that were leaving the building when we arrived.'

'I'm afraid that's not going to be possible. They're busy.'

'So are we, Mr Cuthbert,' said Carruthers, mentally adding obstructive and unhelpful to the growing list of things he didn't like about Barry Cuthbert. 'I'm sure they could spare a couple of minutes. I take it you have a licence for the shotgun one of your gamekeepers was carrying?'

'Course. You wan' ta see it?'

'That won't be necessary, thank you. But I'd like you to call them in. You can start by giving me their names. I'd also like a word with your estate manager.'

'Pip McGuire's day off today. Our estate manager.' Cuthbert turned his back to the two officers, picked up a mobile that was lying on a nearby nest of antique tables and barked an instruction into it. When he was finished he replaced the mobile back on the table. Within minutes the two men Carruthers had seen outside walked through the door. The older and burlier of the two still carrying the shotgun.

'Names please?' said Carruthers.

The older one spoke. Pointing to the boy who looked about as terrified as a school leaver starting a new job he said, 'This is Joe McGuigan, and I'm Derek Sturrock.'

Carruthers brought out his police ID. 'Have either of you gentlemen been anywhere near the Kinsale beach at Pinetum Park Forest recently?' He caught the pimpled younger man casting quick glances at his weather-beaten colleague. The boy scratched the angry looking acne on the side of his neck. It was the older man who spoke.

'Nah, why would we?'

'Would you mind putting the shotgun down, Mr Sturrock? Guns make me nervous.'

'It's not loaded.'

'Even so.'

Derek Sturrock did as he was requested and placed the gun down on a nearby table.

Fletcher took out her black notebook. 'We're interested in talking to anyone who was in the location recently,' she said. 'We believe bird poisoners were out on the cliffs overlooking the beach on which a young woman's body was found. We're not here about the poisoning. That's not our department. We want to know who called the police.'

Carruthers silently congratulated Fletcher for getting straight to the point.

'It wasnae us,' said the younger man. This time he glanced across at Barry Cuthbert.

'Mr Cuthbert, would you mind waiting outside whilst we conduct this interview?' said Carruthers.

Cuthbert looked as if he was about to complain but grabbed his mobile instead and started walking towards the door. 'Don't keep them too long. They've got work to do.'

Carruthers waited until Cuthbert had left before fishing out the bagged binoculars. 'Belong to either of you?' he said.

They both shook their heads although he could see the younger of the two looking nervously at the glasses.

'They were found on the cliffs overlooking the spot where we discovered a young woman's body.'

'What did she die of? Did she drown?' said the younger man, his eyes still on the binoculars.

'We don't know yet but we don't think it was an accident,' said Carruthers. 'We haven't yet ruled out foul play. What are your duties as gamekeeper?' Carruthers asked the older man.

The man shrugged. 'Whatever Mr Cuthbert needs us to do.'

'Can you clarify that?' said Fletcher.

Carruthers watched the younger man glancing at his colleague with quick darting eye movements. *He knows something. Young Joe McGuigan knows something and ten a penny the binoculars are his.* Carruthers scrutinised him. The boy couldn't be more than eighteen. *Someone has told him to keep quiet. But who? The older gamekeeper or Cuthbert?* Carruthers watched the younger man carefully. The man winced. *He's scared of something. Or someone. And I mean to find out what and who it is.*

'Organising shoots,' said Sturrock. 'Keeping records of what is shot or caught, training gun dogs, controlling predators like foxes and rats; repairing equipment.'

'And a lot of this would be done on your own and in remote areas, wouldn't it?' said Fletcher.

There was silence from both men.

'Answer DS Fletcher,' asked Carruthers.

'Aye, I suppose,' said the older man, Sturrock.

'I'll ask you one more time,' said Carruthers. 'Have either of you been anywhere near Pinetum Park in the last few weeks or seen anything suspicious as you've gone about your duties?'

Whilst the older man shook his head, the younger stared at his feet.

Carruthers decided to try a different tack. 'Would you be prepared to come to the station so that we can take a set of your fingerprints? It's just routine. We'd like to be able to eliminate you from our enquiries.'

A red flush was spreading up from Joe McGuigan's angry neck. Carruthers was reminded of molten lava.

'Are you arresting us?' the younger man said.

Christ, the boy looks about to piss himself.

'Course he isn't, ya eejit,' said Sturrock. 'We havenae done anything wrang.'

'Like I said it's just routine.' As he said this, Carruthers calmly turned the bag over in his hand. *Nothing like putting the wind up them,* he thought. '*If* you haven't done anything wrong you won't have anything to worry about, will you?'

'He's just bluffing,' said Sturrock. 'He knows he cannae ask us to come down the station to give a set of prints.'

Carruthers put the bagged binoculars back in the carrier bag.

'OK, let's go back to your duties for a moment,' he said. 'I'm assuming you'd also protect game from poachers by patrolling the beat area at night? It's your job to keep the guns clean, too?'

'Yes, and it's in the job description that we'd be working with the police to deal with crime such as hare coursing and badger baiting,' said Cuthbert, walking back into the room.

Clearly his curiosity got the better of him and he couldn't keep away, thought Carruthers.

'We're all law-abiding round 'ere,' said Cuthbert. 'We ain't the bad guys.'

'Glad to hear it,' said Carruthers, handing the plastic bag to Fletcher.

Carruthers looked over at Fletcher, who nodded. 'OK,' he said, 'you can go. If you do think of anything you can call us on this number.' He brought out two business cards and gave one to each man.

'Will there be anything else?' said Cuthbert.

'We'd still like to have a word with your estate manager, Pip McGuire, Barry. Let him know, will you? He can ring us at the station.'

They walked off. Carruthers threw a backwards glance to see a glaring Cuthbert. The two officers headed back to their car.

Fletcher slipped her black notebook back into her shoulder bag. 'What are your thoughts, Jim?'

'Cuthbert's definitely one to watch. Don't trust him an inch.'

Fletcher laughed. 'That much was obvious. You know you're not very good at hiding your feelings.'

'That's why I make a lousy poker player. What did you think of him, Andie?'

She tucked a tendril of dark hair behind her ear. 'I'm not sure. I'll say this for him, though. He's got good taste. That room was beautiful. Did you notice the furniture? It was all antique. And what about the artwork? Stunning. I really liked the painting of the horse. It looked like a Stubbs.' She was quiet for a moment. 'I'd quite like to have a nosey around his estate,' she said.

'Just what I was thinking,' said Carruthers. 'We'll just have to think of a reason to come back.' Their feet crunched on the gravel drive. 'I'll say something though. East Neuk of Fife's not short of a bob or two.'

'Those two gamekeepers know something,' said Fletcher. 'The McGuigan kid's scared.'

Carruthers unlocked the car doors. 'I thought so, too,' he said.

Fletcher grinned. 'And it definitely put the wind up them when you suggested they come down the station to be fingerprinted.'

'Pity we didn't find any prints.' Carruthers grinned. 'They weren't to know that, though.'

'Any plans tonight?' asked Fletcher, opening her door.

'A few phone calls.' Carruthers opened his door and climbed into the driver's seat. 'Watch the *News at Ten* for the report on our dead body on the beach.' Fletcher shut her door and Carruthers started the engine. 'Hopefully we'll get a few leads through that and with a bit of luck a positive ID on the body. Doesn't look as if she's local. Nobody's come in to report her missing. Pity door-to-door yielded nothing.'

'I'd really like to know her story.'

'Me too,' said Carruthers, pulling out down the drive. 'She must have a family out there somewhere that's missing her. We just have to find them.'

After dropping Fletcher at the station Carruthers drove home. Once he'd had a quick chat with his mum on the phone about the family dinner she wanted him to attend on Sunday he settled back in his favourite old chair to watch the *News at Ten* with a whisky. Swirling the amber liquid of the ten-year-old Laphroaig around his glass gave him a satisfied feeling. He was drinking less these days. Enjoying nothing but the occasional glass. Being in control of his drinking felt good. There'd been a couple of times, just after his wife left and also right after his brother's heart attack, when he'd really struggled and turned to the drink again. It hadn't been easy watching his fitter older brother struck down by a heart attack and finding out that heart disease ran in the family. He'd been told to get his cholesterol tested. He still hadn't. Perhaps he just didn't want to know. He watched as the police artist's impression of the young woman came on the screen. Wondered who the dead pregnant woman was, how she had met her death and why on earth she'd had to end up on his patch. He fell asleep in his chair, waking around two in the morning with a sore back and the empty crystal glass still in his hands. Putting the glass down carefully on the table he climbed the creaking stairs to bed.

Five

Carruthers managed to get to the station by eight the next morning. He'd hardly had time to take his jacket off when his desk phone rang.

It was his contact at the National Crime Agency, John Stevenson. Carruthers was surprised to hear his voice.

'I thought you'd want to know as soon as possible,' Stevenson said. 'We caught the gang I was telling you about.'

'You're joking?'

'Nope. Had a tip-off about a lock-up off the M25. Apparently there was all manner of comings and goings. Folk got suspicious and gave us a buzz.'

'Go on,' urged Carruthers.

'We recovered only one painting. A little-known eighteenth-century watercolourist. They managed to move all the other pieces. They're being interviewed at the moment. The only thing is, Jim, they're not admitting to any other thefts. We're pretty sure they're responsible for the thefts down south and one in York but I'm starting to have grave doubts they would have got as far north as Scotland.'

'OK, thanks for telling me,' said Carruthers. 'With the gang caught I'm just wondering where that leaves us. MO was virtually the same. It's either a massive coincidence or copycat.'

'Like I said, it's unusual for a gang to steal high-end artworks. Our lot are the real deal. They're going for lesser-known artists, which makes them professional art thieves.'

Carruthers sat listening. 'You said with the well-known names it's near impossible to sell them on, especially in the normal market.'

'Yep. They're literally too hot to handle. What have your lot got away with?'

'A Constable, a Sisley and a Vettriano.'

Carruthers heard the man whistle. 'I wonder if they're amateurs.'

'Well, if they are, they're being very professional about it. Look,' said Carruthers, 'I hear what you say about masterpieces and paintings by well-known artists being too hot to handle. What about selling on the black market?'

'It can be just as difficult for criminals on the black market as the open market. As a general rule, stolen artworks' black-market value is around ten per cent of the actual value, but with paintings worth tens of millions of pounds, you can see that even that mark-down is way out of most criminals' price range. The kind of people who are able to get their hands on that kind of money by and large aren't interested in owning something that they could possibly go to jail for possessing. And remember that they wouldn't be able to sell the pieces on easily, either. However, that said, to play devil's advocate, you can also see the attraction of art theft for criminal gangs. Stolen art can easily be carried across international borders.'

'I suppose you wouldn't have to worry about currency conversion,' said Carruthers.

'That's just what I was about to say. Size is important too. Some smuggled paintings are smaller than an A3 sheet of paper. It might be worth contacting Interpol. It's possible these paintings have already left the country.'

Carruthers sat deep in thought. He could certainly see the attraction of becoming an art thief.

'What else can you tell me?' asked Carruthers.

'Worth bearing in mind it isn't always about profit,' continued Stevenson. 'I know I said earlier that criminal gangs wouldn't generally steal high-end art but let's not forget that there will still be wealthy private individuals who want to own a piece of exquisite and rare art for the sake of it. Even if they can't show it to anyone.'

Once more Carruthers thought of the Paris heist.

'There have also been cases of organised criminals stealing valuable works of art to be used as collateral.'

'Care to elaborate?'

'Right, well, just say our art thief is caught – when faced with prison, criminals have been known to try to broker shorter sentences in return for information leading to the discovery of the famous piece of stolen art.'

'Does it work?' said Carruthers.

'Most European courts do accept these type of plea bargains. Generally what you've got to remember is that art theft is a big deal. Moving away from the high-end pieces of stolen art for a moment – thousands of lower value works are stolen every year and are simply never found. We just don't have the resources to go after them all. Did you know that Scotland Yard has just three people working in its arts and antiques unit?'

Carruthers was surprised. 'Why so few?' he said.

'Art retrieval is largely left to the private sector. Two reasons, really. First, it's because victims' insurance covers the majority of losses and secondly, most thefts traditionally haven't involved violence, although as we know that now is changing.'

Carruthers moved a cold half cup of coffee off his notebook. He flicked open the notebook to a clean page and picked up a pen. Poised with the pen mid-air he said, 'Tell me a bit more about it. What happens if an artwork is stolen?'

'The first thing to do would be to check with the Art Loss Register which is a London-based company part owned by Sotheby's, Christie's and Bonhams. They maintain a database of over 400,000 missing works. Before each sale, dealers and auction houses have a duty to check the item against the register. If it's listed as lost or stolen, the ALR will then handle negotiations leading to its return in exchange for a fee.'

'What happens when an item is found?' asked Carruthers, curious to learn more about an area of police work he was unfamiliar with. He looked down at his scribbled notes.

'Often, when an item is found, it's owned by someone who has no idea it's been stolen because it's already been sold on,' said Stevenson.

'That must be tricky. I take it the new owner doesn't get to keep it? Or does it end up going to court?'

'Too expensive. It's in the interests of both parties involved to try to negotiate privately. It's different in every country, but generally if someone has bought it in good faith, not from the thief but from someone who has bought from the thief, and they've held it for six years, they may have a chance of holding on to it – but the whole business is complicated.'

Carruthers could feel his brows knit together as he listened. He asked a few more probing questions then thanked Stevenson and hung up. He stood up to get a fresh coffee whilst he digested the latest news. Picking up yesterday's dregs he headed to the bin with it. He had just started to walk away from his desk when his phone rang again. He doubled back and snatched the receiver.

'Detective Inspector Jim Carruthers,' he said. He winced as he said it. His demotion still rankled him. Thank God due to budget cuts the station hadn't yet got a new DCI and Carruthers was, for the time being anyway, allowed to keep his office. Felt a pain somewhere in his chest every time he thought about his demotion that had nothing to do with a family propensity to heart disease.

'Inspector Carruthers?' The faltering voice on the phone was female, heavily accented and sounded Eastern European.

'Yes, speaking. Who am I talking to?' He pulled his chair up and sat down on it. Placed the cold coffee back on the table.

'I don't want to give my name. I watched the news last night. I think I know who the girl in the picture is.'

'Where are you calling from?' He wondered how she'd got his number. The number given out on the TV had been for the incident room.

'Please, I don't want to say. I'm scared. Just listen. I think her name is Marika Paju.'

He grabbed a pen and paper. He asked her to spell it out to him. 'How do you know her?'

'We worked together. I was lucky. I got away. I can't tell you any more. It's too dangerous. I'm sorry for Marika. She was my friend.

But I told her they would never let her go. You should tell her family. They are good people.' The line went dead.

Carruthers swore. Putting the phone down he bolted out of his office shouting for Harris. 'Quick, we need to put a trace on a call that's just come in.'

At that moment Fletcher passed. Carruthers called her into his office. 'We've got a possible name for the dead girl. Marika Paju.'

'Marika Paju?' said Fletcher. 'I'm pretty good with names but I have no idea which country that name comes from. Sounds Eastern European, though.'

'The voice of the girl I spoke to was heavily accented. Could it be Polish?' said Carruthers.

'Hang on.' She reached for his phone and made a call.

As he waited, Carruthers sat again at his desk. Playing with his pen as he waited.

'It's Estonian,' Fletcher said when she put the phone down. 'Just spoke to that new girl in records, Paulina. She's Lithuanian but her boyfriend, Daniel, is Estonian and started in records a couple of weeks ago. As luck would have it he was standing right next to her.'

'How on earth do you women find out all these things about colleagues?'

Fletcher laughed. 'We listen. And ask questions. Lots of questions.'

Carruthers digested this. For once he was grateful for Fletcher's nosiness. 'OK, Andie, this might be a long shot but I want you to get in touch with the Estonian authorities. See if they have anyone by that name reported missing and send the dead girl's photo over to them. The woman on the phone sounded scared. I need to ring the NCA again. A request for data on a missing person like this normally moves through Interpol.' He repeated the brief conversation to Fletcher. 'It's not much to go on but it's all we've got.'

'Oh, I don't know. We have a possible name, at least,' said Fletcher.

'Might be a false one.'

The phone on Carruthers' desk rang. He picked up.

It was Dougie Harris's voice. 'That call you wanted traced. It's come from a phone box a couple of miles outside Castletown. I know the one. Unfortunately being rural there's no CCTV on it.'

Carruthers thanked Harris and ended the call. He threw his pen down. Took his glasses off and cleaned them. Carefully laying them down on his desk, he pinched the bridge of his nose.

'You look tired,' said Fletcher.

He looked at her without moving his hand. 'I am tired.'

She walked round his desk and put her hand on his shoulder. 'I'll make that call to Estonia,' she said. Carruthers sighed, stood, grabbed his wallet. He'd slept later than he'd meant this morning. Hadn't had a chance for breakfast. Or even coffee. He couldn't function without a hit of caffeine first thing in the morning. He left his office and went to the canteen. Took his bacon roll and double espresso back to his desk. He had just put the scalding cup to his lips when Harris stuck his head round the door.

* * *

'Well, at least we have something to go on, now,' said Fletcher. She turned to Watson. They were standing on yet another doorstep. So far even with the extra information, the door-to-door had drawn a blank. She was starting to feel tired. 'Looks like the girl may be Eastern European after all,' she said. 'Jim got me to phone the Estonian authorities about her. They're looking into it and getting back to us. And Interpol are on the case.'

Despite the blue sky there was a strong easterly bringing a welcome cool wind. Fletcher always enjoyed getting out of the office but especially now as the air con still hadn't been fixed. However, this was the twentieth doorstep they were on. She hoped the weather might be turning a bit cooler. Hadn't had a chance to listen to the weather forecast.

'Yes, but nobody seems to know who she is,' said Fletcher. 'Neither the name Marika Paju, nor the photograph has rung any bells.'

'Perhaps she hadn't been in the country long,' said Watson, knocking on another door.

Fletcher pulled a face. 'Or perhaps somebody kept her hidden away. Nobody knows the extent of sex trafficking in the UK. You know how it is. Girl from poor family promised well-paid au pair or bar job in another country. Ends up working as a prostitute. It happens, and more frequently than we like to think. Perhaps she managed to get away from her captors.'

'To end up dead on a Scottish beach,' said Watson. 'I wonder if her pregnancy had anything to do with her death? Mackie wasn't able to rule out suicide, was he? She wouldn't be the first to top herself in those circumstances. And if she is that girl, Marika Paju…'

Fletcher nodded. 'She may well have been in Scotland without family, without the support network of people to look after her. If she was working as a prostitute and found herself pregnant she'd more than likely be made to have a termination, although according to Jim, she was early stages of pregnancy.'

As she spoke, Fletcher thought of her own circumstances the year before. She had only just managed to get her head around the fact she'd fallen pregnant when she'd found out that Mark was not the solid, dependable man she hoped he'd be. He'd left her when she'd lost the baby. She'd recovered down at her parents' place in East Sussex. What would she have done had she not had their support? She swallowed hard. Had suicide ever entered her mind during those terrible months? No, she couldn't say it had, although she'd still been a mess when she'd finally returned to work.

There'd been a couple of incidents when she'd lost control. She felt the heat rise to her face when she thought of how she'd slapped Jim at work. What had she been thinking? What had she said when he'd told her to go for counselling? That she'd rather poke her eyes out with a stick. The situation hadn't improved. She'd come dangerously close to completely losing all sense of perspective. In the end he'd given her an ultimatum. See a counsellor or take a further extended period of time off work. Finally she'd seen a counsellor.

'Andie?' This from Watson. 'You OK? You seem miles away. I know it can get to you. You have to build some sort of wall. Not get too involved.'

Although Fletcher smiled at Watson the smile didn't reach her eyes. She was picturing the dead girl on the windswept and lonely stretch of beach, and despite what she'd said to Carruthers about being OK, she knew that it would be an image that would haunt her for a long time, especially now she knew the girl had been pregnant.

* * *

Several hours later, Carruthers and Fletcher were standing in his office. Carruthers spread out the photographs of the stolen paintings in front of him and looked at each in turn. *Where would these paintings be now,* he wondered?

Fletcher echoed his thoughts. She picked up a photograph of the Vettriano. 'I wonder if this is still even in the UK? Perhaps it's already been shipped overseas.' She turned to Carruthers. 'Where would it most likely go, do you think?'

He shrugged. 'The US? If it *is* overseas I wonder how they transport works of art?' That was something he hadn't considered. Who would buy such well-known pieces and how would they be transported? John Stevenson had said something about briefcases but Carruthers wondered about other methods of transport. A question played on his mind. As he leant across his desk to pick up his phone, Harris walked in.

'Boss, like I said earlier, I've been going over the various tradesmen again that the victims used. I think I might have something. The roofers the McMullans used were Forth Roofers. They were also used by the Warristons.'

Carruthers put his coffee cup down. His earlier cup had grown cold so he'd had to fix himself another. 'Good work. As soon as Gayle gets back, go over and interview them, will you? Find out what sort of outfit they are. How many do they employ? Where they were when the McMullans were getting robbed? In the meantime find out all you can about them.'

He returned to look at his photographs. Frowning, he picked up the phone and rang John Stevenson.

'I've got a question,' Carruthers said. 'How would works of art generally get transported out of the country?'

'A number of ways. We've known them to be carried in diplomats' bags.'

'Diplomats' bags?' said Carruthers.

'Think about it,' said Stevenson. 'Makes perfect sense. Diplomats don't get their luggage searched. They can take the paintings out of their frames, roll them up and get them out of the country that way. And it's not just artworks we're talking about, Jim. Drugs, guns, diamonds.'

Carruthers scratched his chin. Lurking somewhere in the back of his memory he did remember hearing about a diplomat being stung by a hidden camera whilst in the throes of negotiating a fee for taking stolen items out of the UK. Was it a diplomat from one of the African countries? He couldn't remember the details except when it came to light the staff of the embassy of that country had distanced themselves from the man arrested claiming that he was just a junior member of staff.

Brown walked in, interrupting Carruthers' train of thought. 'Boss,' he said, 'we've just had a phone call. Lad from Windygates has gone missing. It was his grandfather on the phone. Says it's totally out of character.'

'How long's he been missing?' asked Carruthers. His ears pricked up. The first anonymous call had come from a phone box in Windygates.

'They last saw him yesterday morning. Didnae come home after work.'

Carruthers wasn't unduly worried. Most mispers turned up and the boy hadn't been missing that long, no more than twenty-four hours. 'Where does he work?'

'Boss, yer going to love this. Barry Cuthbert's estate. He's an assistant gamekeeper.'

Carruthers' gut twisted. He knew the answer to his next question. 'Name?'

'Joe McGuigan.'

* * *

'That's the lad we interviewed yesterday.' Carruthers leapt up and grabbed his mobile, jacket and bagged binoculars. He felt alarm bells ringing. 'Right, tell Andie to meet me round the front. Fill her in. We'll go straight to the grandfather's home. In the meantime make some enquiries about this Joe McGuigan, will you? And I want a list of all those who work at the Cuthbert estate.'

'We don't normally do this,' said Brown. 'He's no' been missing that long.'

'I realise that but I've got a bad feeling. And, Willie, whilst we're gone, check out whether McGuigan or Sturrock are on file.'

Carruthers ignored Brown's grumbling about being overworked, thinking he'd been in the company of Harris too long, paid a quick visit to the Gents then headed out into the car park. Fletcher came running out of the building, her shoes clacking on the gravel, black shoulder bag over right shoulder, bottle of water in hand. She brushed a tendril of hair away which had been blown across her face as she opened the driver's side door.

'What's going on, Jim? How's this all connected? There is a connection, isn't there?'

Carruthers jammed his mobile into his shirt pocket, climbed into the passenger seat, slammed the door, buckled up and passed the bagged binoculars to Fletcher. 'Put these in your shoulder bag, will you? I wish I knew. C'mon. Let's get going. As you drive, you can fill me in on the research you've done on local airfields and flying schools.'

* * *

Carruthers brought out his police badge and held it up to Mrs McGuigan. 'We're here about your grandson. Can we come in?'

He assessed the older woman as he spoke. Comely and homely were two words that sprang to mind. She was wearing a patterned apron and had her grey hair swept up in a bun.

'Oh lord,' she said running her wet hands on her apron. 'Have you found him? Is he OK?'

'May we come in, please?'

Mrs McGuigan opened the door wider and, taking off her apron, stepped aside. Carruthers and Fletcher walked into a carpeted hall that looked like it was something out of a 1970s film set. *Perhaps they didn't have much money to do it up,* he thought. They were taken into a small cosy sitting room. The furniture was dated but the room was spotless.

'You said he didn't come home after work yesterday,' said Fletcher, remaining standing, taking out her notebook. 'When did you last see him?'

'About seven o'clock in the morning.' Mrs McGuigan dabbed at her eyes with a screwed-up tissue. 'He had breakfast with us.'

Mr McGuigan appeared from another room. The thin stooped man put his arm round his wife. 'We're early risers.'

'Does he live here permanently with you both?'

'Yes, his parents got killed when he was five,' said Mrs McGuigan. 'We've looked after him ever since. He's a lovely boy. Really, no bother.'

'I'm very sorry to hear that,' said Carruthers. 'How old is Joe, Mrs McGuigan?'

'Nineteen. It's his first proper job. We're so proud of him.'

'How did he seem when you last saw him?'

'Look, sit down, will you?' Mrs McGuigan pointed to a couple of battered old armchairs.

Fletcher and Carruthers both sat. The McGuigans sat on the sofa.

'That's one of the reasons we're so worried,' said Mrs McGuigan. 'He's not been himself for a few days. Bill here got the impression it was something to do with his work but he was very tight-lipped about it. Wouldn't say what was bothering him. He used to tell us everything but not anymore. Instead of talking to us he just got on with his chores.'

'Chores?'

'We find it a bit more difficult to keep the house clean. My husband's eyes aren't so good and my hip plays up. Can't afford a cleaner. Joe does a lot for us.' Carruthers was starting to form the impression that Joe McGuigan was a decent young man thanks to the love shown him by his grandparents.

'Why did you think it was his work that was bothering him if he didn't say?' said Carruthers. 'Could he not have had a falling out with a pal?'

'No. It was definitely work. He's normally so chatty about it but… well, the last few days he stopped talking about it. And then a couple of days ago he came home from work and he was really quite upset. He also seemed anxious.'

Around the time the girl was killed. 'And you don't know what had upset him or made him anxious?'

'No.'

'How long had he been working on the estate?' asked Fletcher.

'About five months.'

Not long, thought Carruthers. He was starting to put two and two together and he wasn't liking the result.

Changing tack he asked, 'Does your grandson own a pair of binoculars, Mr McGuigan?'

'Well, yes, being a gamekeeper…'

'He's also a keen birdwatcher,' said Mrs McGuigan.

'Is he?' Carruthers turned to Mrs McGuigan. 'If he was ever asked to take part in killing birds of prey he'd be upset?' *Upset,* thought Carruthers, *if he was indeed a keen twitcher the boy would have been devastated.* He thought of his own lapsed RSPB membership.

'Of course he would.'

'He's not in any trouble, is he?' said Mr McGuigan. 'I mean, you're not accusing him of something, are you?'

Carruthers ignored the question. 'This is a sensitive question but do you know whether your grandson has ever been asked to do anything illegal whilst working on the Cuthbert estate?'

'Like what?' asked Mrs McGuigan.

'Well, like poison birds of prey? We're not accusing him, Mrs McGuigan, we would just like to know how he would feel if he were asked to?'

Mrs McGuigan looked at her husband before answering. Carruthers could tell they were both genuinely shocked. 'He'd be terribly upset,' she said.

'He's never been in trouble with the law before?' asked Fletcher.

'No, of course not.'

'Can we see his binoculars now please, Mrs McGuigan?' asked Carruthers.

Mrs McGuigan stood up, smoothed down her skirt and left the room. Carruthers could feel the pulse in his neck throb. What was the betting she'd come back with an empty case? For once he hoped he was wrong. Carruthers tried smiling at Mr McGuigan but all he got in return was a worried look.

A few minutes later the door opened and Mrs McGuigan re-entered the room. 'He must have them with him,' she said. 'It's not unusual. He often takes them to work. All I've found is the empty case.' She held up the black casing.

Fletcher fished the plastic bag containing the binoculars from her bag and passed them to Carruthers. Carruthers with sinking heart handed them to Mr McGuigan. 'Are these your grandson's binoculars?'

Mr McGuigan took them, turning them over in his hands. He gave a puzzled look first to Fletcher then to Carruthers. 'They look like them. I don't understand. Where did you find them?' He then passed them to his wife who fitted them snugly into the empty case.

'Top of the cliffs, yards from where we discovered some poisoned meat,' said Carruthers. 'We found them the day we got an anonymous call about a girl's body on the beach over by Pinetum Park,' he continued.

Fletcher gave Mr McGuigan a copy of the artist's impression of the girl. The older man looked at the likeness but shook his head. Reaching up he passed it to his wife.

'They can't be Joe's,' was all Mrs McGuigan said.

'Mrs McGuigan,' said Carruthers, 'would Joe be likely to phone the local police station if he came across a crime?'

'Yes,' said Mr McGuigan.

Once again Carruthers wondered if their grandson had come across the woman's body when he'd been out laying contaminated meat to poison birds of prey. And been talked out of reporting it to the police, only to make an anonymous call instead.

If Joe McGuigan was a keen birdwatcher then clearly he would be greatly upset at being asked to do something not just illegal but, in the boy's eyes, immoral too. And if he'd come across the woman's torn body whilst doing that… well, he'd quite rightly be anxious. He didn't say any of this to the McGuigans. All he said instead was, 'Look, we interviewed your grandson yesterday afternoon–'

'So he got to work alright, then?' said Mrs McGuigan.

'Yes,' said Carruthers, 'but like I said, we interviewed him and we felt he knew a lot more than he was saying.'

'You think he might be in danger, don't you?' said Mr McGuigan.

Mrs McGuigan let out a cry, looked as if she might collapse. Fletcher sprung up and guided Mrs McGuigan back onto the sofa. Mr McGuigan reached out and put a comforting hand on his wife's arm.

'Find our grandson for us, will you,' said Mrs McGuigan.

'Can you give us a list of his friends? Phone numbers if you have them?' said Fletcher.

Mrs McGuigan nodded.

Carruthers stood up. 'Can we see his room? Would that be OK? It might give us something to go on.'

Mrs McGuigan looked over at her husband. He shrugged. 'I don't know why you'd want to see it, but I can't see that it would hurt. It's the second on the left up the stairs.'

Carruthers and Fletcher took the stairs. The door to the boy's room was shut. Carruthers turned the door handle and walked in. The room felt stuffy. As he switched the light on, they looked round. It was a small room, crammed full of belongings. There were children's board games in one corner with a bunch of football magazines. Carruthers flicked through them. Some were very old. Carruthers imagined that Joe McGuigan had had the room since being a wee lad, perhaps since he arrived as a bewildered five-year-old orphan. He guessed the McGuigans were in their eighties which meant they would have been in their sixties when they took Joe in. A hell of an undertaking for a couple of that age to take in a five-year-old child.

He looked around him. There was a bookcase. He went over and ran his finger over some of the books' spines. Most of them were about birds and wildlife, some were on fitness. A painting of a Lancaster bomber was on the wall. He opened a few drawers. Socks and pants. Then he looked under the bed. He found a really old copy of *Nuts* magazine. No doubt Joe had had to smuggle that into the house some time back. He was surprised. Most young men nowadays looked at that sort of stuff on their mobile phones.

Nothing in the room to help us. It was an ordinary room of a young man who had left his boyhood behind and was now navigating the sometimes treacherous waters of young adulthood. But what must it have been like for Joe to have grown up with people two generations older than him? Especially after losing his parents the way he had? If he had gone off the rails a bit would it have been surprising? But Joe McGuigan did not sound like a young man who was going off the rails. He sounded like a thoroughly decent lad.

Carruthers and Fletcher went back downstairs. Mr and Mrs McGuigan were standing close together at the foot of the stairs. Mrs McGuigan gave Carruthers a sheet of paper.

'The list you asked for, of his friends. We don't know his most recent friends very well but he's still in touch with his school friends and we know them.'

Carruthers took the sheet of paper, folded it and put it in his shirt pocket. 'We'll do our best to find your grandson,' he said. 'And if he turns up make sure you give us a ring, will you?'

Mr McGuigan nodded.

They said goodbye to the older couple. As the door shut on them Fletcher turned to Carruthers. 'What do you think?' She had to raise her voice over the sound of the wind. Carruthers didn't remember the weather being quite so breezy earlier in the day.

Carruthers shook his head, rubbing the stubble on his chin. 'I don't know, but I don't like it.'

'I don't want to jump to conclusions,' said Fletcher, walking towards their car, 'but do you think this boy could be one of our poisoners? Out laying poison. Seen something he shouldn't. Left in a hurry, dropped the binoculars and made the anonymous phone call to us?'

'It's a theory. Why do you think he's disappeared?' said Carruthers.

'Either he's scared and in hiding or someone's caught up with him and silenced him before he could blow the whistle.' She opened the car door.

Carruthers was silent for a moment. He had his hand on his door handle. 'It's possible. It would make sense, although if he's been silenced it's unlikely to be over birds of prey.'

'Perhaps he saw what happened to the dead girl.'

'There's also numerous other things that could have happened,' said Carruthers, climbing into the car. Fletcher did the same. He shut the door. She followed suit. 'Perhaps he's gone out on a bender with friends and is sleeping it off somewhere?'

'Do you really think so? That sounds out of character. He sounds like the sort of person who would have at least phoned his grandparents. Stop them from worrying. What's our next plan of action?'

'Back to the estate. Interview Barry Cuthbert and Derek Sturrock again and get hold of the elusive estate manager.'

Six

They found Cuthbert out in his garden practising his golf. He was struggling against the wind which was tearing at his trousers. He looked up at them. 'The best golfers are the ones who can play in all weathers,' he said.

Carruthers looked at the man with disdain; salmon pink trousers and purple striped shirt. *He might have money,* thought Carruthers, *but he has no idea how to dress himself.* He wondered if there was a regular woman in Cuthbert's life. He suspected not, although he also suspected there wouldn't be any shortage of beautiful, disposable females.

Laying his club down, Cuthbert asked, 'What is it this time?'

'We're here to make enquiries about Joe McGuigan. He hasn't been seen since yesterday afternoon,' said Carruthers. Cuthbert looked at them blankly. 'We interviewed him yesterday,' confirmed Carruthers.

Cuthbert selected another golf club from his caddy. 'I have a good number of staff on my books. Some are temporary, often seasonal.' He dropped a golf ball on the ground. It rolled away from his feet. He bent over, picked it up and dropped it again. He took a practice shot. 'Name isn't familiar.'

'Like I said, we interviewed him yesterday. He was with Derek Sturrock. Remember? The two gamekeepers you didn't want us speaking to.'

'I know them by face. Not all their names. How long did you say he'd been missing?'

'Since yesterday, Barry. Is there something wrong with your hearing or is this a stalling tactic? You don't sound too worried if I may say so.'

Cuthbert took a swing at the ball and drove it 250 yards or so. Shielded his eyes to see where it had fallen. 'Not bad in this wind.' He looked over at Carruthers. 'He's not been missing long. Don't you normally wait forty-eight hours after someone's been reported missing?'

Carruthers ignored the question. 'We have reason to believe that one of the bird poisoners saw the body on the beach and rang it in anonymously. The call came from Windygates which is where Joe McGuigan lives. He's now missing.'

'I've already told you my gamekeepers don't poison birds of prey. It didn't even happen on the estate. You have absolutely nothing that links me or anyone here to poisoned meat, the body on the beach or a missing gamekeeper.'

'Except Joe McGuigan works for you, Barry,' said Carruthers. 'I find it a bit of a coincidence that the day after I come to talk to you one of your gamekeepers goes missing.'

Carruthers cast his eye over to the golf club lying on the grass. He picked it up. Felt its weight. 'Nice golf club. Expensive. Belong to a club, do you?'

'All my things are expensive,' Cuthbert said. 'I like nice things. It's not a crime.'

'Which golf club do you belong to?' asked Fletcher.

'Carrockhall.'

Same as Bingham and McMullan, thought Carruthers. 'Do you know a man called McMullan?' he asked. 'Belongs to Carrockhall Golf Club, too?'

Barry thought for a moment. 'Victim of a recent robbery?'

Carruthers nodded.

'I know him.'

'Do you know the other victims, Barry?' Carruthers consulted his black notebook. 'The Ashburtons and the Warristons?'

Barry Cuthbert shrugged. 'It's a small place.'

'There seems to be a spate of art thefts in the area, Mr Cuthbert. I couldn't help but notice you have some half-decent paintings. If you have any tradesmen in the house, keep a note of who you use, will you? And if your gamekeeper turns up will you let us know, please?' said Fletcher.

'And your elusive estate manager hasn't been in touch with us yet,' said Carruthers. 'We still want to speak with him.'

'I'll pass the message on,' said Cuthbert.

'Just one more thing,' said Carruthers. 'Have you heard of a woman named Marika Paju? She may be Estonian.'

Cuthbert shook his head. 'No. I don't know any Estonians.'

Carruthers drew the artist's impression out of his jacket pocket and presented it to Cuthbert. 'Have a proper look, Barry. I want you to call a meeting of your staff, show them this photograph and ask them if they know this girl or know the name, Marika Paju. Call it your civic duty, Barry. After all, yours is the nearest estate to where her body was found and you're this area's largest employer.'

He motioned to Fletcher and they walked off, leaving Barry Cuthbert to select another golf club from the caddy. Cuthbert gave the impression of nonchalance but Carruthers knew Cuthbert would be digesting every word said.

'Oh, Barry,' Carruthers shouted over his shoulder, 'don't go far. Chances are we'll need to talk to you again.'

* * *

'Did you notice how evasive he was?' said Fletcher. 'But he's right. We're clutching at straws. We've got nothing on him and apart from some poisoned meat we don't even know if a crime's been committed. The girl may have been suicide, the boy might turn up, after all he's only been missing since yesterday afternoon and the bird poisoners may not even be from this estate.'

They opened the car doors. 'Get on to the station, Andie, will you?' said Carruthers. 'Set up a team brief for later today. I want to know if anyone's made a connection in the cases of all these different art thefts.'

'Do you think that's going to help us with the missing boy?'

Carruthers shrugged. 'No idea.' He buckled up, shutting his door.

Some thirty minutes later Carruthers was standing by the incident board scanning the room. He'd gone straight from his car into the stuffy briefing room. No coffee. No bathroom break. 'Dead girl, missing boy, poisoned birds, high-end art thefts,' he said. 'It's a bit of a coincidence that so many things have happened in such a small place like this. What's the connection?'

He looked round at the expectant faces. Harris with a pen behind his ear, Gayle Watson fanning her face with a file, Fletcher, poised with legs crossed, notebook on lap. They were getting so used to the broken air conditioning it wasn't even being mentioned in conversation anymore. Two days ago they would have all been moaning about it.

'We're getting nowhere fast,' he said. 'We need to start bringing in some results.' He consulted his own notebook. 'The Ashburtons robbed on the 13th July; the Warristons robbed on the 27th July and the McMullans robbed on the 7th August. What have they all got in common?'

'All rich and well connected,' said Fletcher. 'But,' she flicked through her notebook, 'in terms of tradesmen, none had the same tradesmen in common. The Ashburtons had a new drive put in on 20th to 23rd June by a company called Dream Drives, the Warristons had window cleaners in May 27th and a plumber on 5th June and the McMullans had roofers in on 30th June. Same roofers used by the Warristons. All companies have been checked, all are legit and from what we can see, they're all clean.'

Carruthers sighed. He raked through his short greying hair. 'What about hobbies?'

He remembered Cuthbert swinging his golf club in his grounds. 'I've just had an idea. All these victims are people of a certain age and class. Without generalising, what would their hobbies be?'

'Bridge is popular amongst a certain class,' said Fletcher.

'Gayle, what are Mr Ashburton's hobbies? Is he a bridge player?'
'I don't think so.'

'No,' said Carruthers. 'What about golf? The McMullans are members of Carrockhall Golf Club as is Cuthbert. Andie, I want you to check the Ashburtons and Warristons. See if they're members, too.'

At that moment Detective Constable Brown put his head round the door. 'Boss', he said to Carruthers, 'you've got a call.'

Carruthers frowned. 'You can see I'm leading a brief. Take a message, will you?'

Brown didn't budge. 'Think you'll want to take this. It's the Policja on the phone.'

'The who?'

'Estonian police.'

Fletcher stood up. 'That's my call.'

'I'll get it,' said Carruthers. He left the room and followed Brown to the station phone. He took the phone from Brown. 'Inspector Jim Carruthers here.'

'Hello, this is Olev Lepp from the police in Tallinn. I was told you are interested in a girl called Marika Paju. As I just told Interpol we have a girl of that name known to the police. A runaway from home. Reported missing by her parents.'

Carruthers felt a shiver of anticipation.

'As I'm sure you are aware we ordinarily give very little information over the phone but your details have been verified and in this instance we are happy to proceed. We have had a few sightings of Marika Paju. Think she may have become a lady of the evening. We have many gangs here that run girls. Unfortunately, although she's known to the police as a runaway we don't have her DNA on our files.'

'A lady of the night, you mean? A prostitute?' said Carruthers, disappointed that they didn't have her DNA. 'She turned up in Scotland.'

'Oh well, this is good news. She made a new life for herself.'

'Oh no, you misunderstand me. She's turned up dead on a beach in Fife.'

'This is terrible news.' He sounded genuinely upset, thought Carruthers, wondering if perhaps he had a daughter the same age.

'She has blonde hair, a tattoo on her ankle,' said Carruthers. 'Does this sound like the same girl? I'm afraid her face is a bit of a mess.'

'I'd have to double check. I don't remember hearing about a tattoo but she had blonde hair. Can you describe the tattoo?'

'I'll email you a copy of the photograph we took alongside pictures of the dead girl and the artist's impression we had done; like I say, the face was a bit of a mess. We'll also send in a sample of her DNA to you. If you can give us a positive ID on her we'll need to get someone to fly in to formally identify her.' Carruthers took note of the email address he'd been given and finished the call.

He left the station desk and put his head round the briefing room door. 'We're one step closer to establishing the identity of the dead girl. There's a girl called Marika Paju, a runaway, known to the Tallinn Police. A possible prostitute. I need to wait on a call back from Tallinn. But this tallies with our mysterious phone caller and what she said about her friend, although we still need to keep an open mind. Team briefing over. We'll resume it at 8am tomorrow. Andie, can I borrow you for a moment?'

Fletcher stood up and walked towards him. 'I need the details, including the photograph of the dead girl's tattoo and the artist's impression, emailed to this address. Can you do it now?'

'Yes, boss.'

'Oh Dougie,' Carruthers said as Harris was set to pass by him. 'Any joy on the criminal records front?'

Harris looked sheepish.

'Just get it done, OK?' Carruthers strode over to the coffee machine and fixed himself a double espresso. As he was taking his first sip he heard a shout behind him and swung round. Brown was walking down the corridor.

'That's Tallinn on the phone again, boss.'

Christ, that was quick, he thought. Taking another swig at the coffee, and in the process burning his mouth, he strode after Brown.

* * *

It was a clear line. 'I have the picture of the tattoo in front of me,' said Lepp. 'I had to call you straight back. You know what this tattoo means?'

'No.' Carruthers could feel his pulse quicken as he held his breath. 'So the tattoo is familiar to you?'

'Yes, indeed. We have seen this tattoo many times recently.'

'Go on,' said Carruthers. He had picked up a pen and motioned for Fletcher to find him something to write on.

'It's the mark of the Haravere gang in Tallinn. They're a particularly vicious gang of pimps. Brand their prostitutes like cattle. The eye and tear drop is a symbol of Lucifer. The leaders of the gang are brothers, Aleks and Marek Voller. The older, Marek, calls himself, Kurat – the devil.'

'Can you give me a positive ID on the girl?' asked Carruthers.

'Looks similar to the girl reported missing. It may be Marika Paju,' said Lepp.

'We need to get in touch with her parents,' continued Carruthers, feeling excitement mounting. At last. A breakthrough. 'See if they can fly over to identify her.' *If it is her.* 'Can you give me any other information on the Vollers and their gang?'

'They don't just run high-class prostitutes. They are involved in people trafficking. Very nasty. Also drugs.'

Carruthers swallowed hard. People traffickers. And they'd arrived in Scotland. Or at least one of their victims had. Carruthers glanced at his watch. After a short exchange of conversation Carruthers thanked Lepp, who promised to stay in touch. Bypassing the coffee machine he made a beeline for Harris.

'No joy, boss,' said Harris. 'Computer systems are down. It'll have to wait til morning.'

'Shit,' said Carruthers. 'Bring back the good old days, eh. We could have found that information out by now. First thing tomorrow, Dougie. Hear me?'

'I'm only as good as the computer systems, boss,' Harris said in an aggrieved voice.

Which is fucking useless, thought Carruthers. Harris was, in fact, even more useless than a temperamental computer. Finally though, he felt, they were starting to get somewhere in the investigation. He'd left Olev Lepp and the Tallinn Police to contact Marika Paju's parents so that was one monkey off his back.

He did three more hours of work. Feeling tired, he shut his computer down. His stomach growled. He should get some supper. He looked at his watch. Knowing she often ate late, he picked up the phone and called Gill McLaren.

* * *

Carruthers brought the pint up to his lips. Took a deep drink of it. It left a foaming moustache above his top lip, which he wiped away with the back of his hand. He was sitting in his new favourite chair in a corner of the Waterfront. There was a live folk band playing. He had only meant to go in for one but ended up having three. He remembered the night he'd taken Jodie Pettigrew, the pathology assistant, to the Dreel Tavern for a meal. A wave of sadness came over him. That hadn't ended well. Much like all the other relationships he'd had.

The front door of the pub opened. Carruthers looked up. In walked Gill McLaren.

'Glad you could make it,' Carruthers shouted over the noise of the band.

'I got delayed,' she mouthed. 'Forth Road Bridge again. It was a bit hairy coming over in this wind.'

'It's still blowy.'

She nodded taking a seat. 'See you've made a start without me,' she said glancing at his pint.

The song came to an end to generous applause and the band announced they were taking a break. 'So tell me about this conference you're attending tomorrow, then,' said Carruthers.

'It's a seed science conference in Castletown. I'm deputising for a colleague who's fallen ill. Thought I'd make a weekend of it.

I'm in a B&B here in Anstruther.' She picked up a menu. 'How are you getting on in the investigation?'

Carruthers pulled a face.

'Oh dear. As well as that? That why you on the booze?'

Carruthers grimaced. Putting his pint once more to his lips he asked, 'No more news on the meat laced with poison, I suppose? Sorry, I'm forgetting my manners. Would you like a drink?'

'Diet coke, please.'

Carruthers fought his way to the bar, bought the diet coke then walked back to their table, handing the drink to Gill, who smiled her thanks.

'You were just about to tell me about the poison?' said Carruthers.

'It's a common enough toxin,' said Gill. 'Meat was fresh so had only been out there a day or so. I've found something of interest for you, though.'

'Oh yes, what's that?'

'The RSPB organises walks around Pinetum Park dunes on the lookout for sea eagles. They've been hugely successful. They usually see at least one sea eagle. That's not all though. These sea eagles or white-tailed eagles, as they're also known, are fitted with transmitters. Sometimes you can see them actually being released into the wild.'

'So it's more than likely they were after sea eagles?'

'Indeed. Beautiful birds. We got one into the SASA lab once. A few years ago, now. That was a case of poisoning. The wingspan is simply enormous. It caused quite a stir. I think everyone who was in the building that day came to take a look. Even the on-site massage therapist. Anyway, as much as we both love birds, you don't want to talk sea eagles all evening. Have there been any developments in the body on the beach case?'

Carruthers thought back to when the body on the beach had been found.

'There has been one development,' he said.

'Oh yes?'

He stared into Gill's blue eyes. 'We've been making enquiries at the nearby Ardgarren Estate. It's a shooting estate so an obvious starting point. We reckon whoever laid the meat may have left the binoculars and called in the body. Anonymously. It's a theory anyway and at the moment we don't have much else to go on. We interviewed the two gamekeepers of Cuthbert's.'

'Sounds sensible,' said Gill. 'So what's the development?'

'One of them, the young lad, has disappeared.'

Gill whistled. 'Foul play?'

'Let's hope not. We already have one body to deal with. Don't want two.'

The waitress came over. A thin girl with dyed pink hair Carruthers hadn't seen before. 'We're just taking last orders for food,' she lisped. He noticed she had her tongue pierced. Wondered if the piercing had been recent. He had heard that the tongue swelled when pierced and could imagine it might cause a temporary lisp. He wondered if it hurt. After studying the menus for a few moments they ordered their meals. Gill plumped for scampi and chips. Carruthers went for a favourite dish of his – steak and ale pie.

'So what is the latest on the body on the beach?' Gill prompted.

Carruthers unravelled his knife and fork from its red paper serviette and placed the serviette on his lap.

'You're keen,' said Gill with a laugh. 'Are those pot noodles really that bad?'

Carruthers smiled then looked serious. 'We may have identified the girl. She's possibly Estonian.' He didn't tell Gill that Marika, if it was the same girl, had been known to the Estonian police, was in the early stages of pregnancy or that her presumably heartbroken family were flying over from Estonia to try to identify her.

'Did the tattoo help identify her?'

'Yes, in a manner of speaking, it did.' Again, he didn't want to impart too much information, even to a friend. 'We still don't know what the link is between the cases yet…' Perhaps they didn't know the link, he thought, but having spoken to the Estonian police they'd found out the meaning of the tattoo. It had been the tattoo that had given them their breakthrough. And it had meant something. It had been a mark of ownership.

'You really think there is one?'

Carruthers laughed. 'We don't believe in coincidence in the police. But we do believe in cause and effect.'

'I'm not sure I follow you.'

'Sorry. Just ignore me. Thinking aloud. I'm not sure I know what I'm talking about myself.' He laughed. But as he said that he was thinking about the disappearance of young Joe McGuigan. He was sure the boy hadn't gone on a bender. Was convinced something more sinister had happened to him. Perhaps because of something he'd seen. There it was. Cause and effect.

The steaming plates of food arrived. Carruthers could feel the saliva building in his mouth. He was seriously hungry. As he speared a piece of meat, the band took their positions once more on the stage, making further conversation impossible. Instead they shared a smile and ate in companionable silence.

Once the band had finished their final set, Carruthers fell into easy conversation with Gill. They chatted like old friends. Carruthers watched her as she talked, so bubbly and full of life. He liked the way her cheeks shone with a rosy glow in the warmth of the pub and loved the way her blue eyes sparkled. He was surprised to find he was still thinking of her long after they'd called it a night and he had gone to bed.

* * *

The following day Carruthers was at his desk by 8am again. By 8:30am he was leading the team brief. That morning he'd put on the lightest shirt he could find, short-sleeved white cotton. It was already sticking to his back. Despite it being overcast the weather was still humid and if it kept up like this he knew he'd need another shower by lunchtime.

'Right, we're finally starting to move with the investigation into the body on the beach,' he said. 'The Estonian authorities have been in touch to say that twenty-six-year-old Marika Paju was reported missing on July 18th from a suburb just outside Tallinn. Her parents are flying over to ID the body.'

'What was she doing in the UK?' asked Harris. 'Come to scrounge, like the rest of 'em?'

'Oh, shut up, Dougie,' said Fletcher.

'It seems she was a prostitute,' said Carruthers. 'Being run by a bunch of human traffickers in the Tallinn area. Tallinn Police managed to speak with a couple of the girl's friends. Seems she wanted to make a new life for herself in the UK. Had always wanted to live in Scotland. Felt we were more welcoming of immigrants than other parts of the UK.'

That at least had the effect of shutting Harris up. Carruthers hadn't been unaware of the glare Fletcher had given Harris.

'This,' said Carruthers, lifting up the photograph of the girl's tattoo and tapping it, 'has meaning.' He'd got their attention. Even Harris seemed interested and had stopped glancing at his *Racing Post*, which he clearly thought Carruthers couldn't see under his file. 'The Estonian police identified it as being a tattoo that a particular group of pimps use to brand their prostitutes.' Even as he said it he started to feel sick again. And sick that someone should have been subjected to that lifestyle. 'Apparently one of her friends gave her money. Enough to get across from Estonia, at least. What happened between the time she left Estonia and when she ended up on a Fife beach, we don't yet know.'

There was a momentary quiet in the room as the officers considered the point.

'We need to find out,' Carruthers continued. 'And we still don't know whether it was an accident, suicide or something altogether more sinister. There is a chance her pimps might have tracked her down.'

'All the way to Scotland?' asked Harris. 'Seems unlikely.'

'Dougie is right,' said Fletcher. 'Unless she had information about them and they wanted her silenced.'

'Gayle, I want you to speak with immigration,' said Carruthers. 'See if you can find any record of a Marika Paju coming into the country. Could be a flight or ferry. Anything. See what you can find.'

'Do we know how long she's likely to have been in Scotland?' asked Watson.

'Police think she may have left Tallinn in the middle of July, and her parents reported her missing earlier in the month, so not long.' Carruthers looked around the room. 'OK, I'm taking it nobody's come forward locally to say they knew the girl?'

There was a shaking of heads. 'OK. Keep asking around. Once again, I'd like you to extend the area.'

'Andie,' said Carruthers, 'I want you with me when I talk to Marika Paju's parents.' Fletcher nodded. 'Right,' he said, pulling open another notebook, 'let's move on to our art thefts. Andie, what did you find out about the airfields and flying schools?'

Fletcher opened her black notebook and read from it. 'I've spoken to Fife Flying Club, based in Glenrothes. There's also a flying school here in Castletown. I'm getting a list of everyone who's attended or who's taken up a plane in the last twelve months. I've got to be honest. I've spoken to both managers and neither remember any unusual requests to circle particular areas or to take photographs. They're asking all the trainers.'

'OK.' Carruthers squeezed the back of his neck. It felt tight and sore. Maybe he'd slept at a funny angle. 'We seem to be drawing lots of blanks at the moment. Keep at it. How are we doing on the golf club membership?'

'There might be something in that,' said Fletcher. 'All three victims were members of Carrockhall Golf Club.'

Carruthers glanced at Harris and said, 'Dougie, have you managed to run checks to see if anyone working at Carrockhall has a criminal record?'

'Derek Sturrock's got a criminal record for theft.'

Carruthers looked questioningly at Harris, who had a broad smile.

'Has he now?' said Carruthers.

'There's more,' said Harris.

'Are you going to share it with the rest of us?' asked Carruthers.

'Barry Cuthbert. Breaking and entering from when he was a teenager and a short stint inside when he was in his thirties. For burglary.' Dougie Harris sat back, placing his hands above his head, looking pleased with himself.

'Well, well, well,' said Carruthers. 'We keep coming back to Mr Barry Cuthbert, don't we? So our illustrious Barry "I-like-expensive-things" Cuthbert not only has a criminal record for theft, he is also a member of the same golf club as our three art theft victims, likes his expensive works of art and employs a gamekeeper who is currently missing. Not only that, but the senior gamekeeper has also got a criminal record for theft.'

'Was there anything on the elusive estate manager, Pip McGuire?'

'Nothing under that name.'

'And nothing on Joe McGuigan?'

'No. He's clean.'

'Back to Cuthbert's, sir?' asked Fletcher.

'We've got nothing on him,' said Carruthers. 'But I want him watched closely. I want a tail put on him.'

'We don't have the manpower,' said Harris. 'Will Bingham give us more muscle?'

'Leave Superintendent Bingham to me,' said Carruthers.

Suddenly Brown put his head round the door.

'You're developing a habit of interrupting team briefs. What is it this time, Willie? Had better be good.'

'I just thought you'd want to know that Pip McGuire has arrived. I've put *him* in your office.'

'Thank you, Willie.'

Brown disappeared after he'd winked at Carruthers. Carruthers wondered what the wink was all about.

Carruthers wrapped up the meeting and headed back to his office. He opened the door and found himself surprised and face to face with Barry Cuthbert's estate manager.

'Philippa McGuire.' As she said her name the woman rose to her feet. 'Everyone calls me Pip.'

Carruthers tried not to stare but it was difficult. She was about five foot nine inches and wearing jodhpurs and a riding jacket. A smell of horse clung to the air. A partly drunk cup of tea sat on the edge of his desk, Carruthers wondered where on earth Brown had found a china cup in this station. But then Brown was a sucker for a pretty face. And he lived very close by. Carruthers wouldn't be surprised to hear that Brown had dashed home just for the cup and saucer.

'You've been very elusive, Ms McGuire. But thank you for coming to the station.' Carruthers wanted to add the word 'finally' but resisted. 'Please,' he gestured for the woman to sit. 'Take a seat.'

As she sat down demurely, Carruthers assessed her. She looked only late twenties but surely she must have been older. Perhaps she had one of those ageless faces that some women were graced with. *Yes,* Carruthers decided, *she must be early thirties.* But even so, he found it an odd appointment. He couldn't imagine her getting involved in anything or with anyone dodgy, and Barry Cuthbert had 'fake' written all over him.

'Why did you want to see me?' She broke the silence and his thoughts were that she had a cut-glass English accent. Carruthers got the impression this was a woman far from timid. He took in her manicured nails, blonde hair swept up in a ponytail and expensive looking diamond earrings. And she most certainly had what the upper classes called 'breeding'.

He cleared his throat. 'Ms McGuire, how long have you been Barry Cuthbert's estate manager?'

Pip appeared amused by the question.

'A little over a year.'

Carruthers realised that they were each sizing the other up. He could tell that she had already worked out that he was surprised by her age and gender.

'Ms McGuire, how much do you know about Barry Cuthbert?'

'I have a very close working relationship with Barry but that's as far as it goes. We're not friends outside work.'

Carruthers chose his next words with care. 'I imagine you would need to have in order to manage the running of his estate.' He noticed though that she hadn't actually answered his question.

She smiled at him but Carruthers could see that the smile was false. There was a coldness in her eyes. She was most certainly ambitious, thought Carruthers. Of course, nothing wrong with that. He wondered what salary she commanded in order to be able to buy herself the diamond ring and expensive earrings. It was of course also entirely conceivable that they were family heirlooms.

'What are your duties?' he asked.

'I am sure you know what an estate manager does,' she said. 'My official title is CEO of Cuthbert Estates.'

'I would assume you are responsible for hiring staff?'

She nodded.

'In that case did you hire Joe McGuigan?'

'I did.' Her face suddenly clouded. 'I hear he's gone missing. He's expected back on duty tomorrow. I'll have to find someone to replace him if he doesn't turn up.'

Carruthers wondered if Pip McGuire had a bit of a callous streak.

She seemed to sense the thought. 'Has he been found?'

'Not yet. You don't know why he'd go missing?'

'No, of course not. Why would I?'

Carruthers reached over to his desk. Brought out a buff file and took out the photographs of the dead girl. He passed them to Pip. 'We left copies with Barry but just in case he didn't show you them…'

She took the photos. He scrutinised her face as she looked at them. She leant forward and gave the photos back to Carruthers. She didn't flinch. Why was that? Wouldn't that be the normal reaction? He had the feeling she'd worked hard at making her facial expression unreadable. He wondered why.

'No, I haven't seen them, but I've been pretty tied up the last day or so,' she said. 'I haven't had a chance yet to have a proper meeting with Barry. We try to meet up every few days to touch base,' she explained. 'I've never seen this girl before. Who is she?'

Carruthers wasn't entirely sure whether he believed her but he didn't push it.

'We think she may have been an Eastern European prostitute run by a gang of people traffickers from Tallinn. She had a tattoo on her ankle of an eye with a tear drop. Apparently that's the mark of the Haravere gang. But what she's doing over here in Fife and what, if any, connection she has with your employer, is a mystery. A mystery I mean to unravel.' Carruthers held Pip McGuire with his unblinking gaze. 'If you know anything at all about this girl or any illegal activities that Barry Cuthbert is engaged in, including poisoning birds of prey, now is the time to tell me.'

Pip in turn fixed Carruthers with a steady gaze. 'To the best of my knowledge Barry is not involved in any illegal activities, certainly none to which I am party.'

To the best of my knowledge, thought Carruthers. He did not like that expression. It told him the person in front of him was probably lying. 'Did you know he has a criminal record?' he asked.

She frowned. 'No, I didn't. I take it the police record is not recent?'

Carruthers had to admit that it wasn't. 'The past doesn't interest me,' Pip said. 'It's what a person is like now that matters.'

'And you said you don't socialise with Barry Cuthbert outside work?'

'I work long hours but no, I don't. I like to keep my work and my personal life separate.'

In other words, don't ask me any questions about what Cuthbert gets up to in his free time as I either don't know or I'm going to pretend I don't know.

Well, that's me told, thought Carruthers. He looked at this assured young woman in front of him. Decided she was a very cool customer. She had an interesting choice of words. When she spoke, she sounded much older than her years. He decided for now she was off the hook but she was definitely someone to keep a close eye on.

He changed tack. 'You will be aware of the recent spate of art thefts in the area, Ms McGuire, and as estate manager I'm sure it won't have escaped your notice that Barry has some very expensive pieces of art. I would recommend making sure they are fully insured and it might even be an idea to review your security.'

'I'll bear that in mind.'

'You said you worked for Cuthbert Estates. That implies Barry has more than one estate?'

'Just the one. The Ardgarren Estate.'

'Yet his business is called the Cuthbert Estates.'

Pip shrugged. 'You'd have to ask Barry.' She stood up, confident that she could terminate the meeting with Carruthers.

Carruthers followed suit.

'I need to get back to my hack,' she said. 'Do you ride?'

Carruthers shuddered. He was a little scared of horses but of course would never admit it. 'No. What's a hack?' he asked feeling a little stupid.

'A ride. I need to get back to my ride.'

As he escorted the glamorous woman out of the station, Carruthers wondered if she was riding more than just the horses.

Carruthers returned to his office and shut the door. He could still smell the scent of horse above the lingering perfume worn by Pip McGuire. He wondered what her story was. There was something that intrigued Carruthers about her. She certainly wasn't your average estate manager, that was for sure. He sat back at his desk steepling his hands, taking in her faint citrus perfume. He hadn't been sitting there more than five minutes when he heard running down the corridor and a sharp knock at the door.

'Come,' he shouted. Brown put his head round the door. Carruthers noticed the man was out of breath. And from the look on his face it seemed he had a big secret to share. Carruthers didn't think he had come to tell him the air conditioning man had arrived.

'Thought you'd want to know as soon as possible. Just had a phone call from a member of the public. Body's just been pulled out the water down by West Castle Beach.'

'Shit,' said Carruthers. 'Does it look like a drowning?'

'Well, he might have drowned,' said Brown, loving every moment of imparting an important piece of news. 'But he's also been shot. Bloody big hole in his chest.'

* * *

Carruthers could feel the wetness of the sea spray on his face as he ran down the wide expanse of sandy beach. The wind had picked up once more, buffeting the already choppy waves, creating white froth and foaming puddles of seawater. The sky was a stormy grey, a definite weather front pushing in from the north. Carruthers tasted salt, wiped his gritty stinging eyes. Sometimes these summer storms in Scotland were worse than winter ones.

In the distance he saw coverall-wearing figures huddled over an object on the sand. He saw one of them shout out, but the cry was lost as another gust of squally wind stole the sound away. As he drew closer he saw the body of the man, partially covered with sand and moss-green fronds of seaweed. The man was lying on his back. There was a gaping red hole in his chest.

Carruthers looked at the face, what was left of it. Skin and flesh were torn away in the cheeks where the body had been battered by rocks.

'Jesus Christ,' said Carruthers, stopping short.

Dr Mackie was on one knee, struggling to maintain his balance as the wind sent another gust up the beach. Liu, the police photographer, setting up his camera, was muttering about the weather conditions. He started to take a series of photos of the body from different angles, the startling white flash of his camera contrasting with the brooding darkness of the glowering sky.

'There's not time to erect a tent, Jim,' shouted Mackie over the noise of the wind, 'tide's still coming in. We need to get the photos and take him back to the mortuary. I can tell you one thing, though.

This one hasn't fallen from rocks. He's been in the water a fair few hours.' Carruthers saw Mackie glance at the churning sea. 'You couldn't survive in that sea for long but then again from the state of his chest I'd say it's almost a certainty it was the shot that killed him. With this amount of damage you might be looking at a shotgun.' As he spoke another enormous wave broke and one of the uniforms, who was nearer the sea, had to make a run for it as the advancing water snapped at his trouser legs.

Carruthers heard a noise behind him and swung round to see a damp-looking Fletcher arriving. Her hair was in rats' tails. He had forgotten all about her. She doubled over, holding her stomach, rain dripping off her dark hair.

'Are you OK?' he asked.

'Stitch. Is it him? The McGuigan boy?' She was still bent double and breathless.

'I don't know. Any ID on him?' Carruthers addressed this question to the uniform he took to be first on the scene, who was in the process of shaking off his soaking black trouser legs.

'Haven't touched anything, sir. Thought it best to wait for you.'

'The report we had was he got pulled from the water. Is that true?' said Carruthers.

'I'm not sure, sir. I wasn't here when he was found. It was PC McNeil.'

'Where's McNeil now?' said Carruthers.

The dark-haired police officer ran the back of his hand over his wet nose. 'Answering another emergency call that came in.'

Carruthers swore. 'Get him to phone me at the station as soon as, will you?'

The terrified PC nodded.

'Who found him?'

'A woman in that group of dog walkers over there.' The PC pointed to a knot of people standing in the grassy dunes.

'I want you to take statements from all of them.' The PC galloped off to do as ordered.

Kneeling down, Carruthers took a latex glove out of his trouser pocket. Wiped his wet hand down his damp trouser leg and fitted the glove over his hand.

'Oh no, you don't,' said Mackie. 'Don't want you to corrupt my crime scene. Here, let me.' He rummaged in the trouser pockets of the body. Brought out a few coins and a bit of fluff. The fluff immediately blew away. 'Nothing,' he said. 'No ID, if that's what you're after.'

'Could be our man,' said Fletcher, sinking to her knees oblivious of the wet sand beneath. 'Young enough. About the same height and build. Looks like him.' Carruthers looked again at those battered features. It could be McGuigan, but he couldn't swear to it.

'When you're ready, get him back to the mortuary,' said Carruthers. 'When can you do the post-mortem?'

'I'll need to check a few things but should be able to start it within an hour.'

'OK. I'll meet you there.' He looked across at Fletcher who had stood up but was struggling to stay on her feet. 'Do you feel comfortable coming to see his grandparents with me? We'll need to get them to the mortuary.'

She shouted to him over the wind, 'I'd be pissed off if you asked anyone else.'

Carruthers nodded. 'Good,' he said. Carruthers unpeeled the glove and stood up. His knee was soaking from where he had been kneeling in the wet sand. He glanced up at the sky. The brooding clouds were advancing, growing darker by the minute. 'There's going to be a downpour,' he said, noticing that Liu had already packed away his expensive camera equipment. He looked across at Fletcher. 'Let's get back to the car.'

They got back just as the rain started to lash down. Sitting behind the steering wheel, Carruthers stared out through the blurred windscreen at the increasingly choppy grey waves. Tonelessly he said to Fletcher, 'We'd better make a move to Joe McGuigan's grandparents. It's not something I'm looking forward to doing.'

Seven

Carruthers and Fletcher stood on the doorstep of the McGuigans. Carruthers hesitated before pressing the bell.

'Shit,' said Fletcher. 'I hate this part of the job.'

'You never get used to it,' Carruthers responded.

The weather front had closed in. Torrential rain was falling with the sort of wind that knocks old people off their feet. Damaging gusts of sixty miles an hour were due later that evening. Rain beat against the McGuigans' door, dirty streaks running down the blue paintwork. Carruthers heard a crash as a green household bin toppled over. Thankful for his waterproof jacket he looked down at Fletcher whose face and hair were soaked.

'When I moved up to Scotland I didn't think I'd have to wear waterproof trousers and Gore-Tex in summer,' she said.

Carruthers rang the bell again and waited. He could hear voices inside. Snatches of conversation greeted him as the door was opened by Mr McGuigan.

Carruthers took in the drawn and anxious face. He didn't want to prolong their agony.

'Have you found him?' Mr McGuigan asked.

'Can we come in, please?' said Carruthers. He ushered Mr and Mrs McGuigan into their living room and told them to sit down. Carruthers watched as stoic-faced Mr McGuigan guided his wife to the sofa. She sat down and once she was settled he took his place beside her. She looked up at Carruthers with worry etched in every facial line.

'The news isn't good, I'm afraid.' As he spoke he searched their faces. 'A body of a young man has been pulled out the water at

West Castle Beach, Castletown. We don't yet know what exactly killed him or if it's definitely Joe, but he'd been shot.'

A heart-rending scream filled the air as Mrs McGuigan half-collapsed against her husband. The sound she made was neither human nor animal, a deep primal sound of keening. Mr McGuigan bent over his wife and tried to lift her from her half-collapsed position. Carruthers helped him.

'It'll be the shock,' said Fletcher. 'Can we lay her out on the sofa with her legs up?' Mr McGuigan stood and walking round his wife lifted her legs onto the couch. Fletcher grabbed a cushion from a chair and gently placed it under the woman's legs and feet. Mr McGuigan knelt by his wife's side.

Carruthers looked at Mr McGuigan. 'I hate to ask this, but we need someone to accompany us to ID the body.'

Looking up from his kneeling position Mr McGuigan said, 'I'll come to the mortuary with you. But can I call the doctor for my wife first? I can't leave her like this.'

'Of course,' said Carruthers. 'Is there a relative or friend who can be with her?'

'I'll phone Mary. She's Sarah's best friend and only five minutes' drive away. She's a capable woman. She'll know what to do.'

As Mr McGuigan was making his calls Carruthers had a quiet word with Fletcher. 'Keep an eye on the wife,' he said. 'I'm going into the hall to call Mackie.'

Fletcher nodded.

'Are we scheduled to start the PM on time?' Carruthers asked the pathologist as soon as the man answered the phone.

'You're in luck,' said Mackie. 'Nothing more pressing has come in. I'll get it done straight away. Where are you now?'

'With the grandparents of a young gamekeeper who's gone missing. We're just waiting for the doctor to attend the man's wife then I'll drive the boy's grandfather over. Can you hold off til then?'

'No bother. You thinking he's our victim?' said Mackie.

'Could be. I have a bad feeling… Can we do the ID first then get straight on and do the PM?'

'OK, I'll check over the facial injuries and prepare the body for viewing. If I know you, you'll want to stay for the PM. I'll have the fags to hand.'

'You know I've given up.' Carruthers finished the call and turned to Mr McGuigan.

'Mary'll be over in five minutes,' he said. 'She'll sit with Sarah until the doctor arrives.'

* * *

Forty minutes later they were at the mortuary with Mr McGuigan. Fletcher took the man's arm and guided him into the viewing room. Dr Mackie hung back. Carruthers could see Mr McGuigan's Adam's apple bob up and down as he swallowed hard.

'Take your time, Mr McGuigan,' said Carruthers. The man remained silent but nodded.

The only part of the corpse visible was the victim's face, a white sheet having been draped over the torso. Mr McGuigan, who appeared to have visibly aged in the last hour, shuffled up and leant over the body. As soon as he laid eyes on the face he looked away, taking a sharp breath as he did so but not before Carruthers saw the grandfather's agonised expression. The hoarse voice came out just above a whisper. 'It's him. My grandson. That's Joe.'

'I'm so sorry, Mr McGuigan,' said Carruthers. He squeezed the man's shoulder. Mr McGuigan turned to Carruthers, tears in his eyes. Carruthers hadn't known Joe McGuigan personally, wasn't a parent himself, but looking at the pain in the old man's face, he still had a lump in his throat.

'Just find who did this to my boy. And why,' he said to Carruthers.

My boy, thought Carruthers. Reinforcement that they had been closer than the average grandfather and grandson.

Carruthers nodded.

As Fletcher led a numb-looking Mr McGuigan away Dr Mackie joined Carruthers in the viewing room. 'PM after a fag and caffeine break. Coming?'

'I won't say no to a coffee.' Once again Carruthers thought about his brother's heart attack. He was finally taking heed and starting to live a healthier lifestyle.

Whilst Mackie nipped outside to smoke, Carruthers sat in the canteen, hand wrapped around his coffee. He stared into the cup, trying to piece together the events that may have led to a nineteen-year-old local being shot in the chest. He glanced at his watch. Lunchtime but he didn't feel like eating.

He could see Mackie outside, apparently oblivious to the rain but Carruthers knew the Highlander was a hardy soul. The only concession to the foul weather was that the old boy had put his waterproof jacket on and turned up the collar. Mackie tossed the cigarette butt to the ground. The doctor's habitual littering habit normally irritated Carruthers but this time it registered only as the end of his coffee break. He stood up.

* * *

The body was laid out naked, covered only by a sheet. Mackie took the sheet away and the post-mortem started. The pathologist began by examining the hands, picking each up in turn. Carruthers found it hard to tear his gaze away from the gaping hole in the boy's chest. There was also livid bruising on McGuigan's torso and gashes to the legs and upper right arm. Mackie caught him looking at the gash in the arm.

'Jagged. Most likely caused by the body coming into contact with underwater rocks. Been in the water for a while. Likely twenty-four hours.'

'Can you tell me when he died?' Carruthers was wondering if he died soon after disappearing.

'Hold your horses, laddie. All I can tell you at the moment is that it wasn't self-inflicted. As I said at the locus I've every confidence it was the shotgun blast that killed him, but we need to be thorough. There's procedures to be followed. And it's definitely a shotgun that's been used on him, by the way,'

Mackie picked up a scalpel. He looked at the edge, shifting it in the light and making Carruthers wonder if the man was malicious or just hamming it up for the audience, knowing Carruthers wasn't keen on this sort of thing. 'Physically he's in good condition. Excellent muscle definition. Must work out.' Carruthers remembered the books on keep-fit in the bookcase of Joe McGuigan's bedroom. He also remembered the lads' mag found under McGuigan's bed. Funny how death often made people think about sex. Why was that?

The sharp edge of the scalpel easily made the standard Y incision, though with a gaping hole in McGuigan's chest there was a large section he didn't have to cut. Next came out the small circular saw. Again the shot had blasted most of the sternum apart but enough remained, mostly the top inch or two, that the pathologist had to separate. He usually cut the costal cartilage at this point, but the shot had made enough mess of the sternum that it was the easiest to separate. The smell of bone burning under cutting knife churned Carruthers' stomach: just as well he hadn't had lunch. The way Mackie pulled back the ribs was practiced if not easy. Carruthers had never lost the ability to feel queasy at a post-mortem. A nauseating stench of body fluids and decaying flesh greeted him. Reminded him of an old meat market he knew in London that had long since closed down. Saw the doc take a sly glance at him.

'Regretting not having had that fag now, eh?' he chuckled.

'No,' said Carruthers stoically. 'Every ciggie takes six minutes off your life,' he added.

'Bollocks. Where d'you hear that stat?'

'My mother.'

Glasses perched on the end of his nose and without looking up, Mackie asked, 'How's your brother now?'

Carruthers shrugged. 'On meds for life.'

'Well, at least he's got one. A life, that is,' Mackie said. 'See much of him?'

Once again Carruthers felt a pang. 'No.'

'Where does he stay?'

'Glasgow.'

'Not far away.' Mackie took a glance at Carruthers. He chuckled. 'Don't fret, laddie. I've got a sister I haven't seen in over seven years.'

Carruthers didn't want to ask Mackie where his sister lived in case he said Australia.

Mackie dug his gloved hand into the dead man's chest cavity and brought out the heart. Carruthers tried to ignore the squelching sounds.

'Talking of hearts,' said Mackie, cradling it in his hand, feeling the weight of it as you might a paperweight. He dropped it onto the weighing scales. Carruthers had to focus hard to not gag. Suddenly his mobile cut through the squelching noises. He fished it out of his trouser pocket. It was the station.

'I'd better take this,' he said to Mackie, backing out of the cut-up room.

Mackie chuckled again. 'If I didn't know better I'd swear you set it up so that your mobile would ring right in the middle of the PM.'

Carruthers lifted an eyebrow.

'Sorry to call you in the middle of the action,' said a familiar voice, that of Fletcher. 'I've found something you need to see.'

'Important enough to leave the PM for?' asked Carruthers, surprised.

'Definitely.'

Carruthers couldn't imagine what that might be, but anything that would give him a legitimate reason for leaving a PM: he'd take it. He'd never had that strong a constitution. 'Right, give me twenty-five and I'll see you back at the station. This better be good.'

'Oh, it is,' said Fletcher. 'I may have established a link between Barry Cuthbert and the dead girl.'

Carruthers felt a frisson of excitement. 'I'm on my way.'

* * *

The earlier heavy rain had left rivulets of water running down the streets. Carruthers drove carefully, trying to avoid the flooding by the side of the road. The destructive winds that had been forecast had mercifully not materialised. At least not in Fife. Carruthers wondered if some other poor bugger further north was getting it. He remembered a visit to Shetland he'd once made with his ex-wife. That had been in August. Another summer storm. The weather had been so bad that the ferries had all been held in port for safety and theirs had been the last flight allowed in before the airport had to be shut too. He remembered the ferocious gale that had nearly knocked Mairi off her feet as she set foot on the tarmac and tried to make her way to arrivals. She managed as far as the disabled toilets in the airport building and had thrown up. Another lifetime ago.

He wondered how long it would be before he stopped thinking about his ex-wife. He still thought about her far too frequently but at least it wasn't with the terrible searing pain that it had been in the early days of their separation. He put all thoughts of her resolutely out of his mind. An image of another woman came into his head instead.

The dead girl on the beach.

He hopped out of the car and half walked, half ran into the building. He grabbed a coffee from the vending machine before going to find Fletcher. No thoughts about lunch. He was being fuelled by caffeine and pure adrenaline. *So much for healthy living.* Knew it would catch up with him sooner or later but in the meantime…

He found Fletcher at her desk, head bent over some newspaper cuttings and photographs.

She had a grin on her face. 'This is what I want you to look at,' she said. 'I've been doing some research on our Barry Cuthbert. Being a local bigwig and self-styled celeb I thought he's bound to have made it into the newspapers at some charity event or other. I wasn't wrong. Take a look at this.' She pushed a picture towards him. It showed Cuthbert centre stage dressed in a tux with a stunning and young woman on his arm. The girl was wearing a short silver dress and high heels.

'When was this photo taken?'

She pointed to the date. 'Six months ago.'

Carruthers took the photograph. 'Likes them young then, our Barry, does he?'

'Looks like it,' said Fletcher. But that's not what I'm showing you. What else can you spot?'

Carruthers' eyes took in the girl. She really was very beautiful. Scandalously beautiful cheekbones, long neck, tiny waist, long tapered legs. Just looking at the picture made Carruthers' pulse quicken. Carruthers glanced at Fletcher. She was looking at him. Looking at where his eyes were on the picture.

'Keep going,' she urged.

He gazed at the girl's calves for a nanosecond too long and then he saw it as his eyes travelled towards her feet. Tattoo on left ankle.

'That's it. You've got it.' Fletcher said it with a touch of victory in her voice.

Carruthers held up the paper closer so it was almost at his nose. 'Is that–? We need an enlargement of that tattoo. It's the same size, looks like the same shape…'

'Already onto it.' She handed him another photograph. 'Speccie Techie owed me a favour.'

Carruthers eagerly grasped the photograph. Studied it. And there it was. A close-up of the tattoo. An open eye with a teardrop and a strange curved line. The same tattoo as the dead girl. But not the same girl.

'Shit,' he said.

'Told you it was good. The question is what does this all mean? We now have two girls with the same tattoo. Have we got people traffickers from Eastern Europe operating in Scotland?'

'I wouldn't have thought anything other than this is a popular tattoo, if it hadn't been for the information from the Estonian police,' said Carruthers. 'But then I know nothing about tattoos.'

'We've found a link between the dead girl and Barry Cuthbert,' said Fletcher. 'Through a tattoo. And if we've found one link there's bound to be others. We just have to find them. How are we going to play this?' she asked. 'Do we tell Bingham? And what about Joe McGuigan's body? When do we confront Cuthbert? We need to interview him again. Even if he wasn't involved in McGuigan's death, Cuthbert was McGuigan's employer.'

Carruthers looked at Fletcher's earnest face. He was glad she was back to her old self. At least on the surface. But her miscarriage hadn't really been that long ago. Not in the grand scheme of things. She must still be hurting. *Losing a baby must be like an open wound that won't go away,* he thought. He wished she'd opened up to him a bit more at the time. But he knew she'd say that of him, too. Sometimes they had more in common than he wanted to admit.

'Almost a certainty McGuigan was killed by a blast from a shotgun, although I'm still waiting for Mackie's final PM results. Who do we know that keeps shotguns, Andie?'

'Cuthbert. And the last time we saw a shotgun it was being carried by Derek Sturrock.'

Carruthers shook his head. 'We need to interview both Cuthbert and Sturrock as soon as possible. I want to start with Cuthbert. Put some pressure on him. And get a home address for Sturrock, will you? He may have been the last person to see Joe McGuigan alive.' Carruthers touched Fletcher's shoulder. 'Also, find Gayle. She's dealing with the press. Tell her to get them to hold off making the discovery of McGuigan's body public. At least for twenty-four hours.' He wondered if he should interview Pip McGuire again but decided she could go on the back burner. She would just deny any knowledge.

'Right you are, boss,' said Fletcher.

Carruthers picked up the plastic cup and drained it of the lukewarm coffee. 'In the meantime, I'll talk to Bingham. I'll see him now. Give me anything you've got on Cuthbert, including this photograph.'

Fletcher handed over a folder.

'And, Andie,' said Carruthers, 'fine work. You've done a good job.'

* * *

Carruthers tapped on Bingham's door. Put his head round. Bingham was sitting at his desk immersed in paperwork.

'Ah, Jim. I take it you've got those forecasts for me? About bloody time. Hand them over.'

Carruthers' heart sank. He walked in. Thought he could detect cigarette smoke again, faint but there. Was starting to wonder if Bingham was defying the smoking ban. He closed the door behind him without looking. His hand came into contact with polythene.

Bingham made a tssking noise with his tongue. 'Mind my suit.' Carruthers glanced behind him seeing a recently dry-cleaned dinner jacket.

'Going somewhere nice tonight?' Carruthers said, feeling a stab of resentment that this man was allowing himself the evening off.

'Dinner party at the home of one of the golf club members,' Bingham said at last. 'Not that it's any of your business. Now where's the paperwork? And stop changing the bloody subject.'

Carruthers had a bad feeling. Call it a sixth sense. 'Which member?'

Bingham took his glasses off and rubbed his eyes. Putting them back on, he said, 'Barry Cuthbert.'

'You're not serious?' said Carruthers, suddenly realising he hadn't been keeping Bingham up to date about the developments. So much had happened in such a short space of time. 'Listen, sir, before you go to that dinner party I need to speak to you urgently about Cuthbert. There's something you need to know.'

Bingham sighed. 'Is this more of your stalling tactics? Because if it is—'

'With all due respect, this is more important than forecasts and paperwork.'

Bingham cracked the knuckles of his left hand. 'Don't take that tone with me, Carruthers. I'm your bloody superior. And if you've got something on Cuthbert, let's hear it.'

Eight

Carruthers left Bingham's office fuming. Bingham wouldn't countenance one of his golf club members having any part to play in any illegal activities, let alone the possibility of murder. Even managed to excuse the fact Cuthbert had a criminal record. And refused to put a tail on Cuthbert, citing budget restrictions.

As he strode away from Bingham's office, Carruthers' mobile flashed up Mackie's number. He accepted the call.

Carruthers immediately recognised the Highland lilt of the voice. 'I've just finished the PM, Jim. As expected he was definitely killed by the shotgun blast unless toxicology comes back with anything else. The most important thing you need to know, though, is that he's been dead between twenty-four and forty-eight hours. Closer to forty-eight hours by my reckoning, although we both know it's not an exact science.'

'Most likely he was killed sometime late on Wednesday then,' said Carruthers. *The day he went missing.*

'Agreed. However, he hadn't been in the sea that long so you can make your own deductions from that.'

Whoever killed McGuigan had kept his body somewhere before disposing of it.

Carruthers listened to the pathologist. 'Thanks for giving me a ring.' He ended the call. Glancing at his watch he realised the day was getting away from him. It was near on five o'clock.

Carruthers walked back to his desk. It dawned on him he was famished, that he hadn't eaten anything since breakfast. However, he had no time for food. He was on a mission. He grabbed his jacket and picked up Andie. His thoughts were on Barry Cuthbert.

Wondered how the man would react to the discovery of his young gamekeeper's body and brutal death. Not to mention how he'd react to the discovery of the photograph of himself with the young woman bearing the same tattoo as the dead girl, the mark of a prostitute. How would he be able to explain that one away?

Carruthers selected a car pool key and he and Fletcher headed to the station car park. The weather was still gusting and the wind made it feel ten degrees colder than it actually was. Nobody would think this was the height of summer – except the Scots. It was only as he climbed into the Corsa that he realised for the first time in a couple of days he didn't feel as if he was covered in a fine sheen of sweat as he'd left the building. The air conditioning must have been fixed and he hadn't even noticed.

* * *

'For crying out loud, what is it now?' asked Barry Cuthbert.

His housekeeper had taken them through to the drawing room. Carruthers took out the photographs of the dead gamekeeper and slapped them down on Cuthbert's mahogany table.

'The body of Joe McGuigan was discovered this morning on West Castle Beach. He'd been shot at close range in the chest with a shotgun. His body ended up in the sea.'

Cuthbert stopped dead in his tracks and just stared at Carruthers. 'What did you say?'

'You heard. McGuigan's been found dead. Blasted by a shotgun. Let's hope for your sake it wasn't one of yours. Whoever did it obviously thought the body would be taken further out to sea. No such luck. Tide brought him back in. Not a pretty sight.' Carruthers paused whilst watching Cuthbert carefully for any reaction. If Carruthers had to name an emotion he would have said Cuthbert was in complete shock. But then again the man might be a good actor.

'I'd like to start by asking you where you were from about 6pm Wednesday evening and then I'd like to see your firearms licence, please,' said Carruthers.

Cuthbert stared for a moment, mouth open, then said, 'You're not seriously suggesting I've murdered one of my own staff?'

'Just answer the question, please, Mr Cuthbert,' said Fletcher.

Cuthbert smiled. 'As it happened I was with Derek Sturrock until about eight.'

'And then?' said Fletcher.

Cuthbert shrugged. 'I changed for dinner and went to friends.'

'We'll be asking for their names and address,' said Carruthers, 'but in the meantime I take it you were on your own at some point that night?'

Cuthbert grinned at Fletcher but Carruthers could see there was worry in his eyes. 'Normally I don't go to bed alone but that night I did.'

He hasn't got an alibi and he's worried.

'I also want to examine all your shotguns,' said Carruthers. 'They may have to be taken away for forensics.' Carruthers knew fine well that shotguns could only be matched to the mark left on the expelled casing by the firing mechanism. To do this the casing was required, yet in this case no shell casings had been found because the body had been discovered distant to the site of death. Still, no harm in putting the wind up Cuthbert. He continued talking. 'Then I want to talk to your estate manager and senior gamekeeper again. And I want to know the movements of all your staff in the last seventy-two hours.'

Barry Cuthbert turned white. Started playing with the gold signet ring he was wearing. Carruthers knew a nervous habit when he saw one.

'And when we've done all that I want you to tell me what you know about Marika Paju.'

'Who?'

Carruthers brought out the photograph of the dead girl. 'The girl found dead at the foot of the cliffs. And I want to know what your link is with Eastern European prostitutes.'

Barry Cuthbert did a good job of trying to look mystified and outraged all at the same time but it didn't wash with Carruthers.

He knows about the prostitutes, thought Carruthers, *but he genuinely did look shocked at the mention of McGuigan's death. Interesting.*

'Come on, Barry,' urged Carruthers, 'you're in it up to your neck. We also know about your criminal record and that of your senior gamekeeper.'

Cuthbert took the photograph from Carruthers, pretended to study it. 'I have no idea what you're talking about. I've never been to a prostitute. And as for having a criminal record, well, let's just say I had a bit of a misspent youth.'

'So you're also saying you have no link with Eastern European prostitutes?' said Fletcher.

'On my life, I have no idea what you're talking about.'

Carruthers stared at Cuthbert until the man looked away. He had a strong feeling Cuthbert knew more than he was saying.

'Well, in that case how do you explain this?' Carruthers pulled a folded up piece of paper out of his jacket pocket. He unfolded it and handed it to Barry Cuthbert. It was a copy of the newspaper clipping Fletcher had showed him. Cuthbert stared at the image in front of him.

'It's not a crime having a pretty girl on your arm, is it?' he said.

Carruthers looked at Cuthbert's blank expression. 'It's not so much the girl that interests me, Barry, as her tattoo.' Carruthers delved into his pocket again, bringing out a second photograph. 'It's incredible what the IT guys can do nowadays. This is a blow-up of that tattoo. Take a look at it. Then take a close look at this second photograph.' Carruthers handed him the photo. This time the image was of the dead girl and her tattoo blown up. The tattoos were identical.

'The tattoo on the ankle of the girl on your arm is identical to the tattoo on the dead girl,' said Fletcher.

'So what? Tats are popular. Doesn't mean anything.'

'No?' said Carruthers. 'Well apparently this tattoo does. I've spoken with the Estonian authorities and this tattoo is the mark of a notorious group of pimps in the Tallinn area. The Haravere gang. Heard of them? They tattoo their prostitutes, Barry. It's a sign of ownership. They're also people traffickers. And this symbol refers to Lucifer. Bit more than just a coincidence that the leader of the Haravere gang calls himself Kurat – the devil. Who was the girl on your arm, Barry? I want to know how to contact her.' Carruthers could see Cuthbert's Adam's apple bob up and down as he swallowed nervously.

Barry Cuthbert gave the photographs back to Carruthers. He shifted his weight from his right to his left foot. He resumed playing with his signet ring before running a finger round the inside of his collar. Carruthers took a step closer to him so Cuthbert would feel the hot breath in his ear. 'Look, she was just a girl I met. To be honest, can't even remember her name.'

'Easy come easy go, eh, Barry? Is she a call-girl? I need to know where you met her. I want the name of that agency. You knew Marika Paju, didn't you? Were you her lover, Barry? The father of her unborn child?'

'No, of course not. Like I said, I don't know any Marika Paju.'

Carruthers sought Cuthbert's eyes with his own. Looked down on him. 'I have no idea what part you played in the deaths of Marika Paju or Joe McGuigan, Barry, but I swear, if you were involved, I'll bring you down.' Cuthbert remained silent but Carruthers had noticed the colour had drained from him. But as he said it he realised that they still didn't know for definite that this girl was Marika Paju.

'Nothing to say, Barry? That'll be a first.' Carruthers looked around him. 'Now I believe you were going to fetch me your shotgun licence. I'm afraid I'm going to have to look at your guns.'

'I haven't killed anybody,' said Cuthbert.

'Shotguns. I'd like to see them, please. Now.'

Barry Cuthbert led Carruthers and Fletcher through the drawing room to a study situated towards the back of his house. He took a key from his pocket, used it to open the desk drawer and produced a bunch of keys on a key ring. The two police officers followed Cuthbert through the hall to a small door at the end of the corridor. Cuthbert unlocked the room and stepped back to allow Carruthers and Fletcher to enter first.

'As you can see I'm strict about security. This is the gun room. Have a look round. I have nothing to hide.'

As Carruthers walked to the centre of the room he saw a large glass cabinet filled with shotguns. Although the cabinet was locked the gun on the far left was missing.

'Where's the missing gun, Barry?' asked Fletcher.

Cuthbert was frowning. He looked genuinely surprised. 'I've no idea. It should be here.'

'Who has a key to this cabinet and to the room?' asked Carruthers.

'Only myself and Derek Sturrock.'

'Is he around at the moment?' asked Carruthers.

'Day off.'

Carruthers turned to Fletcher. 'Let's get ourselves over to Sturrock's.' He turned back to a flustered-looking Barry Cuthbert. 'Don't leave Scotland anytime soon, Barry. We'll be back. And I'd appreciate it if you didn't give Sturrock the heads-up that we're on our way.'

'Do you think Cuthbert will warn Sturrock?' said Fletcher as they reached the car.

Carruthers was grim-faced. 'We're about to find out.'

Twenty minutes later Carruthers and Fletcher were rapping on the gamekeeper's door. Fletcher was brushing the water off the bottom of her black trousers. They'd had had to wade through a stream that was rushing past Sturrock's front door, way over the stepping stones. The rain had stopped but the wind was still picking up. Grey clouds were scudding across a darkening sky. The home was in a row of old cottages that reminded Carruthers of miners' cottages. The door was opened by a pale middle-aged woman. She looked as washed-out as her faded summer dress. Hugging her ankles were a couple of young children. They looked like twins.

Both Fletcher and Carruthers fished out their badges. 'We're here to see Derek Sturrock. Is he in?'

The woman turned her back on them for a moment. 'Deek,' she shouted.

Derek Sturrock came down the stairs of the cottage tucking his T-shirt into his blue jeans.

'We need to talk to you,' said Fletcher. 'About Joe McGuigan.'

Sturrock licked his lips nervously. He didn't invite them in so they stood on the doorstep. 'What's he done?'

'Joe McGuigan's been found dead, Mr Sturrock. On West Castle Beach. The tide brought him in. He was killed by a single shot to the chest from a shotgun.' Carruthers handed the photographs to Sturrock that had earlier been shown to Cuthbert and waited for his response. 'You ever seen the effects of a shotgun blast? Course you have. You're a gamekeeper. It's not pretty. But perhaps you've never seen the effects on a human body before. Unless, of course, you were the one who fired the shot that killed Joe.'

Sturrock pushed Carruthers roughly aside and vomited into the shrubbery. Carruthers had the impression Sturrock hadn't been warned by Cuthbert. Perhaps they weren't particularly close, Sturrock and Cuthbert. Or maybe Cuthbert wanted to throw his gamekeeper to the wolves.

'Sorry,' Sturrock managed to say. He spat onto the ground. As he wiped his hand over his mouth, his eyes kept returning to the photographs. On his face was etched a mixture of horror and revulsion.

'When did you last see Joe?' asked Carruthers.

Sturrock thought for a moment. 'About six o' clock on Wednesday. Knocking off time.'

'Was he going straight home?' said Fletcher.

'No idea. We don't tend to talk about stuff unless it's work-related.'

'At the moment you're the last person to see Joe McGuigan alive,' said Fletcher.

'We want to know what's going on, Derek,' said Carruthers. 'Second dead body on a Fife beach within a week. It's making us look bad.' Carruthers paused for a moment before continuing. 'There's a shotgun missing from Cuthbert's gun cabinet,' he added. 'Where is it? Have you got it?'

'No,' said Sturrock. 'I keep my own. I dinnae use the boss's.'

That's not what Cuthbert said, thought Carruthers. 'We need it. Your gun.'

'Oh no,' said Sturrock, 'you're not planting this one on me. I havenae killed him.'

'Then who has?' asked Fletcher. 'Barry Cuthbert?'

Sturrock remained silent.

'We know it was you and Joe up on the cliffs that day when the girl's body was found,' said Carruthers. Of course he didn't know any such thing, but Sturrock didn't need to know that. 'You were out laying poison on Cuthbert's orders. What part has Barry played in the girl's death? We already know he's up to his eyes in it. What's more, he knows it, too.' Carruthers allowed the pause to stretch a few moments longer than necessary before continuing. 'What do you know about Cuthbert running prostitutes?' Carruthers knew he was on very thin ice. After all, they had no evidence that linked Cuthbert to prostitutes except for a newspaper cutting. At least not yet. Whether he was linked to the dead girl, well, that was another matter.

'What? Look I'm just a fucking gamekeeper. I ken nothing about hoors.'

'But it *was* you laying poison that day, wasn't it? On Cuthbert's orders. We'll find your prints on the binoculars. The binoculars that were at the scene of the crime.' Of course, Carruthers knew no prints had been found on the binos. 'It doesn't look good. We also know about your criminal record and your boss's criminal record. What's your involvement in the girl's death? Did you kill her, Derek? Is that what you did? She found you spreading poison, didn't she, high up on those cliffs? Worked out what you were doing. She may have been Eastern European but she still knew that poisoning birds of prey is a crime, punishable by a prison sentence. Of course you already had a criminal record, didn't you? You wouldn't want to go back inside.'

Even as Carruthers said it, it sounded like nonsense to his ears. You wouldn't kill a woman to stop her reporting you for trying to poison birds of prey. The best she could give was a description to the police, by which point you'd be long gone from the scene. So why had she been killed and what, if anything, did McGuigan and Sturrock have to do with her death?

Carruthers felt something wet land on his hand and then something on his head. The rain was coming back on. He turned up the collar of his jacket. He was aware of Fletcher buttoning up hers.

'Where does Joe McGuigan's murder come in?' said Fletcher. 'McGuigan made the anonymous phone call, didn't he? Wanted to tell the police. Became a loose cannon. After all, what else did he know that he might just tell the police about? Considered too much of a threat so he was taken out?'

Sturrock was silent.

'I would start by telling us everything you know about Barry Cuthbert,' said Fletcher.

'He's not likely to protect you, is he?' said Carruthers. 'We've just interviewed him. Asked him not to contact you and give you the heads-up. And by the look on your face when we told you of McGuigan's death he didn't, did he?' Carruthers paused, to allow time for this to sink in. If he hoped Sturrock would crack, he was disappointed.

'We want names of all his associates, but first of all we want to know where you were Wednesday evening. You can start by telling us where you were from the moment Joe McGuigan left work.'

'I was with Barry and then I came home to my wife.'

'How convenient. Two old lags together.' Another heavy raindrop splattered by Carruthers' feet. He hoped they'd be able to finish the conversation with Derek Sturrock before the heavens opened fully.

* * *

They left a jumpy Sturrock and headed back to the car. The drops of rain had turned into another downpour. Carruthers could hear the rain bouncing off the roof as they opened the car doors.

'Well, you've got Sturrock's cage rattled, that's for sure,' said Fletcher as she climbed into the driver's seat. There was a deafening noise as hail like marbles started to hit the car roof.

'Shit,' said Fletcher pulling her door quickly closed. 'Looks like we got in just in time. This weather's unbelievable. One day blazing sunshine, the next a hailstorm. Don't think I'll ever get used to Scottish weather. How on earth do we manage hail in the middle of summer?' She turned to Carruthers. 'Do you think Sturrock's responsible for McGuigan's death?'

'By his reaction, I'd say no,' said Carruthers. 'I find it interesting Cuthbert didn't try to contact him before we got there.' He stared out of the window at the blanket of white appearing as if by magic as the layer of ice-balls covered the ground.

'I get the feeling Barry Cuthbert knows how to look after Barry Cuthbert,' said Fletcher. She started the engine to the sound of the battering hail.

* * *

Carruthers stirred his coffee. An idea was coming into his head. He kept batting it away but it just kept coming back. It sounded ludicrous, even to himself. And yet… Looking at his watch he made a decision. Grabbing the detested paperwork Bingham wanted him to do, he pulled his jacket off the back of his chair, swept up his mobile and car keys.

'Is this weather set in for the rest of the day, do you know?' he said to Brown on the way out.

Brown shook his head. 'Don't think so. Think it's due to blow itself out. Supposed to be dry later.'

Good, thought Carruthers. *One less obstacle.*

Once back in his cottage he showered, changed his clothes, pulled on hill-walking trousers and a T-shirt and headed out to the award-winning Anstruther Fish Bar. Settling himself in a seat by the window he people-watched while tucking in to haddock and chips washed down with a mug of tea.

He looked at his watch once more. It was seven o'clock. No doubt Bingham would be at Cuthbert's by now. He wondered idly which external caterers the man would be using. A dark-haired waitress collected his plate and while he waited for another mug of tea, he pulled the paperwork out of a rucksack and made a start on Bingham's figures.

Just after eight, he gathered his belongings and squeezed past a queue of people waiting to be seated. He walked towards the cobbled harbour to his car and opened the driver's door. While looking at the bobbing boats, he threw his rucksack onto the passenger seat then got into the car and set off with one aim in mind. Stake out Cuthbert's estate.

He pulled up in a country lane just yards from the main entrance. Brown had been right. The rain had finally stopped. Carruthers reached over for his rucksack. Dragged it over to his lap, unzipped it and grabbed his binoculars. Trained them on the house. The wall was obscuring all downstairs rooms. Swearing, he started the car up again and drove round the estate looking for a gap in the wall, anything so he could get a better view. He finally settled for a layby, parked up and got out. Immediately he planted his foot it went cold. He'd stepped straight into a deep puddle. 'Fuck,' he said. He walked to the back of the car, opened the boot, leant in, pulled out a pair of latex gloves from a box and stuffed the gloves in his trouser pocket. You never knew when they might come in useful. Shutting the boot, he walked away from the car. Nicked through a hole in the old stone wall and positioned himself behind a clump of trees.

Training the binoculars on the downstairs drawing room he had a good view of the guests. There were maybe twenty people in the room. Cuthbert had plumped for a buffet rather than a sit-down meal. People were standing talking in groups of threes and fours. The men wearing evening suits, the women long evening dresses. No sign yet of Bingham. And no sign of estate manager, Pip McGuire.

A light suddenly switched on in an upstairs room. It looked like a study. A familiar figure came into view. Barry Cuthbert. And who was that with him? Could it be Derek Sturrock? It looked like him. Carruthers licked his lips. The men were arguing. That much was clear. Sturrock was angry, he appeared to be shouting. Cuthbert was calmer. Carruthers could hazard a guess at what they were discussing.

Carruthers craned his neck, putting the binoculars to his eyes. He edged closer but the closer he got the less he saw as his view was now being blocked by trees. He needed to hear what they were discussing. Saw a window open on the second floor. Wondered if he would be able to access it by climbing up the outside of the building. A bat flew low overhead making him aware twilight was falling. From somewhere far off he heard the hooting of an owl. He was also aware he was out of shape, wasn't as young as he used to be and that this endeavour was nothing short of foolishness. He hesitated for a few seconds, wondering what this would do to his already dented career.

Finally he decided this was the best opportunity he was going to get and at least it wasn't as bad as punching a fellow officer… was it? He made his move.

Pulling the latex gloves out of his pocket he carefully put them on. Taking a deep breath he stealthily climbed up a drainpipe, grateful for his decision not to wear jeans. Despite not having the best diet he had twenty years of hill-walking and scrambling behind him. His one concession to fitness. He was also as lean as a whippet. He ignored that one foot felt heavier than the other because it was wet. The gloves seemed to hold so that was fine.

Suddenly he heard voices outside the building and immediately beneath him. He froze. The smell of cigarette smoke drifted upwards. Not daring to look down, hardly daring to breathe, Carruthers clung to the drainpipe. He stayed there motionless, praying that the men wouldn't look upwards. They didn't. But they said nothing interesting either. Carruthers cursed to himself. It was only when their voices became more distant that he allowed himself to expel a long anxious breath. Realising this was utter recklessness, he attempted to climb back down the drainpipe.

He didn't make it. He lost his grasp of the pipe then his footing and as he fell he made a desperate grab for the piping, a section of which came away in his hand. He felt himself falling through space, landing on a rhododendron bush that broke his fall. He bashed his arm on a branch, felt a sudden sharp pain. He fell from the branch onto the ground, landing awkwardly, banging his knee. He gave an involuntary cry. He got onto his feet as quickly as he could and stood behind an old oak tree, ripping the latex gloves off and nursing his bleeding arm.

'I'm telling you, I heard something outside.' The voice belonged to Barry Cuthbert. 'Go outside and 'ave a look. I'm not 'aving gate-crashers. We're accommodating a special guest soon.'

Carruthers stayed sitting behind the tree. Wasn't sure how long for. Long enough to notice twilight turn to an inky darkness, giving him some much-needed camouflage. He suddenly heard voices coming closer. Took a few slow, shallow breaths.

A gruff male voice said, 'Told him there's no one out here. It's foxes. He's fucking paranoid. Still, no harm in having a quick look. At least this way we've done our job.'

'So, do you ken who this special guest is, then?'

'Nah. And best not to ask questions. You've seen what happens to people who ask too many questions. All I know is, he's flying in.'

Carruthers was listening intently. Cuthbert accommodating a special guest? Flying in? At last, something interesting to be heard. Carruthers frowned. Where would he be flying in to at this time of night? And what about the other bit? What exactly did he mean by that? Well, one thing was certain, he wasn't going to have an early night. His curiosity was piqued – he would have to stay here until this VIP arrived.

He hobbled back to his car still holding the gloves. Opened the car door and threw them on the passenger seat. Knew he had some tablets in the glove compartment. Popped two from the blister pack then looked round the car for a bottle of water. He was in luck. Underneath some empty crisp packets and the remnants of a takeaway he found a half-drunk bottle of Highland Spring. With difficulty he unscrewed the top, popped the two painkillers in his mouth and took a slug. He sat in his car surveying the damage. His hill-walking trousers were ripped where he'd fallen.

Gingerly he examined his arm. There were lacerations from the branches and a large gash with congealing blood. He looked down at his chest. His T-shirt was splattered with blood. Knew he should get his arm cleaned up but didn't have the luxury of time and certainly had no intention of sitting in casualty for hours on end. His knee was throbbing. He took a look at his watch. Eleven already. Agonised over what to do. He sat motionless in the car for another thirty minutes waiting for the painkillers to kick in. As time went by he heard car engines and saw the big gates swing open as guests began to leave.

Starting to wonder how he was going to drive himself home, he opened the car door to answer a call of nature. No sooner had he left the car and had undone his fly than he heard another noise. This time it was no car engine. Growing louder it seemed to fill the whole sky. And then he saw it. A helicopter. Circling. Carruthers could almost feel the trees sway. At one point he felt he was so close he had trouble remaining standing. It disappeared behind the trees. Carruthers limped towards the noise and within minutes of pushing his way through undergrowth was rewarded with the sight of the helicopter, blades still rotating in a large clearing.

Under cover of darkness it was difficult to see the occupants of the copter. Carruthers was just able to make out a man alighting holding the hand of a giggling woman in a short dress. A second woman got out, then a third and a fourth. But it was when Carruthers saw them illuminated by the lights of the aircraft that he got a better view. All the women were scantily clad in short dresses and ridiculously high heels. Carruthers wondered how in God's name these women were going to manage the wet grass wearing the most inappropriate shoes he had ever seen.

He edged ever closer, trying to get a good look at the man in the party. He was tall and slim, that much was obvious. Dark hair, which he wore in a ponytail, and a hooked nose. He had a deep accented voice. But it was when the girls started to talk to each other that it got interesting. As he caught only snatches of conversation from his safe distance, one thing became clear. They weren't speaking English.

Carruthers struggled to work out what language they were speaking. To his ear it sounded Eastern European, perhaps Russian. The party cut across the manicured lawn and disappeared inside. Carruthers limped back to his car. Opening the driver's door he sat behind the wheel while he decided what to do. Despite the painkillers his knee was throbbing. He felt he had got about all he was going to get. Couldn't see how he was going to get closer to the guests with his injury. He had committed the man's face to memory and was pretty sure if he worked with a police artist he could get a good likeness. Decided to call it a day, go home, tend to the wounds, take some more painkillers and try to get a good night's sleep. The following day he'd go and pay Derek Sturrock a visit. He started the engine, straining his body to put his seat belt on.

Back in Anstruther, Carruthers climbed out of his car with great care. The Anstruther Fish Bar had long since shut up shop. A couple passed him walking arm in arm. They gave him a strange look and moved further away. He realised he must look a sight with his arm covered in blood and his trousers ripped at the knee. Bringing out his front door key from his rucksack he suddenly heard his name. Looked up and was surprised to see Gill McLaren. She was accompanied by two men. She left the two men and hurried over.

'Oh my God, Jim, whatever's happened to you? Why are you limping?'

'I fell. I'm just going inside to clean myself up.'

Brushing a stray tendril of blonde hair off her face she said, 'I think you should go straight to emergency. Look, I'll drive. I've got the car.'

'No, no, I'll be fine. I think they're superficial wounds. You can give me a hand to get me indoors though, if it'll make you feel better.'

She turned to her concerned looking colleagues. 'Jim's in the police. He's a friend. I'll see you guys tomorrow. OK?'

'Are you sure?' said one of the men, looking rather doubtfully at Carruthers.

She laughed. 'Yes, I'll be fine. It was a lovely evening. Good night.'

Out of earshot, Carruthers said, 'I think he had designs on you. Wasn't at all happy you were going off with me instead.'

'If only.' Patting his hand she said, 'Now I smell a story coming on. We'll get you inside, get you cleaned up and I want to hear everything.' She suddenly stopped, looking serious. 'I still don't like the look of your arm. Are you sure you wouldn't rather me take you to hospital?'

He looked down at her, saw the concern etched on her face. Felt warmth spreading through him. Thought how nice it was to have someone care about him again. Even if it was only because he was covered in blood.

Inside, she was gentle as she washed his wounds in hot soapy water. Making him take off his ripped T-shirt at the basin sink, so he could feel her breath on him. Her lightness of touch made him tingle. Told himself to get a grip and hoped he wasn't about to get an erection. She prodded his cut and bruised arm. He flinched.

'Not as bad as first feared,' she said. 'Think you're right – the injury's pretty superficial, thank goodness.'

He shook his head. 'It'll be fine. If you can put a plaster on it that would be a help. There a first aid kit in the cabinet there.'

When they'd finished with his arm she said, 'How's your leg?'

'Sore, but I'll live.'

'I think you should take your trousers off and let me take a look.'

He put his hand on her shoulder. 'Gill, that's really not necessary.'

She smiled and it lit up her face. 'Let me be the judge of that. Come on. If you show me where the bedroom is you can sit on the bed whilst you take your trousers down. It'll be easier that way.'

'Has anyone ever told you how bossy you are?'

'Many times,' she said with another smile. 'That's probably why I'm not married.'

'I think you'd make a wonderful wife.' The words were out before he even thought about them. What on earth had made him say that? He blushed.

'Do you know it's been a long time since I saw a man blush? I didn't think people blushed anymore. It's an endearing quality, Mr Carruthers. Especially in a man.'

There was a moment, just a moment when he wondered if something was about to happen. He waited, uncertain, cursing himself for his hesitancy. Not being sure what he wanted to happen.

'Come on. To the bedroom.'

Carruthers led the way. It wasn't often he got a request like that.

Having unbuckled his belt and pulled the trousers down to his hips he sat down on the bed. Gill knelt down before him and tugged at his trousers. He felt like a child.

'C'mon, I need to get these over the knees.' Somewhere in the house a door slammed. He wondered if he'd left a window open. As if to echo his thoughts he heard a windowpane rattling. The wind had clearly picked up again. *This weather front is relentless,* he thought.

Suddenly he felt shy. A final tug meant the trousers came down and he felt very silly sitting on his bed with his trousers around his ankles in front of this beautiful, vivacious woman.

He heard a sharp intake of breath. 'Ouch. Look at your knee.' He looked down. Purpling, and cut. 'Don't think you need to go to hospital, but we'll get some ice on it.'

'Just as well. I don't have time. The cases…'

'Ah, yes, you were going to tell me about how you ended up in this mess. First I need to find some ice.' She stood up.

'If you're sure?'

She nodded.

'I have some ice in the freezer. Kitchen is downstairs, second on the left.'

'Won't be a tick.' She disappeared out of the bedroom to return a few minutes later with some ice cubes wrapped in a dishcloth. She knelt down and administered the ice pack over the knee for a few minutes. 'You'll need to elevate that leg,' she said. 'How's it feeling?'

'A lot better.' Carruthers smiled. 'Do you fancy a whisky while you're here?'

'You know how to tempt a girl, but I'd better not. Clear head needed for tomorrow and all that. If you're OK to leave, I'd better be getting back to the B&B.'

'Fair enough.' Carruthers tried to stand up.

Gill laughed. 'Before you start trying to walk you might want to pull your trousers up.'

Nine

At 9.30 the next morning Carruthers pulled up outside Sturrock's house. Overnight another weather front had pushed in. He'd awoken at five, unsure if the wind rattling the window pane or the throbbing of his knee had robbed him of sleep. He'd had to get up to shut the window, popped two more painkillers and hobbled back to bed but he'd struggled to fall back to sleep. Eventually he'd got up and had put the news on. Listened to the damage the severe weather had done further north. Was mightily glad he wasn't living on Shetland, where the storms had caused severe structural damage and had knocked out broadband for some users in Vidlin and Burravoe. Before leaving for work he'd had to help his elderly neighbour upright her fallen bins. He wondered if his bird table was still standing in the back garden. It had fallen over that many times that he'd had to tie it to the washing line with rope.

* * *

Carruthers could see Sturrock's wife through the window doing the washing up. He wondered if she had much of an existence. Suddenly the front door opened. Out came Sturrock, black holdall slung carelessly over one shoulder. Carruthers opened his car door and, grimacing with pain, limped, head down into the wind, across the road to meet the gamekeeper.

Sturrock appeared startled, as well he might.

'Mr Sturrock?'

Sturrock kept walking. 'Fuck, what is it now?'

'What were you and Barry arguing about last night?' Carruthers found himself shouting. He had to make himself heard over the noise of the gale. 'You were seen having a heated debate during the party.'

Sturrock opened the boot of his car, threw the holdall in and slammed it shut. Walked round to the driver's side. 'Look, I don't know what you're talking about,' he said, jumping in.

'I know enough about Barry Cuthbert, Derek, to know that he's not going to save you if it means, by dropping you in it, he can save himself. That's all I'm saying.' Carruthers caught the driver's door as Sturrock tried to shut it. He stooped down and leant into the car. 'If you know anything about Cuthbert's illegal activities you need to tell us.' Carruthers took a deep breath. Decided to go out on a limb. He had long been an exponent of the means justifying the end as long as, of course, he could get away with it. He wouldn't tell Fletcher his thoughts. She wouldn't approve. He wondered just how much trouble this case would get him into. 'Cuthbert's going down, Derek. It's only a matter of time before we find evidence he's involved in the trafficking of Eastern European prostitutes and my gut tells me he's involved in the art thefts. The question you need to ask yourself is, are you going down with him? At the moment you have the choice. You won't always have that. What we also know is that he's ruthless, as are the people he works with. Two people have already been murdered. Do you want to be the third?'

Remaining silent and without looking at him Sturrock slammed the door, turned the ignition and drove off at speed.

* * *

Carruthers stared at the phone on his desk. Picking it up, he made a call.

'Get me the police artist, will you?' Out of the corner of his eye he was aware of the door to his office opening.

'Glad you decided to grace us with your presence.' Superintendent Bingham moved around Carruthers' office with the speed of light. Carruthers wondered what had brought the man out of his room. No doubt he was on the prowl for his wretched forecasts.

'You look awful, man,' said Bingham. 'You alright?'

'Fine.' Carruthers didn't feel fine at all. He was waiting for Bingham to leave so he could open his desk drawer and pop another couple of painkillers. He tried to remember how many he'd already taken and when he'd taken the last lot.

'Well, I hope you're not getting this summer flu that's going around. Can't afford for you to be off.'

Carruthers was just wondering how to tell Bingham about the argument between Cuthbert and Sturrock without giving away his own activities when Bingham spoke first.

'I need to talk to you. There's been another art theft.'

'What?' said Carruthers. 'When?'

'Overnight. Christ, I was only there a few hours before. It's unimaginable.'

Carruthers found himself standing up. 'Are you telling me it was Barry Cuthbert's estate that got hit?'

'Yes. Bastards got away with the Stubbs.'

Carruthers felt completely poleaxed. He was starting to feel nauseous and didn't think it was anything to do with the throbbing pain from his knee. Thank God he'd worn the gloves otherwise his fingerprints would have been everywhere. He thought quickly. Had Derek Sturrock known anything about it? He decided he couldn't have, which meant he must have left the party before it occurred.

'There's more. This time they got violent. Cuthbert's in hospital.'

'How bad?'

'He's got a fractured cheekbone.'

'I need to interview him.'

'Not possible at the moment, I'm afraid. He's severely concussed. Apparently he lost consciousness for a few minutes.'

Carruthers tried to swallow. He had been starting to form a theory. His theory had placed Barry Cuthbert right at the heart of the art thefts. Cuthbert had known all the victims. Liked expensive works of art. The man even had a criminal record for theft, for

Christ's sake. So, if Cuthbert wasn't responsible for the art thefts then who the hell was? Carruthers' blood ran cold. Could it be the Estonians? He remembered the girls who had got out of the helicopter with the dark-haired man. He'd just left Sturrock, and the man hadn't said anything about Cuthbert being in hospital. Perhaps he didn't know.

He needed to draw up a likeness of the man in the helicopter whilst he still remembered. Then get it sent off to the Estonian police as soon as possible. He was kicking himself for not asking the Estonian police for a picture when he last spoke to them. Still, that was easily remedied.

'I've sent Fletcher and Watson off to the Cuthbert estate to take statements,' said Bingham. 'Apparently some of the staff were still on site and got threatened.'

'Do you know if Cuthbert's estate manager, Pip McGuire, was there?'

'No. I don't think she was. I didn't get introduced to her at the party.'

'Did those that were still at the party see the gang?' asked Carruthers.

'Wearing balaclavas. There were three of them. I want you to meet Watson and Fletcher over at the Ardgarren Estate.'

Carruthers pushed his chair back and made a grab for his jacket. Limped from his desk towards the door.

'Whatever happened to your leg?' asked Bingham.

'It's nothing. Had an accident, that's all. What do we know so far?'

'They weren't quite so professional this time. Tried to gain entry by shimmying up the drainpipe. It's come away from the building. Robber must have fallen into a clump of rhododendrons. You're probably looking for a man with a number of injuries.'

Bingham looked at Carruthers, frowning, but didn't say anything. The older man gave Carruthers one last quizzical look then left the office.

Carruthers swore. Ran his hands through his short hair. Never mind his fingerprints. His footprints would be all over the estate. There was something else on his mind, though. It was Mackie's mention of his brother. He'd agreed to a family meal on Sunday, just the three of them, him, Mum and Alan. How was he going to take the time off to go to Glasgow with two suspicious deaths and now this? He was going to have to cancel. He hoped his mother would understand but since his brother's heart attack… His mother would be really upset. Perhaps she'd accuse him of not wanting to spend time with his brother. He had to force these thoughts out of his head. Now was not the time to be thinking such things.

Carruthers arranged to see the police artist that afternoon at the station. In the meantime he hurried to join Fletcher and Watson at the Ardgarren Estate. It wasn't an easy journey. The torrential rain had flooded several minor roads so Carruthers had to take a detour which added another twenty minutes on his journey.

'I want someone ready to take a statement from Cuthbert as soon as he's able to be interviewed,' he said to Fletcher. Catching sight of Fletcher staring at his leg he said, 'Don't ask. Long story.'

'Uniform have an officer standing guard outside Cuthbert's room. They'll notify us as soon as there's any change to his condition.'

'Do we know what happened?' asked Carruthers.

Fletcher shrugged. 'Same MO as the last three robberies – except it looks like they attempted to gain entry by shimmying up the drainpipe. It gave way. Assailant landed in those bushes over there.' Fletcher pointed to the clump of rhododendron.

'Already dusted the drainpipe for fingerprints. Nothing to send to the lab unfortunately.'

Thank fuck.

'But we've found footprints in the soil underneath one of the windows.' Carruthers prayed they would have been footprints of the two men who had stolen out for a ciggie break. Not his.

'So,' said Carruthers, walking around the building, 'how did they gain access?'

'Different MO to the McMullans, which is interesting. Begs the question, is it the same gang? Back of the property. This time they rammed a Jeep through the French windows. Before you say anything, there was a Jeep stolen last night in Kirkcaldy. Could have been used as the getaway vehicle.' She caught up with him. Laid a hand on his arm. 'Watch your step. There's broken glass everywhere.'

'And Cuthbert?'

'Put up a fight. He was punched in the face. Looks like he hit his head against a chest.'

'What time was the break-in?'

'Just after five in the morning.'

So Derek Sturrock must have left before five. 'I wonder what time the party finished?'

'Party?'

Carruthers thought quickly. 'Bingham had a freshly laundered dinner suit hanging on his office door, yesterday. He said he was attending a black-tie event over at Cuthbert's.'

Fletcher frowned. 'Didn't realise they were so chummy.'

'Know each other through the golf club, apparently. Come on. Let's walk around the grounds first before we enter the house.'

He directed a confused looking Fletcher away from the building, towards where he had seen the helicopter deposit its occupants.

'What are we looking for?' said Fletcher.

'You'll see.' They walked through the undergrowth and came out at the clearing. 'I knew it. There it is.' Carruthers pointed to an enormous 'H' marked in the clearing.

'Wow. A helicopter landing pad,' said Fletcher. 'How did you know this was here?'

'Let's just say a little bird told me. I have it on good authority that guests arrived last night by helicopter.'

'Whose authority?' Fletcher said frowning. 'What guests?'

'C'mon, let's get back to the house. I've seen what I needed to see.'

They walked back to the house and made their way to the back of the property where the robbery had taken place. Mud tracks showed where the Jeep had slid in, stopped and then fishtailed back out again. Accessing the house through the remains of the French windows, Carruthers saw shards of broken glass everywhere. There was a massive scuff mark in the black leather couch.

'What happened there?'

Fletcher shrugged. 'Not entirely sure, boss. Think that gang might somehow have caught the frame on the leather.'

'Guess his insurance will cover it all,' said Fletcher, watching the fingerprint team working on dusting the walls. 'Can't imagine someone like Barry Cuthbert being underinsured.'

Unlike the McMullans, thought Carruthers. He tended to agree. He gazed at the dirty space over the fireplace where, until a few hours ago, the Stubbs had hung.

'Easy enough to find out.'

'What now?' asked Fletcher.

'I think I need to pay Barry Cuthbert a visit. I have a lot of questions for that man.' He looked at his watch. *Damn. Mustn't forget I'm meeting the police artist later.*

'Well, he's not fit to be interviewed yet. He's still concussed.'

'Indeed. We also need to interview Derek Sturrock again. Look, Andie, I've got a meeting set up with the Pajus in an hour. Can you cover that for me if I head off to the hospital?'

'Sure thing. You're obviously banking on him being fit to be interviewed soon.'

'I am. The Pajus are staying at the Longstone Hotel in Castletown. Debrief me as soon as you can. I'll be on my mobile. And, Andie, I don't like to ask but—'

'You want me to accompany them to the mortuary?'

Knowing he was going to be tied up first at the hospital then back at the station, he nodded.

* * *

Fletcher and Watson arranged to pick up the Pajus from their hotel. When Fletcher pulled up in her green Beetle there was a blonde couple in their forties already waiting by the front door, clinging to each other like shipwreck survivors. The two female officers got out of the car and went across to them.

'Mr and Mrs Paju?' Fletcher felt it inappropriate to smile under the circumstances but she extended her hand to each of them, thanked them for flying over and tried her best to look approachable. She understood only too well what the loss of a child felt like, for all her circumstances had been very different.

'Erik and Karen, please. Marika is our only child,' said Karen, looking towards her husband. 'What could we do? Of course we would fly over. We need to know what happened to our child.'

Erik nodded before speaking. 'Can we get on with it, please? As you can understand, we are both very anxious.'

'Of course,' said Fletcher.

Watson held open the back door for the couple while they climbed in the car. She shut the door then took her seat next to Fletcher.

'It will only take us about fifteen minutes,' said Fletcher, starting the engine. She looked for a break in the traffic and then manoeuvred the car into the road.

'We are a bit unclear how this girl died,' said Erik. 'We still have a hard time accepting it might be Marika.'

Watson turned round to speak with them. 'Understandable. The circumstances are not yet clear. What we do know is she fell from a cliff.'

'Fell?' said Erik.

'As I said, we're still not yet clear what happened to her,' said Fletcher.

'Is there anything else you can tell us?' asked Mr Paju.

Fletcher and Watson exchanged a look.

'Not at this stage.' It was too soon to share the information that the girl had also been pregnant. The woman's ID first needed to be established. Fletcher glanced at the Pajus in the rear-view mirror. She could see Erik reaching for his wife's hand and giving it a squeeze.

Inevitably the details of this woman's death and pregnancy would be disclosed in the fullness of time. Fletcher swallowed a lump in her throat. Thinking about the dead girl's pregnancy was bringing back unpleasant memories and difficult feelings.

Fletcher pushed away all thoughts of her own pain. Now wasn't the time. In all likelihood these poor people were about to see the body of their dead daughter. 'Had Marika been unhappy at home?' asked Fletcher.

'Like many teenage girls she is headstrong,' said Erik.

Fletcher noticed the use of the present tense. *They still don't think it's going to be the body of their daughter,* she thought. 'Teenage?' asked Fletcher, frowning. 'How old is Marika?'

Mrs Paju looked confused. 'Eighteen.'

Fletcher lowered her voice and hissed to Watson, 'The Estonian police told Jim Marika Paju was twenty-six.'

'Is there a problem?' asked Mr Paju.

'No, no,' said Fletcher quickly. The conversation halted. Fletcher was busy trying to work out how this discrepancy had arisen. She knew mistakes happened, but still… Wasn't sure whether to phone Carruthers. She decided to wait. They were now only five minutes away from the mortuary.

'How had your daughter been in the last few weeks before she went missing? Was there any change in her moods or had she met anyone new?' Fletcher hoped the answers to these questions would assist the investigation.

'We had a couple of rows,' said Karen. 'She wasn't always happy with the decisions we made for her, but running away? No.'

'You made her decisions? At eighteen? What sort of things did she want to do that you disapproved of?' asked Fletcher.

'She wanted to travel,' said Mrs Paju. 'We thought she was too young. What did she know of life? There are so many dangers out there. She had dreams of coming to the UK to be a nanny. She loves children. But like I said, we told her, she was too young.'

Fletcher knew that an increasing number of young women were being lured to countries like Britain with promises of cleaning or nannying jobs. Instead they ended up being trafficked for sex. Karen stifled a sob. Fletcher was starting to get the impression of loving if over-protective parents. Had Marika felt stifled? Probably.

'Did Marika have a boyfriend when she went missing?' asked Watson.

Probably not, thought Fletcher, otherwise why would she want to travel, unless he was going to be going with her?

'No. She had been in a relationship with the son of friends the year before but the relationship had finished. They were still friends, though,' said Mr Paju.

They finally pulled up outside the mortuary. As she guided the Pajus out of the car they approached the front door to be greeted by Jodie Pettigrew, the pathology assistant.

'Do you want to go through to the waiting area?' Jodie asked. 'Dr Mackie's just on a quick break.'

Fletcher smiled. 'Sure,' she said. She escorted the Pajus to reception while Watson went to find the toilet. Fletcher wondered if Carruthers knew Jodie was back. Made a mental note to give him the heads-up. Knew he wouldn't be happy. Jodie Pettigrew was another relationship that hadn't ended well for him. What was it about her boss and women?

Once Watson got back from the bathroom and Mackie had finished his cigarette they guided the Estonians to the viewing area. Mrs Paju was quietly sniffling, her husband still holding her arm.

At the sight of the sheeted body through the window Karen started to cry again. Fletcher noticed that Erik's hands were shaking. *What an ordeal for any parent,* she thought. *And how much more difficult when you had to travel to a foreign country where the language wasn't your own.*

Mackie asked the couple if they were ready. Mr Paju said something in Estonian to his wife and she nodded. As the sheet was gently lifted back the Pajus both leant over and looked at the face of the young woman.

With a shriek Mrs Paju collapsed into her husband's arms. Fletcher caught sight of the expression on his face. It was relief.

He turned to her. 'Thank God,' he said. 'It isn't little Marika. It isn't our daughter.'

Fletcher, shocked, could only watch as the Estonian couple clung on to each other, laughing and crying at the same time.

* * *

The dark-haired uniformed police officer stood and moved aside as Carruthers approached him, flashing his police badge. 'He's a lot better than he was.'

'Since when?'

'A short while ago.'

Carruthers scowled. 'Why didn't you ring me?'

The young officer turned red. 'Doctor wants to run some more tests before he gets interviewed. Told me to wait.'

'And who do you answer to? Him or me?'

'You, sir.'

Carruthers could feel a muscle twitching in his cheek. 'Might be worth remembering that in the future.'

The dark-haired man hung his head. 'Yes, sir.'

Carruthers peered through the window in the door at Barry Cuthbert. He was lying in bed with his eyes closed. Half his face swollen. Head bandaged. He was on his own. The doctor must be still doing his rounds. Carruthers knocked once and entered the room.

'Are you up to answering some questions?' Carruthers didn't wait for an answer. 'Who did this to you, Barry?'

Cuthbert tried to turn his face away from Carruthers. ''Ow should I know? They was wearing balaclavas.' His words came out in a hiss. And Carruthers could detect a slight slurring of words, probably due to the concussion. It was clear to Carruthers that the man was having trouble speaking.

Carruthers limped across to the other side of the bed, pulling up a plastic chair as he went. 'Did they speak? Did you recognise the voices?'

'I don't remember them speaking.'

Carruthers shook his head. 'I find that hard to believe. You end up in hospital after trying to stop thieves from robbing you and not a word was said?'

Cuthbert just shrugged. He tried to sit up, gesturing that he wanted his glass of water. Carruthers leant over him and moved the straw closer, noticing the man's bloodshot eye on the side of the face with the swelling and bruising. He then saw Cuthbert's bloody and swollen knuckles. Pointing to them, he said, 'Got a few punches in, then?'

'I 'old me own in fights.'

Cuthbert spluttered on the water, gasping for air. 'Take it easy,' said Carruthers. 'What were you arguing with Derek Sturrock about at your dinner party?'

Silence.

'You were seen arguing by a reliable witness.' *Reliable witness my arse,* thought Carruthers. He was acting without permission from Bingham and nothing he said would be admissible in court. But the point was he was there and had seen with his own eyes the two men arguing.

'Derek Sturrock wasn't at the party. Why would he be?'

Carruthers raised his eyebrows. 'OK, have it your way, Barry. So what time did the last guest leave?'

'About two, as far as I can remember. Me memory is a bit fuzzy.'

Carruthers noticed Cuthbert's Cockney accent had got stronger. *Interesting. No doubt he'd been trying to work on losing it but can't keep it up in hospital.* What Cuthbert had said about the time of the last guest leaving, Carruthers knew didn't tally with what he'd been told by Fletcher, but he let that one go. After all, the man had already lied about Sturrock being at the party.

'All drive to the estate, did they?'

Cuthbert tried to prop himself up, half turning to plump up his pillows. Wincing with the effort. ''Ow else would they get there?'

'What about the people who came later by helicopter? For the after-party?'

'What helicopter?'

'OK. If that's the way you want to play it.' Carruthers paused. 'I'll need a copy of your guest list,' he said after some time.

'Is that necessary?'

'It is. Just a minute.' He stuck his head round the door. Found the PC reading the *Daily Record*. Carruthers frowned. 'Find me a pen and paper, will you?' he said.

The PC lowered the paper. 'What, now?'

Carruthers' mouth formed a tight line. 'No, next frigging century. Yes now and quick smart.' Carruthers went back into the room and turned once more to Barry Cuthbert. 'What's the extent of your injuries?'

Cuthbert lifted a bruised and bloodied hand and touched the side of his face. 'Fractured cheekbone's 'bout the size of it.' He winced. 'I hit the back of me head when I fell. They want to run more tests. Keeping me in for observation. Should be out in a couple of days.'

The door opened. The young police officer handed over a pen and paper to Carruthers who in turn handed them to Cuthbert. 'No time like the present, Barry,' he said, 'I tell you what.' He grabbed the pen and paper back, realising how difficult it was going to be for Cuthbert to write, given the state of his injured hands. 'You give me the names. I'll write them down. Let's start with Superintendent Bingham.'

After about twenty minutes Carruthers had written the names of about twenty guests down. Not one of them sounded Estonian.

'Who was the last guest to arrive?' Carruthers asked.

Cuthbert shrugged. Screwed his eyes up. 'I fink it was Dexter Mulholland at about eight but I can't be sure. I can't bloody remember.'

'Nobody later?'

'Why all the questions? Look, can you hurry up and finish. Me 'ead's getting worse and I'm starting to feel sick.' Carruthers opened his mouth to speak but before he had a chance, Cuthbert said, 'For fuck's sake, man, you don't still fink I have anything to do wiv these art thefts? I've been targeted just like the rest.' Cuthbert pulled a face.

'I did wonder that,' said Carruthers. 'And all I can deduce is that you got greedy, wanted a bigger cut so they decided to teach you a lesson.'

* * *

As Carruthers walked away from Barry Cuthbert he checked his mobile. Three missed calls, all from Fletcher. He left the hospital, sat in the car and called her back.

'What's up?' he asked. He needed to get back to the station. He was going to be late for the police artist. He listened to her breathless voice. He knew what she was about to tell him was going to be important.

'Jim, I'm back at the hotel with Mr and Mrs Paju. You're not going to believe this. The dead girl's not Marika Paju.'

Carruthers felt the world tilt. Whatever he had expected Fletcher to say, that wasn't it. He was so sure they'd get a positive ID. He smoothed the creases on his forehead.

'How's that possible, Jim?' said Fletcher. 'The Estonian police were so sure.'

Not just the Estonian police, thought Carruthers. What about the anonymous phone caller also giving the name of Marika Paju? His mind was racing. 'I have no idea,' he said. 'There's no doubt?'

'None whatsoever. Their daughter is eighteen, not mid-twenties. And she doesn't have a tattoo. At least not that they know of.'

'OK, when you're done, get yourselves back to the station. Wait, try to get a photograph of their daughter before they leave, will you? It might prove useful.'

'Already got it, Jim. It's not the same woman.'

Then who the hell was she? thought Carruthers. Instead, he said, 'I'm heading back to the station myself. I'll set up a brief for later.' Carruthers wondered how on earth that mix-up could have happened.

'Oh, I thought you should know. Jodie's back.'

Carruthers' heart sank. They hadn't parted on the best of terms. He didn't have time to respond as Fletcher started speaking again.

'How did you get on with Cuthbert?' she asked.

'Says he doesn't know who beat him up. He's lied about the time the party finished, about Sturrock being there and about the arrival of the late-night guests. Makes me wonder what else he's lying about. Mind you, he was still pretty groggy when I interviewed him.' He paused. 'OK, Andie, keep me posted. I'll be back at the station soon.' He finished the call and drove out of the hospital car park.

As soon as he arrived back, Carruthers went straight to the canteen. Being mid-afternoon there were no sandwiches left so he got himself a coffee and KitKat. Trying to ignore his hunger pangs, he headed back to his desk.

There was a note on his desk. Dougie Harris's scrawly handwriting. 'Police artist delayed til 3.' Carruthers looked at his watch. He had twenty minutes. There was more on the back of the note. 'Inspector Mikael Tamm from the Tallinn Police rung. Can you give him a call back.'

He sat at his desk staring at the note whilst he ate his KitKat. Between mouthfuls he picked up the phone and dialled the number of the Tallinn Police Station. He needed to find out how it was the Estonian police had mistakenly told them that Marika Paju was twenty-six when in fact she was a teenager of eighteen. There was an answer machine. Carruthers didn't understand a word but left a message anyway. Coffee in hand he went in search of Bingham. Found him coming out of the Gents. Uncharacteristically he was still doing his flies up.

'Sir,' he said, 'I need a word.'

'I'm in a bit of a rush, Jim.'

Carruthers decided whatever his superior was in a rush about it was going to have to wait. 'I've spoken to Andie. The girl in the mortuary's not Marika Paju. I don't know how the mix-up has occurred.'

Rushing or not, Bingham pulled up short. 'Where does that leave the investigation?'

Where indeed, thought Carruthers.

'You also had that anonymous phone call, didn't you? Either Marika Paju's the spit image of the dead girl or something else is going on. Have another word with the Estonian authorities?' Bingham said.

'Just left a message for them to call me. Do you remember meeting any Eastern Europeans at Barry Cuthbert's party?'

Bingham pulled up short. 'Eastern Europeans? What sort of Eastern Europeans?'

'Estonians, Lithuanians, Russians?' Carruthers tried hard to keep the impatience out of his voice.

'No, no Eastern Europeans there. At least, not guests, anyway.'

'You mean some of the staff were?'

'I didn't pay much attention. Some of the waiting staff may have been Polish. Honestly, I couldn't tell you.'

'What time did you leave the party?'

Bingham glanced at his watch. 'Are all these questions necessary?'

'I wouldn't ask them if they weren't,' he said, feeling his hackles rising once again. 'Roughly what time? It's important.'

'About ten-ish. Irene had a headache. We left early.'

'How many of the guests were still there at that time?' Carruthers followed Bingham into his office.

Bingham shook his head. 'Party was in full flow. I was one of the first to leave.' He tutted as he tried to wipe a stain off his suit with a handkerchief. He brandished his mobile, which he'd brought out of his pocket. 'Now if you're done with the interrogation I need to make a phone call. It's important.'

Probably phoning his wife about taking the suit to the dry cleaner's, Carruthers thought bitterly.

'Jim, what time does the next brief start? I want to sit in.'

Carruthers was surprised. 'Four.'

'I'll be there.'

Ten

'OK, let's have some quiet,' said Carruthers. He looked at his watch. It was bang on four. He'd managed to put together a reasonable sketch with the police artist. He was happy about that. And the brief had started on time. 'We've got a lot of ground to cover. First thing is that we've not been able to get a positive ID on the dead girl. It's not Marika Paju so we're back to square one. I want us to extend our door-to-door enquiries. Someone, somewhere must know who she is.'

He moved over to stand by the incident board. Put a new dot on the Fife map. 'As you'll all no doubt be aware there's been a fourth robbery. Barry Cuthbert's the latest victim. He's in hospital. Interestingly, the MO is different in that the men broke into the house by ramming the French windows. This time the alarm wasn't switched on downstairs as Barry Cuthbert was still awake. And clearly there was violence.'

'I suppose they waited til all the guests had gone home,' said Bingham. 'Talk about bloody audacious.'

'My concern,' said Carruthers, 'is Barry Cuthbert's guest list. Or more precisely the people that attended who were not on his guest list.'

'What is there to be concerned about, man?' asked Bingham. 'I was there and I knew pretty much everyone. Mostly local businessmen and members of the golf club.'

Carruthers' eyes travelled down the piece of paper he was holding. 'What about the guests who came later? After you left?'

'What guests?' asked Bingham.

'The girls in the helicopter and the man with the ponytail.'

'What on earth are you talking about?' said Bingham. 'And how on earth do you know who turned up after I left?'

'Did you know Cuthbert has his own private helicopter?' said Carruthers.

'Well, yes, but–'

'And you didn't think to tell us? After all, you knew I'd put Andie onto finding out about all local flying clubs.'

'A flying club's a bit different to a man having a private helicopter.'

'Is it?' said Carruthers, starting to feel angry at Bingham's blindness. 'Are you saying aerial photographs of potential victims can't be taken from a helicopter?'

Bingham stood up abruptly. 'I would like to see you outside. Now.'

Carruthers followed Bingham outside. There was deathly hush in the meeting room.

As soon as the two men were outside the room and Bingham had frogmarched him some way down the corridor out of earshot of the incident room, Bingham turned on him. 'What the hell do you think you're doing, Carruthers? You're undermining me at every turn. And in front of the team. I won't stand for it. Do you hear? After the brief I want to see you in my office. That's why you look bloody exhausted. It was you, wasn't it, that climbed that bloody drainpipe? How else would you know who arrived after me? It all makes sense now. That's why you're limping. It was you who fell into the rhododendron.'

Bingham took a step forward. Drew himself up to his full height. All he got for his troubles was to look up Carruthers' nose. 'You are damned lucky they didn't find your fingerprints everywhere. You bloody fool. What the hell were you doing there? I've got a good mind to bloody suspend you again. At the rate you're going you'll soon be back in uniform. This is your problem all over. You're not a team player. You are nothing more than a lone vigilante.' Bingham threw his hands up in disgust. 'My office. As soon as the brief is over.' With that he walked away.

Carruthers wondered if there was any truth in Bingham's words. He knew he could be stubborn and headstrong but he still liked to think he was a team player. A memory came back to him. Of Fletcher saying pretty much the same thing to him on one of their previous big cases. The case that had got him suspended. Perhaps he wasn't as much of a team player as he liked to think. Carruthers took a moment, drew a deep breath and re-entered the meeting. You could have heard a pin drop in the room.

'Superintendent Bingham won't be joining us for the rest of the brief.' He caught Fletcher's quizzical look. Hoped the whole station hadn't heard the exchange. He wasn't relishing the meeting with Bingham later. In the meantime, though, he had a job to do. 'Now, where were we?' he said, trying to ignore his pounding heart and feeling of impending doom.

Carruthers noticed a look between Fletcher and Watson before the former spoke. 'Is it true what you said about a helicopter landing on Cuthbert's estate?' said Watson.

'Yes, it's true.' With a sinking heart he said, 'I suppose you all heard that exchange. Look, however I got that information, it's out there now. And we need to focus on what we know. At 11pm a helicopter landed on Cuthbert's estate carrying five passengers, four young women and one man. All sounded Eastern European.'

'Have you asked Barry Cuthbert about them?' asked Watson.

'Yes and he's denying everything. But he knows he's in it up to his neck.'

'What? In all of it?' said Harris. 'The dead immigrant – if that's what she is; murdered gamekeeper *and* stolen artworks?'

'It all ties in somehow. I'm sure of it,' said Carruthers. 'Just not sure how, yet. We need time to work this all out. Originally I was beginning to think Cuthbert was behind the robberies. After all, he knew all the victims through the golf club; had no doubt been in their homes for dinner parties; likes expensive art himself and has a criminal record for theft.'

'And now?' asked Fletcher. 'Now that he's become a victim himself?'

Carruthers ran his finger around the inside of his collar. 'Part of me believes he may have faked the robbery to put us off the scent.' His face furrowed. 'But since I've seen him in hospital…' He shook his head. 'He took some beating. The fact he was taken in unconscious and with a fractured cheekbone says it all.' He shook his head. 'And there was something else. He seemed scared. That's not to say he's not in on what's been going on. My guess is he's got greedy and they've taught him a lesson.'

'Do you reckon he's the middleman?' said Watson. 'He's got the contacts. Perhaps he's been passing the names to a higher paymaster. The Eastern Europeans, perhaps?'

Carruthers rubbed his chin. 'Whoever got out of that helicopter was important.' As he said this he realised he was admitting to the entire team that he was there with no official backing. It was too late now. Anyway, most likely there wasn't a person in that room who hadn't overheard the exchange between him and Bingham. 'They were talking about an important guest arriving later. Who was the man with the ponytail and who were the girls in the helicopter?'

'Prostitutes?' said Fletcher.

'It's more than likely. We need to find the man in the 'copter. If he's Eastern European we could be in big trouble. I mean, there's no shortage of Eastern European girls living here in Scotland but if the man's Estonian and running his prostitutes from Estonia… We could be looking at a whole different ball game. Anything from the importing of illegals to running a business in sex slaves.

'Derek Sturrock was also seen arguing with Cuthbert at the party,' continued Carruthers, 'so I want us to chase that up. Find out what they were arguing about. Again, Cuthbert is denying the conversation ever took place. Says Sturrock wasn't at the party. But back to the man with the ponytail. I've been working with a police artist to draw up a likeness…' he admitted. 'I got a pretty good look at him in the headlights of the 'copter.'

'Any joy?' said Watson.

'Not yet. I'm going to send it off to the Estonian authorities as soon as I can touch base with them.'

'That's what that phone message was about that Dougie took, wasn't it?' said Watson.

Carruthers nodded.

'So where do the artworks fit in?' asked Watson.

Carruthers ran his hands through his hair. 'Christ alone knows,' he said.

'Where do we go from here?' asked Harris. Carruthers wanted to say that he wished he knew, but the team needed direction from a confident boss. He was already on thin ice. Had to show strong leadership in front of the rest of the team, prove he was a team player.

'I'll phone the Estonian police once I'm free.' Would there be anyone senior at work on a Saturday?

He looked round the room at the expectant faces. His gaze settled on Harris. 'Dougie, Cuthbert gave me a list of his guests.' He handed over a copy. 'I'll run it past Bingham, make sure no one was missed. You grab a willing volunteer and interview all those guests, see what they have to say about anything they saw or heard.'

'Including Mrs Bingham?'

Carruthers considered a moment. 'She will have to be asked at some point, but maybe I'll put someone else on that. One of us in trouble with the Super is enough.'

Harris looked relieved.

'Gayle,' said Carruthers, 'you interview Derek Sturrock again.'

A short while later Carruthers put his head round Bingham's door. As he did so he waved a sheaf of papers like a white flag. The forecasts. He'd also managed to contact the Tallinn Police and had sent off the police artist's likeness of the man he saw getting out of the helicopter.

'Come,' said Bingham.

Looking over his glasses at Carruthers he took the papers off the younger man. Didn't offer him a seat. 'This situation is intolerable, Carruthers.'

Oh shit, calling me by my surname again. I'm in for a serious bollocking.

'Ever since you were demoted back to inspector you've been overstepping the mark,' said Bingham, scowling. 'You're still acting like a bloody DCI. I won't have it.' Bingham stood up and started pacing his office like a caged lion. Always a bad sign. He walked up to Carruthers. Looked him in the eye. 'Of course, I blame myself. I never got another DCI in when I had the chance. You're an excellent police officer in many ways. In fact you make a better DCI than DI. Your demotion was unfortunate but you only had yourself to blame. Throwing punches at fellow officers is not something I tolerate.'

Carruthers felt the injustice of it. Wanted to tell Bingham he had been goaded into the fight by McGhee, who'd been bragging about trying it on with Carruthers' wife. What man would put up with that? Although to be fair, he could have chosen the venue of the fight with a bit more care.

'I've made a decision,' said Bingham, cracking his knuckles. 'I'm getting a new DCI.'

Carruthers swallowed hard. Stared at his feet. Counted to five before looking Bingham in the eye. That's why Bingham had been so keen to get the budget forecasts from him. He'd already decided to start actively looking for a DCI. Just needed to know if it was financially viable and he'd got Carruthers to do all the work. Carruthers had difficulty swallowing the bile. He realised he had missed part of the conversation.

'Can't keep a close enough eye on you myself. And to be frank, it's not my job. You need a DCI to keep a closer rein on you. Anyway, that's my decision.'

Carruthers remained silent.

'Right, now we've got that out of the way. Sit down. I want to talk to you about the art theft cases.'

Carruthers remained standing.

'I said *sit!*'

For once Carruthers did as he was told.

'I've been thinking about the late guests arriving by helicopter. You're sure about this?'

Carruthers nodded.

'I have no idea who those people were,' said Bingham. 'I concede I may have been wrong about Cuthbert. I don't like the thought that a bunch of Eastern European criminals may have been arriving under cover of darkness and right under my bloody nose, frankly. I want you to get to the bottom of who these people are.'

'Already onto it, sir. I've been working with a police artist to draw up a likeness of the man. Feel sure I would know him again. I've sent it off to Estonia.'

'Why send it to Estonia? The dead girl may not even be Estonian,' said Bingham.

'Well, we know that the tattoo on the girl's ankle is the mark of an Estonian prostitution gang so it's most likely she *is* Estonian. Or at least working as a prostitute for the Estonian gang. And to be honest, we don't have that many other lines to follow. It's unfortunate we've been given the wrong girl's details.' Carruthers still wanted to get to the bottom of that.

That seemed to satisfy Bingham. 'OK, keep me posted on your progress. I mean it, Carruthers. I won't have you going off not telling anyone what you're doing. You're part of a team. The problem is you keep forgetting that. Am I the last to know?'

'Do you mean did I tell the others about staking out Cuthbert's place? No, they didn't know. I had a hunch. I didn't want to bring it out into the open until I could prove it.'

Dismissed, Carruthers went back to his office. Switched on his computer. Just as it was booting up his phone rang.

'Detective Inspector Jim Carruthers,' he said.

The line wasn't clear and the voice heavily accented. 'Mikael Tamm of the Tallinn Police. I've been trying to get hold of you.'

'Sorry about that. We've been in a team brief.'

'I would like to email through the information we have on the man in your sketch.'

Carruthers put his ear closer to the phone. His heart was jumping. 'So you do know him?'

'I'm afraid so and it is bad news for you that he is currently in Scotland.'

Finding himself holding his breath, Carruthers gave Tamm his email address. Asked for the heads-up on the man before the information came through. However, he was also wary as they'd already given wrong information out about the dead girl.

'He's Aleks Voller. We think he's Estonian Mafia.'

'Oh Christ,' said Carruthers. So he had been right after all. Bingham would be sick to his stomach. And what would his now being at the same party as a member of the Estonian Mafia do for Bingham's chances of promotion?

Carruthers tuned in to the fact the man was still talking. 'Yes, you had better start praying, my friend. Are you sure it was this man you saw?'

Carruthers thought about it. It had been dark, he had got a sketchy view at best. And yet, he had drawn the profile of someone in the Estonian Mafia. Coincidence? He didn't think so.

Carruthers' words tumbled out. 'What is the connection between the Estonian Mafia and this prostitution ring? And what on earth is the link with Scotland?'

'It makes depressing statistics, I am afraid,' said Tamm.

'Then let me ask you a question,' said Carruthers. 'Have the Estonian Mafia got links with the art world? More specifically stolen works of art?'

'One moment, please.' Carruthers heard Tamm speaking with a colleague. His voice became sharp. Carruthers didn't need to speak Estonian to know the exchange of conversation was terse.

'I'm sorry about this, Inspector Carruthers.'

'Jim, please.'

There was another short terse exchange away from the phone. 'Jim, I'll have to ring you back. I'll pass on all the information I have. We're working on something big at the moment. Things are tense. But I have a feeling that our work may be connected by the questions you are asking. That was my boss. He is, how would you say, rather a stickler. I need to head up a team brief then I have to leave the office for a while. There's not enough hours... I may not be back in tonight. Can I call you first thing tomorrow morning? Shall we say ten am Estonian time?'

Carruthers tried to keep the frustration out of his voice. It didn't seem to matter whether the police force was Estonian or Scottish. They all had the same issues; a strict, inflexible hierarchy, irritating bosses and too much work. Carruthers had a sudden image in his head of lots of mice on wheels, all speaking different languages.

He heard Tamm give a short burst of laughter. Even his laugh sounded nervy. 'Sorry, that was my colleague, Gunnar, making an inappropriate joke.' Carruthers heard Tamm fire off a burst of Estonian. 'I've told him to tell the boss I'll be there soon.'

'Just one thing.' He dropped his voice so Carruthers had to strain to hear him speak. 'Don't talk to anyone but me about this. We must be careful who we trust with this information. I'll explain more when we next speak.'

He hung up. Carruthers was left feeling puzzled. He hadn't even had a chance to ask about Olev Lepp. Nor had he had a chance to talk about Marika Paju and the discrepancy over her age. He stood up, left his office. Went in search of Bingham. The Superintendent's door was locked. He walked up to Brown on the front desk. 'Has Superintendent Bingham left for the day?'

Brown smoothed back the few strands of hair he still had. 'Yep. Said goodnight on his way out.'

Carruthers sighed. He returned to his office and started a search for anything he could find out on Estonia and the Estonian Mafia, even Kurat, the devil.

He was in no rush to get home early. He had nothing to greet him except a pot noodle or a portion of frozen lasagne. He considered calling Gill and dismissed the idea. He briefly wondered if he should get a dog. A dog would be great company for when he went hill-walking. However, as soon as the thought arose he dismissed it. When would he have time to walk it? It wouldn't be fair. Now he knew Jodie was back he thought about ringing her and apologising. But he'd already done that. She hadn't accepted his apology first time round. What would be the point of trying again?

Eleven

At 8am the following day Carruthers was poised by the phone with pen and paper at the ready, eagerly awaiting Mikael Tamm's call back. When half an hour had gone by he thought the man was just late. He stood up, walked over to his office door and stuck his head out. Fletcher had just walked past. He called her over, apologised for asking her to fetch him a coffee but he didn't want to miss Tamm's call.

He drank the coffee slowly, brooding about recent events. Still no call from Tamm. He got Harris to man the phone while he visited the toilet. Met Bingham in the hall.

'I'm waiting for a call back from Inspector Mikael Tamm,' Carruthers said, wondering why Bingham was in on a Sunday and not on the golf course.

'OK, as soon as you have any news… I'll be in my office.'

Another thirty minutes went by. He got on with some paperwork. Carruthers glanced at his watch in frustration. Amazed to see he had been waiting ninety minutes. The time of an entire game of football. In the end he picked up the phone, dialled the Tallinn Police Station and asked to speak with Tamm.

As soon as he made contact he knew something terrible had happened. When he asked for Tamm the woman on the other end of the phone burst into tears. She passed the phone to a male colleague. His English wasn't so good and it was hard to piece together why Tamm couldn't get to the phone. He heard some shouting in the background and a woman crying. A short burst of Estonian mentioning Tamm's name. Then the line went dead.

Carruthers thumped the table top in frustration. *Fuck*. He sprinted out of his office and into the open plan of the DS's.

'Andie!' he called out. 'Can you get hold of that Estonian lad who started in records? I need someone here who speaks Estonian.'

She picked up her phone. 'He won't be working, Jim. It's Sunday.'

'Shit. Of course it is. Ring anyway. There may be someone there. See if they have a home number for him, will you?'

Fletcher lifted the phone and made the call. 'You're in luck, Jim. There's such a backlog they've drafted in staff for the weekend. Daniel Root's one of them. He's coming over.'

Carruthers checked his email – not one of them from Estonia.

The knock pulled Carruthers' attention to the door. He saw a young blond man he didn't recognise.

'Daniel?'

The man nodded as he came in, bringing the scent of coffee, obviously from the mug in his hand. 'Daniel Root. You need my help?'

After explaining what he needed, Carruthers hit redial and passed the phone to Daniel. Listening to one side of a conversation was always odd, even more so when he had no idea what the conversation was about. Nor was he sure why Daniel was frowning. When Daniel started biting his bottom lip and holding his breath, Carruthers feared the worse.

Daniel was ashen-faced when he put the phone back down. 'Tamm's been killed.'

Carruthers took in a deep breath.

'What happened?' asked Carruthers.

'He was following up a lead they had on one of their cases. He, another officer and his boss. Had a tip-off from an informant. They walked into a trap. All three were killed. Shot.'

No wonder the woman had been crying, thought Carruthers. In some ways he felt like crying himself and he didn't even know the man.

'Is there anything else?' asked Carruthers.

'That's about all the information I got. I could tell the man I spoke to was deeply affected by the deaths. His voice was shaking.'

'Well, if all three were based at the same police station, he would be. It's a huge loss. To lose two colleagues and his boss… well…' Carruthers trailed off. He was remembering when his nemesis, Superintendent Alistair McGhee, had taken a bullet for him in the line of duty and how emotional he had felt. That moment had been a turning point for him. Up until then he had blamed McGhee for his marriage going wrong, even for his wife leaving him. When McGhee had saved his life Carruthers had realised something important. McGhee hadn't been the all-encompassing shit he'd made him out to be any more than he, Carruthers, had been the perfect husband. Ultimately it had been his own jealously that had driven his wife away. He wondered if Mikael Tamm had a wife – who would now be a widow.

'Sorry it was such awful news,' Daniel turned to go.

'Wait,' said Carruthers, 'I don't want to intrude on their grief but I need to know what they were investigating. Tamm said something to me about the cases colliding – his and mine. We need to give them a call back.' He re-established the connection and gave Daniel the phone. 'And ask whoever picks up to check Tamm's desk. He was going to send me over some details of a man called Aleks Voller. I also need to try to speak to someone about Marika Paju. I didn't get a chance to tell them she's not our dead girl.'

Carruthers held his breath, praying that Tamm wasn't as untidy as him. 'His desk's been cleared of paperwork,' said Daniel. 'Nobody knows what he's done with the files. I didn't manage to ask about Marika Paju. Sorry.'

'Oh fuck.' Carruthers experienced an uncomfortable feeling. *Why would the man's desk have already been cleared of paperwork?* 'Ask them to stand by, will you? I'm going to send over the artist's impression we've got of our man again and see if anyone else recognises him as Voller. Also see if they can give us anything on Marika Paju.'

Carruthers noticed Daniel glance at his wristwatch, a troubled look clouding his face.

'If you're worried about your boss in records, I'll give them a call,' said Carruthers.

Daniel nodded, a look of relief on his face. 'We're short-staffed. I don't want to get into trouble. It's only my second week.'

Carruthers picked up the phone, made the call, then got a fresh brew of coffee and kept vigil by his computer. Just when he was about to give up, he noticed an incoming mail. From Estonia. It was in Estonian.

'This has been emailed by a man named Janek Kuul, a close colleague of Inspector Tamm,' said Daniel, sometime later. 'It hasn't been emailed from the police station but a private residence. He also said the photograph you sent had the likeness of this Aleks Voller. You're not going to be happy when you hear this…'

'Just give it to me, anyway,' said Carruthers, standing up.

'It seems Kuul was a close colleague of Tamm. The only reason he wasn't with him when he was killed was because he took two days off due to a summer cold.'

So he'll be suffering survivor's guilt, more than likely, thought Carruthers. It was how he had felt after McGhee had been shot attempting to save him. He looked at the young Estonian questioningly.

Daniel said, 'It appears Tamm was investigating Aleks Voller in relation to a drugs and prostitution racket. But he was keeping it quiet from some of his colleagues at the station.'

'Does it say anything about where the connection with the Estonian Mafia comes in?' asked Carruthers, leaning forward, arms resting on the desk.

Daniel scanned the email. 'It hasn't been corroborated but the evidence Tamm uncovered points to Aleks Voller having links with the Mafia through a venture that was netting him a huge amount of money.'

'Any idea what that venture was?'

Daniel looked at Carruthers. 'Again this is uncorroborated but Tamm was convinced it was a series of high-end art thefts.'

Carruthers' heart did a somersault.

Daniel continued, 'When he got killed he was meeting a man who said he had information about the exact connection between Aleks Voller and the Mafia.'

'Oh my God,' said Carruthers. He sat down heavily on his chair, incapable of further conversation.

'He also said one other thing. Not to contact him again or ask more questions. It's too dangerous.'

Carruthers remembered what Mikael Tamm had said. Kuul sounded scared. 'Maybe they don't trust someone at the station? Perhaps someone's leaking information? If that's the case and the Mafia are involved, it could be dangerous for them. I don't know the specifics of what things are like in Estonia but I would imagine a lot of these former Soviet-run countries still have their spies.'

'A lot of these mobster groups in Estonia are of Russian origin. So many different groups are now in operation.' Daniel sighed. 'We have a big fight against organised crime.'

Carruthers ran his hands through his short hair. He turned to Daniel, who now seemed lost in his own thoughts. 'Thank you. You've been really helpful. I'm going out for some air.' He grabbed his jacket and left, thinking he hadn't seen the direction this would go at all.

He knew he should report this to Bingham but instead Carruthers reached over for his car keys and headed out to the parking lot. A light rain was falling. A thick band of cloud was making everything appear dull and lifeless. Carruthers needed some thinking time. Didn't have a destination in mind but twenty minutes later found himself standing at the top of the cliffs overlooking the beach where the girl's body had been found. This was where it had all started. With the discovery of the girl. Or had it started further back, with the first art theft? He didn't know.

Despite it being August he shivered, turning his collar up. He regretted wearing his red lightweight jacket. The wind cut through him. His eyes scanned the beach, the only movement a group of black-headed gulls. The wind picked up and he stood gazing at the waves breaking onto the sand. There was a strong smell of sea salt in the air. Breathing it in, he could taste it on his tongue. The rhythmic motion of the waves soothed him. For a moment he felt at peace; until he remembered that this spot had been the scene of the unknown girl's death.

What was he going to do now Mikael Tamm was dead? He had instinctively felt he understood Tamm, could trust him. Had only spoken to him for a few minutes but it was a blow.

He started to walk over the grassy cliffs towards where he'd found the binoculars. This area had already been searched but he found himself looking for anything that had been missed. He scanned the beach, his eyes remaining on the now deserted spot where the girl's body had lain. *What a lonely spot to meet your end,* he thought. *What was she doing here? And why here? Did she throw herself off the cliffs or was she pushed?*

He scanned the horizon and the sea. Something dark was bobbing up and down in the water. Could it be a buoy? He wished he had his binoculars. He studied it intently. It suddenly disappeared. It surfaced a few metres away. He suddenly got a look at the profile. His heart leaped. It was a seal. A moment of happiness. He watched it bobbing up and down for a few minutes then reluctantly he turned away from the sea and started to walk back towards his car, checking his mobile for messages as he opened the driver's door. He had missed calls from both Fletcher and Bingham. He climbed in and switched on the engine.

Twelve

Twenty minutes later Carruthers was sitting behind his desk tapping his fingers on his desktop. He was feeling edgy. He'd lost a man in Inspector Tamm who could have been a useful ally. His options were now limited. His best bet was to pay Barry Cuthbert another visit and to lean on him. Heavily. He didn't want to admit that Mikael Tamm's death was making him nervous, anxious, depressed.

Harris put his head round the office door. 'The Super wants to see you, boss.'

As soon as Harris disappeared, Carruthers rolled his eyes. He was starting to dread these summonses. Reluctantly he left his office and walked the short distance to Bingham's. The door was ajar. He tapped on the door but didn't wait for a response. As he put his head round he was most surprised to see Bingham pulling open a drawer at his desk and bringing out two heavy crystal whisky glasses. Even more surprised to see him heading to his cabinet and extracting a bottle of Laphroaig. He poured a generous measure of whisky into both and held one out. He offered no water. 'Come in, man. Come in.' Carruthers walked into his superior's office and took the glass.

Instead of sitting in the chair he had grown to despise, Carruthers pulled up another chair from a corner of the office. Since they were clearly declaring some sort of truce he would oblige. He sat balancing the glass on his good knee. He'd been taking fewer painkillers although the knee was still swollen. He wondered if he'd got away with it. Perhaps the knee would settle down on its own. He stared into the amber liquid before taking a deep draught of it, enjoying the burning sensation when it caught at the back of his throat. He took his whisky neat. He hoped he wouldn't have to drive anywhere for a couple of hours.

Bingham ran his finger round the rim of his glass before taking a sip. He looked up at Carruthers. 'Do you know why Mikael Tamm was killed?'

Carruthers cleared his throat before speaking. 'His colleague told me he was working to reveal the connection between Aleks Voller and the Estonian Mafia. He had discovered evidence that links Aleks Voller, not just to prostitution but also to a series of art thefts.'

Bingham gulped his drink back. Carruthers stared into the rheumy eyes of his superior. He had the impression this wasn't Bingham's first of the day.

'Christ,' the Superintendent said.

'With Mikael Tamm out of the picture the only link we've got is Barry Cuthbert. We need to lean on him and hard,' said Carruthers.

'What about this other contact of yours?' asked Bingham.

Carruthers shook his head. He swirled the whisky round the glass, coating the sides in the golden liquid. 'Too scared to get involved.' He took a gulp himself. 'Made it pretty clear he's not willing to give me any more information.'

Bingham nodded. 'I've been blinded by my own stupidity. Never trust new money. God alone knows where it came from.'

'Well, I think in this case we may have just found out.'

'If it is true though, why was Cuthbert targeted?' Bingham continued. 'Unless they were teaching him a lesson. The question is, what was the lesson? And they didn't spare him when they put him in hospital, either.' He put the drink down and looked up at Carruthers. 'How is he, by the way?'

'Looks like he's on the road to recovery. He's going to be kept in for a few days.'

'Best place for him, apart from prison.'

Cuthbert was off Bingham's Christmas card list, then. Carruthers took another sip of whisky. It looked as if Bingham had had an even bigger shock than he had. Remembering the earlier stale cigarette smoke he had smelt in his boss's office and now looking at the heavy crystal glass on the table top, he wondered if the police station was Bingham's refuge from a failing marriage.

'Perhaps stealing his art and beating him up was some form of punishment?' said Carruthers. 'Maybe Cuthbert got greedy. Tried to double-cross Voller. Perhaps Cuthbert was the one who identified the targets, maybe even did the reconnoitring for the art theft?'

'The man's clearly up to his neck.' Bingham took a final slug of whisky. 'Perhaps this gang started to get nervous with Cuthbert being the focus of so much police attention,' said Bingham. 'The robbery might have been staged to make it look to the police like Cuthbert is innocent. After all, we're hardly likely to suspect him of being involved if he's one of the victims.' He set the glass down on his mahogany desk. 'Christ, I can't believe I attended one of his bloody parties. What is this going to do to my career when it gets out?' He stared into space and remained silent for a few moments. 'I'm sure with a bit of work we can get him on supplying prostitutes, if nothing else. I had an interesting conversation with one of my golfing friends who also attended the party. After a bit of persuasion he's prepared to make a statement to say he overheard a conversation about Cuthbert setting up certain select guests with these girls. He's not involved, you understand. Seems it was all organised in advance. Just as well we're getting his statement. The other guests are being very tight-lipped about what they saw.'

'Have you ever, well…' Carruthers didn't know how to complete the sentence. 'Been to a party where prostitutes were supplied?'

Bingham's mouth dropped open. 'Good God, Jim, what do you take me for? Of course I haven't. I've only been to Cuthbert's place once before and that was for lunchtime drinks. Although…'

'Although what?'

'Well, his parties were legendary, apparently. There used to be talk at the golf club. I always wondered why they clammed up when they saw me.' Bingham pursed his lips.

He looks like the boy in the school playground nobody wants to play with, thought Carruthers.

'I've been such a fool.' Bingham seemed to collapse into his chair. 'Have you ever lived a lie?'

Carruthers thought about it. Wasn't sure what Bingham meant. He started to wonder just how much Bingham had drunk.

'I know what you think of me,' Bingham said. 'You think I'm a social climber,'

Carruthers shifted uncomfortably in his seat. 'I–'

'Golf club membership, exclusive parties. It's all bloody Irene. It's what my wife wants. I'm trying to fit in with the type of husband she wants me to be. I despise myself for it and it's not working. I'm not happy.' Bingham seemed to collapse forward, head in hands.

Carruthers was gobsmacked. He didn't know what to say.

Bingham raised his head. 'It was fine until I got promoted to superintendent. Suddenly my wife decided we weren't moving in the right circles. She wanted me to take up golf. I hate bloody golf.'

So Bingham wasn't a social climber at all. It was his wife who was. Carruthers had been right about one thing, though. Bingham really did use his office as a refuge from his marriage.

'I want to take up a hobby of my own choosing,' he continued.

Carruthers was intrigued. 'What would you choose to take up?' he asked.

'Metal detecting. And do you know, Jim?' Bingham picked up his glass and toasted Carruthers. 'I'm bloody well going to. Irene can stuff her bloody golf and parties. Look where it's got me. Cavorting with bloody criminals. That's where. Well, that will be the end of any more dreams of promotion for me. I might as well just count the days to my retirement.'

'Talking of criminals,' said Carruthers. 'What about Barry Cuthbert?'

Bingham shrugged. 'Well, Barry Cuthbert won't be going anywhere for a few days. Don't think it's very likely to have been staged. Do you? I mean the man's got a fractured cheekbone.'

'Do you think they were trying to kill him?' asked Carruthers.

'Well, if they weren't, they might now. After all, they know we're onto him. It depends whether they think he might talk. I'm afraid I agree with you that that assistant gamekeeper... what's his name?'

'Joe McGuigan.'

'Yes, Joe McGuigan has most likely been killed by the Estonians. Still need to find the murder weapon.'

'Maybe it's been thrown into the sea,' said Carruthers. Suddenly he had a thought. 'Would Cuthbert be the sort of man you could strike a deal with? To save his own neck, I mean.' He had no liking for Barry Cuthbert at all, but he was the only link they had to the prostitution ring and the art thieves. He was their only chance to stop both.

'I don't know him that well,' admitted Bingham, 'but I imagine he's the sort of person whose true loyalty is to himself. I'm sure he'd do anything to save his own neck.'

'We could offer him police protection?' said Carruthers, trying to think.

'I want you to go back to the hospital,' said Bingham. 'Interview him again. Lean on him if you have to. In the meantime, I'm going to apply to the Procurator Fiscal for a search warrant for Cuthbert's place. We need to find some concrete evidence linking him to the robberies. The most likely place to start is his estate.'

Carruthers stood up. Nodded. 'Good plan,' he said. He placed his whisky glass on the table. 'I'll head back to the hospital after I phone the police station in Tallinn again.' *Shit, can I actually drive after that whisky?* He wasn't living in London anymore. Scotland had an almost zero tolerance to drink driving. You couldn't have as much as a single pint. So that would be a no then, although his glass wasn't empty. 'I need to talk to someone about this girl, Marika Paju. Maybe they think she's in the UK. Perhaps she was the one who made the anonymous call?'

'That doesn't make sense if she did. Why put her parents through all that misery? She'd have known they would have to fly over to identify the body.'

* * *

Several hours later, Carruthers was sitting slumped over his phone back at his desk. He was exhausted. With young Daniel's help he'd made another call to Tallinn but had got nowhere.

Daniel had spoken to an officer whose English had been perfect so he'd passed the phone to Carruthers. Unfortunately that had been the only positive thing about the whole call. The young officer, who hadn't introduced himself, had told Carruthers that the only case Mikael Tamm had been investigating when he'd been killed had been a local drugs ring. He also told Carruthers he'd never heard of a man called Aleks Voller or a woman called Marika Paju. Carruthers had asked to speak with Janek Kuul to be told he no longer worked at the station. He had been transferred. When he'd pushed the Estonian the man had told Carruthers to leave the matter alone then hung up. Carruthers had sat back, deeply perplexed.

Carruthers phoned the hospital later that afternoon to find that Cuthbert had taken a turn for the worse and had been put into a medically-induced coma.

Edgy and exhausted, Carruthers grabbed his jacket and headed home. Mercifully, the rain had dried up but the wind still buffeted. It tugged at his clothes as he walked to the car. He picked up a takeaway and ate it in his comfy armchair while he drank a beer. He listened to the wind whistling down the chimney breast. He wondered if that was their short summer now over. Taking a slug of the beer, he put the bottle down too heavily. He stared morosely at it as bubbles fizzed out of the glass neck and over the side. He watched it pool on the little wooden table beside him before he stood up with a sigh and walked into the kitchen to grab a paper towel. As he mopped up the liquid he glanced at his watch.

'Aw, fuck,' he said. He put his hand over his mouth. Leapt up and grabbed the mobile that he had left in his jacket pocket in the hall. Found he had three missed calls, all from his mother. He was supposed to be eating supper with them this evening. He'd forgotten to cancel. Letting out a long sigh he gripped the phone and rang her.

Thirteen

His mother's hurt voice was still ringing in his ears the next morning. Carruthers banished it and stared morosely into his black coffee. He knew he should really call Alan himself and explain why he hadn't turned up at the family meal but the truth was that Carruthers didn't enjoy talking to his brother. Since his brother's heart attack he had found Alan unresponsive and sullen on the few occasions he had tried to talk to him.

He forced his mind onto the case of the dead woman on the beach and the link between her and the Estonian Mafia. He puzzled over the conversation he'd had with the young Estonian police officer the day before. He recalled Mikael Tamm's instruction to trust no one and to talk only to him. With Tamm dead and Kuul supposedly transferred, Carruthers wondered who he could trust now.

Surely Tamm must have had friends at the station. Not everyone could be corrupt or too scared to talk. Carruthers picked up a pen and started tapping it on his desk. There must be someone in whom Tamm confided. Then he remembered towards the end of the call Tamm had been laughing with another officer. What was his name? Hadn't he said something about sharing an inappropriate joke with a friend? You wouldn't share a joke like that with someone you didn't trust, would you? What the hell had the man's name been?

Just as he was making the decision whether to get a coffee or go healthy and grab a bottle of water, his phone rang. The voice was familiar but the information unexpected. 'Mackie here, Jim. Toxicology results have come back on the dead woman. I thought you'd want to know straight away. She had a high level of diazepam in her system.'

'Consistent with a suicide?' asked Carruthers, chasing away all thoughts of his brother.

'Or murder. If someone was trying to get rid of her it would have made her pretty groggy.'

The day passed in a flurry of phone calls and paperwork and ended with Carruthers feeling frustrated that there had been no breakthrough.

That night he was restless, he tossed and turned. At least his knee didn't bother him though. He woke up at 5am with the first light of dawn. As he was lying in bed it suddenly came to him. The man's name. At least his first name. Gunnar. It had been Gunnar.

Carruthers got up and started to pack a bag. Threw in pants, socks and a couple of T-shirts. Decided the only way he was going to find out what was going on was to fly to Tallinn. God only knew what Bingham would say, no doubt he'd start banging on about budgets, but Carruthers would worry about that later.

He hardly noticed the change in weather as he drove to the station. The wind had finally abated and the sun bathed the ancient town walls in light.

The first thing Carruthers did when he got to the station was to call the hospital. No change. Cuthbert was still in a coma while the swelling on his brain subsided. Bingham had stepped up security and he had round-the-clock surveillance.

Next, Carruthers called Tallinn Police. Took a punt on getting someone young enough to speak good English. He was in luck. He asked to speak with Gunnar. Hoped there was only one Gunnar at the police station. Surprisingly he was put straight through.

'Gunnar?' Though there was no response, Carruthers knew someone was on the line. He could hear muffled background voices and a phone ringing in the distance. 'I am Detective Inspector Carruthers.'

'Yes, I am Gunnar Aare.'

It was going to be an awkward conversation but Carruthers pushed on. 'I know you are a friend of Mikael Tamm and that he's been killed. I'm calling from Castletown Police Station in

Fife, Scotland. I'm on the hunt for Aleks Voller but when I spoke with a colleague of yours yesterday he said there was nobody known of that name. Mikael believed our two cases are linked and that Voller is currently in Scotland.' Carruthers opened his buff file and spread the photographs of the dead woman in front of him. 'A young woman was found dead on a beach here, a gamekeeper's been shot dead and we have a number of art thefts we're investigating. We believe they are all linked.'

'This woman,' said Gunnar lowering his voice and speaking quickly. 'You think she's Estonian? What did she look like? Did she have blonde hair and a tattoo on her ankle?'

'Yes, blonde hair, blue eyes,' said Carruthers hurriedly. He was sure he was on the verge of a major breakthrough and didn't want to lose the momentum. He stared at the photograph of the dead blonde woman as he gave details of her height and weight to the Estonian.

'Oh, my God,' wailed Gunnar. 'The description does sound like Hanna. How did this woman die?'

Carruthers sat bolt upright. 'What? Do you know her? We don't know who she is. We thought she was a runaway turned prostitute by the name of Marika Paju but it turns out she isn't.'

'Look I can't talk. Give me ten minutes and your phone number. I'll phone from down the road.' Carruthers hurriedly gave the man the number. The line then went dead.

Carruthers waited, anxiously tapping his fingers on his desk. Ten minutes later Gunnar phoned.

'If it is who I suspect it is, she's one of us. Her name is Hanna Mets.'

Carruthers grabbed a pen and made a note.

'She's a police officer with us who's been working undercover on the trail of the Vollers.'

Carruthers felt a fleeting moment of irritation. *Why were the Fife Police not advised?*

'Listen,' said the Estonian, 'I can't be away from the station for too long. We'll have to set up another time for a longer conversation. But at the station I have to be careful. I can't talk to you there.'

If you can't speak about police business at the police station, thought Carruthers, *where else would you be able to speak about it?* This man Aare was every bit as paranoid as Mikael Tamm, as scared as Kuul. Carruthers decided to run the thought of his trip to Tallinn past the Estonian. 'I was thinking of flying over.'

There was a moment's hesitation the other end of the phone. 'Yes. This would be excellent,' said Aare. 'I'll meet you at the airport. If you like, I'll get you booked into the Hotel Viru. It's very central. How soon can you get a flight?' he urged. 'I will explain everything but it's complicated. It's best you are here. And soon.'

Despite it being Carruthers' idea, he felt it was suddenly moving too swiftly. He felt he was being left behind. 'If work allows and I can get a flight, I will be there tonight.'

Once the line went dead, Carruthers Googled the Hotel Viru. He found it had been the Russian headquarters of the KGB during their occupation of Estonia. He supposed that it was the perfect place to book in a visitor. After all, it was the first place to expect to be bugged so presumably the last place for those doing the present day bugging to look. He then Googled flights, found one leaving from Heathrow later that day.

He went in search of Bingham, found him in his office, once again buried under paperwork. If anything the pile seemed bigger than last time. Carruthers tapped on the door.

'Sir, I want to fly out to Estonia.'

Bingham looked up, frowning.

'Hear me out,' said Carruthers, raising a hand to block an objection. 'I know this won't be popular. Something's happening in Estonia and it's affecting Scotland. It's connected to the death of the girl on the beach and the art robberies.' Carruthers went on to detail everything that had been revealed in his conversations with Estonia. 'A man called Gunnar Aare wants to meet with me. He thinks we can help each other. He was a friend and colleague of Mikael Tamm.'

Bingham took his glasses off and pinched the bridge of his nose. 'This is most unorthodox. Why the hell didn't we get informed if there's been an undercover Estonian police woman operating in Fife? I don't like it, Jim.'

'If we do nothing, we'll like it even less. I think this Estonian prostitution gang are trying to get a foothold in Fife. My gut feeling is they're behind the heists. I can get a helluva lot more information about them from Tallinn than I can here in Castletown.'

Bingham cracked his knuckles. 'We have neither proof nor evidence. Surely an Estonian prostitution gang would target Glasgow or Edinburgh. The big cities? Why on earth would they come to Fife?'

'I can't answer that,' said Carruthers. 'However, let's be honest. Scotland generally isn't great at combating this type of crime. It's obvious we lag behind England. We've only had one conviction for human trafficking up here, yet as we both know this country makes up ten per cent of the UK population. Our agencies have got to get a lot better at tackling the problem.'

Bingham put his glasses back on.

'We also both know,' said Carruthers, pushing on, sensing a weakness in Bingham he could exploit, 'that the number of women from Central and Eastern Europe working in Scotland's sex trade has rocketed in the last ten years.' Carruthers could see Bingham was thinking. The thought had occurred to Carruthers that if they brought this gang down what a coup it would be for Bingham. Perhaps this feather in his cap would save his faltering career and he'd be back in the running for promotion.

'You asked why Fife?' said Carruthers. 'Perhaps it's all to do with connections. A lot of these girls will be moved from city to city, town to town. The man who got flown into Cuthbert's estate, Aleks Voller, he's at the centre of it. I believe Barry Cuthbert was working for him and Voller in turn is working for the Estonian Mafia operating out of Tallinn.'

Bingham took off his glasses and put the tip of the glasses into his mouth. 'Carruthers, this is starting to sound like something out of *The Thirty-Nine Steps*. You'll be talking about spies and espionage next. And as I said earlier, if an undercover Estonian police officer was operating here in Fife why the hell weren't we told about it?'

Carruthers' thoughts exactly. He wondered if the dead girl really was an undercover Estonian police woman. Once again his mind turned to the high levels of drugs in the girl's body. If the woman really was an undercover officer, murder was looking much more likely than suicide.

Carruthers thought about Aare talking about walls having ears in the police station over in Tallinn and thought it might come to that. Who did the ears belong to, though? 'Do you know much about the situation in Estonia?' asked Carruthers.

'Had a wonderful city break a few years ago with Irene. There's lots to recommend it as a travel destination but I know organised crime is getting a foothold.'

'I suppose places like Estonia are vulnerable,' said Carruthers. 'Cut off from the Western world for so long. It must be strange suddenly having open borders.'

'And with open borders, social rules are relaxed,' said Bingham. 'Along with an influx of new people come new ideas. All of which seems to have given local and foreign criminal organisations a ridiculous amount of freedom to operate.' Bingham cracked his knuckles. 'There's always danger when you've got countries that have undergone drastic political, economic and social change. On top of that,' he added, 'you've now got corrupt officials and politicians. Criminal networks, I am to understand, now operate at the very top.'

'Look, about me going to Estonia,' said Carruthers. 'It would just be for a couple of days. Three at most. Just until I get a handle on what's going on.'

'You need to leave this to Interpol. And, Interpol aside, how can I say yes?' said Bingham. 'With you gone and no DCI the most senior rank at the station will be a DS. What good's that in the middle of a murder enquiry? Anyway, I need you here supervising the search of Cuthbert's place once the warrant comes through.'

'Fletcher is more than capable of doing that. In fact, we have two highly capable DSs in Fletcher and Watson. And as you said yourself, given your social connections with Barry Cuthbert we now have one superintendent with a flagging career.' He saw Bingham wince. Decided to push his advantage. 'If I can break this case by going to Tallinn, how good is that going to make you look? So, look at it this way – can you afford to say no?'

Fourteen

As soon as Carruthers arrived at Tallinn Airport he was hit by a wave of oppressive heat. Trickles of warm perspiration ran down his back as he presented his passport.

He had been told that he'd be picked up by Aare's brother. The man who pulled up in a silver Toyota and called his name reminded Carruthers of a bird of prey. He had a hooked nose, piercing blue eyes and a bald head. The driver remained in the car whilst Carruthers got in the passenger seat. Aare's brother didn't speak as he drove the short distance to the Hotel Viru in the centre of Tallinn.

During the drive, Carruthers stared out of the window, trying to get his bearings. He decided the journey to the centre of the city was nothing special. In fact he was distinctly underwhelmed. Dull Soviet-style buildings occasionally interspersed with older architecture. The man who had picked him up had his driver's window wound down and Carruthers felt a welcome breeze on his face. He was surprised at how humid it was. Being so close to Russia he just assumed Estonia would be chilly in summer. But then he knew very little about Estonia. Just what Bingham had told him, what he'd read in spy stories and heard on the news. For some reason Russia was always portrayed in the UK as being perpetually cold. Big coats and fur hats. Why was that?

'When will I meet Gunnar?' asked Carruthers, left nervous by the lack of conversation.

The man didn't look at him but simply continued driving as he said, 'Tomorrow at eight. He will come to the hotel.' Aare's brother pulled up outside the tallest skyscraper Carruthers had so far seen in the country. 'This is it. Hotel Viru. Your time is your own until morning. Enjoy Estonia.'

Carruthers said goodbye, got out of the car and stared up at the ugly high-rise hotel. It was the epitome of Cold War Eastern Bloc architecture – functional, soulless and lacking in aesthetic features.

Carruthers checked in to his surprisingly comfortable single room on the seventh floor, dumping his small suitcase on the bed. He walked across to the window, and pulling the curtain further back, looked out. His room overlooked a busy thoroughfare of four lanes of traffic. He watched a blue tram going past. The view was dominated by the glass and concrete structure of the Nordic Hotel Forum. On the skyline there was the distant view of the spires of the Old Town and beyond, the Baltic Sea.

What am I doing here? he suddenly thought. *Will I get to the bottom of what is going on in three days?* It suddenly seemed a tall order.

He checked his smart phone for messages. Finding there were none he placed his phone carefully on the bedside table, took his clothes off, laid them over the back of a chair and slipped into the shower. Emerging a little while later, clean but still exhausted, he opened his case, took out his toiletries, hung up a couple of work shirts, brushed his teeth then climbed into bed. Within minutes he was asleep.

* * *

After a fitful sleep Carruthers rose at seven. After a shower he took a wander to the breakfast bar. As he walked into the vast self-service restaurant he noticed it had a distinctly corporate feel. Many of the dark brown tables were of cheap woodchip, several seating six. He walked the length of the room and threw his jacket onto a chair in one of the small booths near the window. Tried to throw off the sluggish feeling he was experiencing. He had been surprised at how early daylight had begun. He hadn't slept much after four.

He glanced around him. There were a few other early risers enjoying breakfast alone or in small groups. To his left was an elegant blonde woman in her thirties sipping coffee. She caught his eye and smiled. He smiled back.

He walked over to the breakfast bar and loaded his plate with Gouda, a selection of hams and a couple of hard boiled eggs. He couldn't stomach the pickled herring so he bypassed that offering. He fixed himself a black coffee and made his way back to his table. As he sat back down the blonde woman at the next table leant over.

'Did you manage to get any sleep last night?'

Surprised by the Home Counties accent, Carruthers shook his head, unsure what she was getting at.

'Whenever I travel to Estonia in the summer,' she said, 'I always make sure I have my eye mask with me. I won't be able to get a proper sleep otherwise.'

'I didn't sleep well,' he admitted. 'It must have been the light. I'm used to black-out curtains.'

'Are you from Edinburgh?' she said, clearly picking up on his accent.

'Glasgow, but I now live in Fife.'

She smiled. 'First visit?'

Carruthers nodded. He took a sip of his coffee. 'I've never been to Eastern Europe before.'

The woman laughed. 'Don't let Estonians hear you say that. They don't see themselves as being part of Eastern Europe. Many see Estonia as a Nordic country.' She shrugged. 'It's very close to Finland. I know some Estonians who feel Northern European.'

Carruthers was silent, absorbing her words, thinking about how easy it was to pre-judge peoples of another country. After all, hadn't he also assumed they all had bad teeth with terrible dentistry?

'It's a fascinating country,' she continued. Carruthers noticed that she kept one eye on her mobile which was sitting on her table. She smiled. 'I love it here. It's my fifth visit. You do need that eye mask, though. Have you heard of the term "astronomical twilight"?'

Carruthers shook his head. He tried the expression in his head and liked the sound of it.

'Did you notice last night, after sunset,' she continued, 'it's no longer light, but it doesn't get dark immediately either? That phenomenon is known as "astronomical twilight".'

Carruthers speared a piece of cheese and thought about it. He hadn't noticed but then maybe that was because he lived in Scotland. Some parts of Scotland never got dark in summer.

He looked over once more at the woman. She interested him despite her rather formal way of speaking. Her blonde hair fell over her face and she smoothed it away with her hand. Carruthers loved the way the light was catching the highlights. He wondered if she was an academic.

'I didn't sleep very well,' he admitted, 'but I have a lot on my mind at the moment. It must be strange to live here for those not used to it,' he added.

'No darkness during summer and little light during winter. It must affect the psyche, don't you think?' She laughed.

'Have you been here in the winter?' he asked, thinking her description of Estonia sounded a bit like Scotland.

She laughed. 'No. Just summer, although I've been to Finland in the winter. Do you know much about Estonia?'

Carruthers shook his head.

'It's got a fascinating history. You know this very hotel was built by the Russians to spy on foreigners? Some of the bedrooms were bugged.' She leaned closer towards his table. Lowering her voice she said, 'There's a story that the hotel frowned on people having sex in the rooms. Couples were made to keep their beds apart. Apparently if a couple started moving the beds together there'd be a knock at the door within a few minutes and a maid would appear to tell them to move their beds back to where they were.'

Carruthers listened, intrigued. 'How did the maid know?' He wondered if she was trying to pick him up with this talk about sex. He didn't know. Although he prided himself on being adept at reading signals, for some inexplicable reason he was useless at reading women.

The blonde woman laughed. 'The bugging devices in the rooms didn't work so well if the beds were moved away from the wall. That's how the KGB knew what the guests were doing.'

Carruthers tried to imagine the lack of freedom and couldn't. He studied the beautiful woman in front of him, instead.

'When I was here last I got talking to another guest, a wonderful Finnish woman called Bodil,' she said. 'She told me she was a PA and that she and her boss used to get the ferry over from Helsinki for a few days business when Estonia was under Soviet rule. Of course, they stayed in this hotel. They didn't get a choice. According to her, it was an open secret that the rooms were bugged. She said that even the vase of flowers on the reception desk had a bugging device in it. They used to talk into the flowers and a member of staff would appear as if by magic. In the old days the KGB also used to employ little old ladies who would sit on their own having cups of tea looking like they were reading the newspaper. Really they were listening in on conversations going on around them and reporting them back.' Her face changed and she looked serious. 'It all sounds twee, but a lot of people disappeared from the hotel if they were considered a threat. They were taken away and never seen again.' Just at that moment the woman's mobile rang. 'Excuse me. I must get this call. I'll let you get back to your breakfast. Enjoy your stay.'

Carruthers wondered what happened to the people who were taken away. Tortured and killed, he supposed, then buried in a shallow grave somewhere. When he had finished eating he rose, giving the blonde woman a backwards glance. He smiled at her but she was still on her phone and didn't see him. Back in his room he brushed his teeth, then grabbing his wallet and a lightweight jacket he returned downstairs. He was waiting in the hotel foyer when a slim dark-haired man with gaunt cheeks walked in.

'Are you Jim Carruthers?' the man said, reaching out his hand.

Carruthers nodded and took the cool dry hand. As they broke contact the man took out his police ID. As Carruthers glanced at it, Gunnar Aare touched Carruthers' arm lightly.

'Come, let's walk.' They left the foyer and Aare hesitated for a fraction of a moment on the doorstep of the hotel before turning left and walking towards the Old Town. As soon as they were outside in the bright light Carruthers had to blink to get used to it. They crossed the busy main road at the lights and walked towards the main entrance to the Old Town, which was marked by two ancient grey-brown stone towers. The towers were topped with red roof tiles in a cone and it all blended with the old city wall. Between the towers, a wide cobbled street led into the maze of the historic heart of the medieval city as the exquisite stone buildings and narrow alleys baked beneath a cloudless sky. Looking around this breath-taking place Jim unexpectedly felt captivated by it. One day he must return to really enjoy the city.

'I know a good place for coffee,' said Aare.

Dragged back from his romanticising, Carruthers realised he wouldn't mind having a second shot. He wondered if the Estonians were big coffee drinkers. He realised how little he knew of this former Eastern Bloc country. He was going to have to get up to speed fast. He side-stepped a woman pushing a buggy. Aare took a first right onto another cobbled road, Carruthers noticed the street sign, Vana Viru. There was a little coffee shop on the right with an attractive outside terrace under a white awning. They picked a table and sat down.

Aare turned to Carruthers. He said quietly, 'You must understand the politics here to get a grasp of this situation. Unfortunately the police, like all official institutions, has been infiltrated by Estonian Mafia. They are a scourge. This is why I need you here. A well-trained police officer from the UK.'

'What can I do?'

'You must help me flush out the bad guys.'

'You can't possibly be serious,' said Carruthers, starting to feel angry. He felt duped. Had been brought over here on false pretences? 'How can you even think I can begin to help? You said it yourself, I don't know the first thing about Estonia, its history or politics. I'm only here three days. You must be mad.'

Gunnar Aare leant forward. 'Not mad. Desperate, my friend. There is a difference. You forget we just lost three of our colleagues.' He continued. 'But you have something of ours we need and we have something of yours.'

'What do you mean?' said Carruthers.

'You have Aleks Voller. We've been trying to locate him for months. We knew he and his brother were the link between Estonia and the rest of Europe. Marek is still here in Estonia. But Aleks disappeared. We just didn't know where to. Then he turns up in Scotland. You can help flush him out. Where would I start looking in Scotland? I've never been to Scotland. Like I said, you have something we want. And we have something you want.'

'Meaning?'

They paused as a blonde woman with bright blue eyes, wearing skinny black jeans and a white top, came up to take their order.

Aare turned to Carruthers. 'Coffee? Black?'

'Yes, thank you.'

Aare ordered for them, barking instructions in Estonian. Carruthers, although not understanding what he said, felt vaguely uncomfortable at the manner in which the man spoke.

Aare leaned forward. 'You want to put a stop to these art thefts you were talking about and at the same time, how do you say, nip in the bud this gang of pimps who are starting to operate in Scotland. Trust me. They are bad news. These art thefts are helping to fund the Mafia in Tallinn. British artists are very popular in Russia, the States, even Japan. We, you and I, bring down Marek and Aleks Voller, put a stop to the gang of art thieves, cutting off one primary sources of income for the Mafia. It will benefit both societies. But first I need you to help me flush out the bad eggs in the Tallinn Police.'

'Bad apples,' Carruthers corrected, without thinking.

'That's right,' said Gunnar. 'Bad apples. I'm not under any illusion. I know another gang will spring up. But having one lot off the streets is a start, is it not? What do you say?'

'I still think you're mad. I'm only here for three days. What can I do in such a short space of time?'

'Let me tell you about the situation in Estonia and then you might understand a bit better. For fifty years this tiny republic was under illegal occupation by the Soviet Union. Estonia recognised this, the rest of the world recognised it. The Soviet Union did not. In 1940, Soviet troops invaded Estonia installing a puppet government with the backing of the Soviet Union. We paid a heavy price.' He waved his hand. 'Anyway, I won't go into that just now. But back in 1991 when the old Soviet Union was crumbling we peacefully took back what was rightfully ours.'

'Things haven't been easy,' said Carruthers, cautiously.

'Far from it. However, Russia has always looked upon us as theirs. To do with whatever they want. You're right. Things have not been easy. We have a big drug problem here. Since 1991 the Russian Mafia saw opportunity and flooded Estonia and this wonderful city, with cheap drugs. Many of our young people are now drug addicts. Even schoolchildren.'

Carruthers wondered if Bingham knew this.

'They saw big money to be made. We also have a prostitution problem. Those drug addicts needed money to buy their drugs. Many of the Estonian Mafia have connections with their Russian Mafia counterparts. And, of course, many Russian Mafia are former members of the KGB.'

Carruthers nodded. He knew of the connection between the KGB and Russian Mafia. He didn't, however, know about the prevalence of drugs in Estonia.

'I'm sure you've heard a lot about Russian organised crime and its links with the Russian state,' said Aare. 'But it operates not just at home. Its reach is global. They have their hands in everything – theft; drugs; prostitution; human trafficking. However, trafficking is now treated as a serious matter by the Estonian government, which passed a law in 2012 criminalising people trafficking with penalties of up to fifteen years imprisonment. We also have stronger anti-corruption legislation than we used to but still…'

Carruthers nodded. It sounded like Estonia had had a lot of work to do. He then thought of Scotland. Police Scotland had come into effect in 2013 to a lot of criticism. Some said it was nothing more than a cost-cutting exercise when the eight regional forces merged into one. Bingham had been one such critic.

Carruthers shifted his attention back to Gunnar. It was all becoming almost too expansive, too abstract for Carruthers to take in. He realised he needed to talk details. The picture of the mutilated body of the dead woman on a windswept beach back in Fife came into his mind. 'Tell me about Hanna Mets,' he said. 'First of all, do you have a photograph of her?'

Aare placed his briefcase on the table, opened it and drew out a photograph. He passed it to Carruthers. The Scottish cop's heart did a leap when he saw the attractive blonde woman in the picture. He then tried to visualise the torn mutilated face of the dead girl on the Fife beach as he had viewed her. Was it the same woman? Same white blonde hair. Same shape face. He took out a police photo of the woman and studied it. Carruthers nodded. 'I think it's the same woman but I couldn't be certain. Tell me about her.'

'It does look like Hanna Mets,' agreed Aare. What do you want to know?'

'What sort of cop was she?'

Aare shrugged and stopped. Took out a red and white packet of cigarettes from the breast pocket of his shirt. 'A good cop. An honest cop, but she was also a woman haunted. And out for revenge.' He put an unlit cigarette between his teeth. Offered the pack to Carruthers, who shook his head. He saw the pack was Winston. He wondered if this was a popular brand.

'Why?'

'Aleks Voller killed her sister.'

Carruthers dragged his gaze away from the unfamiliar pack of cigarettes to the face of the man sitting opposite him. 'You said she was undercover when she died,' said Carruthers. 'Why weren't the Scottish Police informed?'

Aare extracted a silver lighter from his trouser pocket, lit the cigarette and took a long drag. 'She was working undercover in Tallinn. We didn't give her permission to travel to Scotland. Then suddenly she disappeared off the radar altogether.'

Carruthers kept listening.

'We knew she was probably in trouble,' the Estonian continued. 'We couldn't locate her. We left messages for her on her mobile, in code of course.'

'She never returned any of them?'

'No.'

'When she was found she had no personal effects with her,' said Carruthers. 'We never retrieved a mobile or anything else. It made us wonder if she'd killed herself. Simply walked out of home with suicide in mind.'

Aare nodded slowly. 'I can see why you'd think that.'

Carruthers watched as Aare took another long drag on his cigarette, tilting his head back and expelling the smoke into the warm Tallinn air. Simply dressed in jeans and a grey T-shirt, Carruthers could already feel the sweat beading between his shoulder blades. He was looking forward to a cold shower back at the hotel later. Carruthers leaned into the table as he asked his next question. 'You don't think she committed suicide, do you?'

Aare took another long drag at his cigarette. This time he expelled it between his teeth. 'No. There's no way she would have taken her own life. She believed in what we were doing, what she was doing.'

'So you believe she was murdered? Pushed from the cliffs.'

'She'd got close to him, Aleks, in the six months she'd been undercover. Maybe too close. Her cover was obviously blown.'

'Was she sleeping with him?' asked Carruthers.

'Probably. It was more than just a pimp–prostitute relationship.'

'So he trusted her... confided in her?' said Carruthers, wishing wholeheartedly that they'd managed to get to Hanna Mets before Aleks Voller had.

'She was a professional in every sense. We'll miss her. She was a great asset.'

'Yes, I can see that,' said Carruthers, thinking about Fletcher. Would she have volunteered to go undercover, even subjected herself to being tattooed? Probably. Sleeping with the enemy, though? That was a different matter. Would she go that far? He wasn't sure. He wondered how he'd feel if anything happened to her. He pushed the thought out of his mind. It made him feel sick.

'Did she know what he might be doing in Scotland?'

'All we knew was that Marek and Aleks Voller had a contact somewhere in Europe. We didn't know which country, except we suspected it may be Britain. We knew the man had money, a good knowledge of art and contacts.'

'Barry Cuthbert,' said Carruthers. 'I wonder how Hanna found out. And why she didn't tell you?'

Aare dropped the cigarette butt and slowly ground it into the cobbles. 'I can only imagine she knew we would stop her going. Too dangerous. And on her own she would have no back up.' He looked up at Carruthers. 'How did you know she was Estonian?'

'We didn't,' said Carruthers. 'Although the police pathologist guessed she was Northern or Eastern European. Her dental work for one thing. We had an anonymous phone call from a girl… maybe a prostitute, giving us the name of Marika Paju. We found out that name is Estonian.'

'What girl?'

'She never said. Like I said it was an anonymous call. And all she said was that she recognised the photograph of the girl.'

Aare looked puzzled. 'That wasn't the name she chose when she went undercover. Unless she switched names when she got to Scotland.'

Carruthers frowned. He was trying to get everything clear in his head. 'And Marika Paju. That name belongs to a real girl who's missing. Her parents flew over from Tallinn to identify their daughter.'

Aare fixed Carruthers with a curious stare. 'That was unfortunate.'

'So what happened to the real Marika Paju?' said Carruthers. 'Is she…?'

'Most probably dead.' Aare shrugged. 'Another prostitute who had a drug problem.'

Carruthers felt a tightening in his chest. He felt a knot of sudden pain but it disappeared as quickly as it had come. He thought about Marika Paju. How she had gone from being a runaway whose friends had given her enough money to travel to Scotland to ending up as a prostitute and possibly drug addict. He presumed somehow her path must have crossed the Vollers' before she left Estonia. He then thought of her parents. All the agony the parents had been through then the relief of realising the dead girl wasn't their daughter was to be in vain. Their child was most likely already dead. Perhaps they wouldn't even get a body back. He didn't want to ask Aare. Didn't want to hear the answer. 'When Hanna Mets was found she had a high level of diazepam in her system.'

'Diazepam?'

'Was she on diazepam, as far as you know?' asked Carruthers.

'No, I wasn't aware of it. Perhaps it was used to sedate her before she was killed?'

'Is diazepam used regularly in Estonia and Russia?'

'It is one of the drugs we use, yes. Tell me about this man, Barry Cuthbert,' said Aare. 'What does he do?'

Carruthers was a little taken aback at the turn of Aare's conversation but he tried not to show it. 'He owns a shooting estate in Fife.'

They paused their conversation as the waitress served them their coffee.

Carruthers lifted his cup to his lips and took a sip. It was good. He turned back to Aare. 'Do you really think someone at your station is corrupt?'

Aare lit another cigarette. 'Not just corrupt. A murderer. How else do you think Mikael Tamm would have fallen into that trap? Someone at the station tipped off the Mafia. Must have.'

Carruthers looked at him. 'Any ideas?'

'Not yet, but I'm working on it.'

He drew closer to Carruthers. 'Now tell me, when did you start to get an inkling there was a link between the stolen artworks and the Mafia?'

'I just had a feeling.'

Aare nodded. 'Sometimes feelings pay off.'

'I started to find connections between certain people,' said Carruthers. 'The way cops do. I began at the golf club. All those who'd been robbed were members of the same golf club. I started to wonder if someone at the club was passing on information about the members. Barry Cuthbert was a member. We found out he knew all the members who'd been robbed, he liked expensive art and had a private helipad.'

Aare looked quizzically at Carruthers.

'The National Crime Agency in London told me it's possible whoever planned the robberies would have taken aerial photographs of the targets.'

'Ah yes, I see.'

'Anyway, my own superintendent is a member of the club,' Carruthers continued. 'It just so happened there was a function on at Cuthbert's home. I felt it was too good an opportunity to miss so I staked the place out.'

'Good thinking. Did it pay off?'

'Yes. As I was watching I heard a helicopter approaching. The man now identified as Aleks Voller disembarked, as did four girls. Possibly Eastern European. Or the Baltic States,' Carruthers added quickly, not wanting to offend. 'Probably prostitutes. We have evidence to suggest Barry Cuthbert was involved in supplying prostitutes for select guests at parties. Bingham claims he knew nothing of this.'

'Bingham?'

'Superintendent Bingham.'

'Do you believe him?'

'Yes, as it happens, I do.'

'He must feel pretty foolish to have such friends.'

Carruthers was wondering how Bingham was feeling. He almost missed the fact Aare was still talking.

'Was he OK about you flying out here?' said Aare.

Carruthers cupped his coffee, blowing on it. 'He wasn't exactly ecstatic but he understands it's important to gather as much information as possible and that the seeds of these crimes probably originate in Estonia.'

'And it sounds like Barry Cuthbert's the link?'

'That's what we think.'

'Is there anyone else involved in Scotland, do you know? This is all useful information for us, too.'

'I honestly don't know. I hope it's just Cuthbert and Voller who are the main players, but for all we know there could be a whole network of criminals stretching from Estonia to Scotland. Have you traced anyone else to the UK?'

Aare shook his head. 'I wouldn't rule it out but let's hope the line ends with Cuthbert and Voller. Will he make a full recovery? Barry Cuthbert?' asked Aare, his blue eyes unblinking.

'We hope so. As soon as he's well enough he's to be moved to a safe house.'

'Much better than keeping him in hospital, I think. What will happen to him?'

'There's some talk about him being offered protection and a new identity in exchange for information.'

'A good plan.'

'We like to think so.'

They lapsed into silence. Carruthers wondered how Barry Cuthbert was progressing. Made a mental note to call the station as soon as he could.

'Tell me about these stolen artworks,' said Aare. 'What did this gang get away with?'

'They snatched a Vettriano from a couple called McMullan who were raided a few days ago in Fife just before Barry Cuthbert got hit. Cuthbert lost a painting by George Stubbs. He paints horses,' said Carruthers, not knowing how well Aare would know English painters.

'And this Vettriano. What is it valued at?' asked Aare.

'It was last valued at £200,000.'

Aare whistled. 'That's a lot of money.'

'You're telling me.'

'And the other paintings? How many artworks have you lost in total?'

'A Constable and a Sisley. Total estimated value: just under four million.'

Aare's eyes narrowed. 'Four million. Someone stands to make a lot of money.'

'Yes, I must admit I didn't know much about art theft before working on these cases. The NCA were particularly helpful though.'

'NCA?'

'Oh sorry, the National Crime Agency. They told me that anyone who steals high-end works of art such as a Constable aren't usually professional art thieves. Apparently it's so hard to sell paintings on by really well-known artists.'

'Yes, it's fascinating.' Aare glanced at his watch. Carruthers got the impression Aare was switching off from the conversation. He wondered why. Carruthers glanced at his own watch. It was ten.

'I have some things to attend to,' said Aare standing up. 'Police business. I'll make some phone calls. How are you set for meeting up later? Perhaps a meal in town?'

'That would be great,' said Carruthers.

'I'll book somewhere for tonight. I'll give you a call. What will you do with the rest of your day?'

'I'll take a wander. Get a feel of the city. Maybe see if I can book a tour of the KGB room in the Viru.'

'Ah yes, one of our top attractions. It is a must-see, as they say.' He laid a hand lightly on Carruthers's shoulder. 'Now remember, make sure you keep away from the station. We mustn't be seen there together.'

Carruthers nodded. As Aare stood, Carruthers said, 'I might stay and have another coffee. It's good here.' He called over the waitress and ignored the voice in his head that told him not to have a third cup.

Aare nodded solemnly, shook Carruthers by the hand and left. Carruthers stared at his retreating back. The man was already talking urgently on his mobile.

Fifteen

An hour later Carruthers was back at the hotel. He spoke to the staff about organising a tour of the KGB room on the twenty-third floor. Luck was on his side. A tour was starting within the hour. He settled himself at a seat at the modern-looking bar by reception and asked for a bottle of sparkling mineral water. Sipped it while watching the guests going in and out of the hotel and tried to imagine the type of guests the hotel would have had thirty or forty years ago when Tallinn was all but closed to Westerners. He picked up a hotel pamphlet and started reading.

He glanced at his watch. It was nearly midday. A small number of people had started to gather. Carruthers paid for the mineral water and joined them. He found himself with a bunch of noisy young Finns. There seemed to be a lot of Finns at the hotel. Carruthers wondered if they came over by ferry from Helsinki for a cheap weekend. He was pleased to see that the group had an English-speaking guide who introduced himself as Hendrik.

They all squeezed into the lift and it rattled up to the twenty-second floor. 'Officially, of course, the twenty-third floor doesn't exist,' said Hendrik, a tall blond young man who talked expressively, gesturing with his enormous hands. Carruthers was starting to realise just how many Estonians were blond. The guide got out of the lift at the final floor followed by the Finns and Carruthers. The man opened another door and started to ascend a short staircase. The party followed. They found themselves on a landing.

'The two rooms on this top floor have been left exactly as they looked the day the last KGB agent walked out of them in 1991', said Hendrik. 'See the sign stencilled on the door outside?' said the guide. 'It reads "Zdes Nichevo Nyet": *There is nothing here.*'

Hendrik took a key and opened the door to the first room. Carruthers felt his pulse quickening. As a boy he had always been fascinated by spy stories and this was straight out of James Bond. He peered into the room, taking in the details. It was like a time warp. The floor inside was yellowed linoleum. A sheet of paper was jammed into a cheap orange typewriter. There were two old-fashioned telephones on the wooden table next to a cup and saucer, a white phone and a red phone. Carruthers noticed the mysterious red phone had no dial. Hendrik caught Carruthers looking at this strange phone.

'There was no need for a dial. It went straight through to the KGB Headquarters in Tallinn.'

Carruthers found himself swallowing an uncomfortable lump in his throat. He imagined the little old ladies imparting their information to the men in uniform on the twenty-third floor and what it might mean for those unfortunate guests who were on the KGB's radar.

'Let us go into the second room,' said Hendrik. 'There is more to see in there.'

They trooped out. Carruthers heard a shriek of laughter and took a backwards glance to see one of the Finns sitting posing at the desk, red phone in hand, while others took pictures of her. Carruthers frowned.

They spilled into the second room. When the final Finn had walked in Hendrik shut the door behind him. Carruthers gazed around the larger room. The first thing that caught his eye was the yellowing sheets filled with typed notes spilling off the table and onto the floor. The dial of a light blue telephone on the particleboard desk had been smashed. A discarded gas mask lay on the desk. Carruthers' eyes strayed to the ashtray which was overflowing with cigarette butts. Carruthers peered at them. They didn't look recent. One of the Finns cracked a joke and a couple of the others laughed.

'When the Iron Curtain came down, just after the Second World War,' said Hendrik, 'tiny Estonia, today a population of just 1.5 million people, was absorbed into the USSR and this former republic was cut off from the outside world.'

Carruthers tuned out the conversation of the excitable Finns and imagined the KGB going about their secret business in this room.

'We all know that Tallinn is a top tourist destination now but back in the 1960s tourism was just starting up,' said Hendrik, 'Tallinn received just a few hundred foreign visitors a year. The bosses in Moscow realised that millions of dollars in tourism was just passing the Soviet Union by. This gave them a problem. How could they get their hands on some of the much-needed money tourism brings, but at the same time monitor the comings and goings of their visitors? After all, they didn't want these tourists to spread any new ideas which might threaten the socialist order.'

'The Russians decided,' continued the guide, 'that opening a ferry line from Finland was a great way of getting their hands on some of that money. However, they still had the problem of how to keep track of their visitors. Their solution was to build the Hotel Viru. Within a year of opening, 15,000 people a year were pouring into Tallinn, mostly Finns and homesick Estonian exiles. Everyone entering was made to stay here in this hotel. The reason? Sixty guest rooms were bugged with listening devices hidden in the walls, phones and ashtrays; there were peepholes, too. In the hotel restaurant, ashtrays and bread plates held more listening devices. They even had the sauna bugged.'

'Why would they put listening devices in the sauna?' asked a red-headed woman.

'The Russians knew that the Finns loved doing business in saunas. Clever idea, eh? Believe it or not, they even had antennae placed on the roof which could pick up radio signals both from passing ships and from Helsinki.'

Carruthers was amazed, lost in thoughts about post-war Eastern Bloc espionage.

Hendrik's voice brought him back to the present. 'Yet on an August night in 1991, perhaps unnerved by the imminent collapse of the Soviet Union, the hotel's rarely seen owners simply disappeared. Even after their departure the staff who worked here were too terrified to venture upstairs to the mysterious twenty-third floor. They waited weeks before finally finding the courage. And this is what greeted them. Abandoned uniforms, smashed phones, scattered papers and overflowing ashtrays. Bulky radio equipment was left still bolted to the concrete walls.'

Carruthers wondered what had happened to the little old ladies when the KGB had left. Did they go back to being grandmothers? It occurred to him that not all the KGB had left, or if they had, some of the former KGB were now back as Mafia.

The pitch of Hendrik's voice changed. 'A few years later, the Viru was bought by the Finnish Sokos Hotels chain, having been privatised. If it had been purchased by an Estonian company, it's very likely they would have dismantled these rooms in an attempt to block out any memories of what the Russians did here. As you can imagine there was much suffering under Soviet rule. However, the Finns could be much more objective than their Estonian neighbours. Perhaps sensing a marketing opportunity for making this hotel one of Estonia's top tourist attractions, which it has now become, the new owners left the top floor untouched when they revamped the building.'

* * *

As soon as the fascinating visit was over, Carruthers returned to his room to gather his thoughts. He retrieved his mobile from his pocket and returned calls from Fletcher and Bingham before recharging it. No major headway had been made in Scotland. He hadn't missed much. He hoped to learn more over the evening meal with Aare before reporting back to Bingham. He collected his wallet and mobile and headed downstairs. He decided to go for a walk and have lunch in a café. Then he saw the blonde woman from breakfast speaking to one of the girls behind reception.

On seeing him, the woman headed his way, smiling.

'I'm just heading out to find a café for lunch,' he found himself saying. 'Would you like to join me? Our conversation got interrupted this morning.'

'Yes, I'm sorry about that. My husband. Or, should I say, ex-husband, making things difficult as usual. Let's just say we're still thrashing out the financial cost of getting divorced. I have a few hours free before a meeting. I would love to join you for lunch.'

They headed out into the Estonian sunshine.

'It's not easy,' said Carruthers, thinking about his own failed marriage. He'd been lucky in that respect. Mairi hadn't tried to take his money. The woman raised an eyebrow and looked at him. 'Divorce, I mean.'

'You, too?' she asked.

''Fraid so.' He felt a moment of sadness but then it passed as quickly as it had arrived.

'Forgive me for asking such a personal question,' she said, 'but are you over it, the relationship?'

'As long as I don't see a sunset.'

She laughed again. 'Sorry. I don't understand.'

He laughed, too. 'My wife used to love sunsets. Well, I'm pretty sure she still does. We used to watch them together. That's one of the things I miss most about her, about us as a couple, watching sunsets together. I'm afraid our splitting up has killed my love of sunsets.'

'You're a romantic. I like that.'

Carruthers smiled. He retraced the steps he had taken that morning with Aare. They cut across the road and into the Old Town. He turned to her. 'To be honest, you probably know the Old Town better than me. I've only been once and that was this morning to a café down Vana Viru.'

'Then let me show you around. The Old Town is very compact. It won't take long. How long can you spare?'

'I shouldn't really be more away more than an hour,' said Carruthers, thinking of the paperwork he would need to be doing back at his room. Instead of taking a right at Vana Viru the woman kept walking and took the second right instead onto another cobbled road, Muurivahe.

'If you haven't been down this street, you really must. It leads, in my opinion, to what is the most beautiful street in Tallinn,' she said. 'As you can see it's right next to the old city walls.' Carruthers gazed up at the ancient walls. 'Ah, here it is. My favourite street. We can get something to eat in one of the lovely cafés down here.' They took a left and turned into the beautiful narrow medieval street of Katarinna Kaik.

There was a table for two free on one of the outside tables of a traditional looking restaurant so they sat down. Carruthers looked at the menu. He liked the look of the wild boar in red wine but, knowing he'd be out for supper too that evening, plumped instead for the lighter pancake with minced beef. He looked longingly at the beer selection, ordering a diet coke instead. Carruthers watched this beautiful blonde order a coffee and traditional Russian dumplings.

'Oh,' he said, 'I hadn't realised this was a traditional Russian restaurant.'

She looked at him. 'Does it matter?' she asked.

'No, not at all. I'm just surprised.'

She laughed. 'Well, don't be. There are plenty of Russian restaurants in Estonia. After all, 300,000 Russian-speaking people live in Estonia.'

Carruthers realised that the more he found out about this fascinating country the more he had to learn.

'Sorry, I'm completely forgetting my manners. I haven't introduced myself yet.' She thrust her hand out. 'Sadie. Sadie Andrews.'

He shook her hand, liking the feel of it in his. 'Jim Carruthers.'

'It's interesting,' said Sadie. 'One of the organisers of my work trip is Estonian. It's rumoured she won't take us to a Russian restaurant.'

'Oh?'

'The older people in particular have long memories. They suffered greatly under Soviet rule.'

* * *

A couple of hours later, after a most enjoyable lunch, Carruthers was lying on his side in bed next to the naked Englishwoman. It had seemed such a natural progression to invite her back to his room. She was lying on her back half-wrapped in the crumpled white bedsheet. Her tousled blonde hair fanned out on the pillow, a sheen of perspiration on her lightly tanned body. He traced her collarbone with his finger. She tilted her oval face towards him, mischief and laughter in her eyes. He felt sexually relaxed in a way he hadn't been for a long time. His right hand trailed lazily over her shoulder and down her arm. Cautiously at first he started caressing her again, squeezing her buttock. He was surprised to find himself starting to get another erection. He edged closer so she could feel his body next to her skin. Her cool breath was on his face as she spoke.

'Have you got time?' she asked in between kisses. They never lost eye contact as they spoke.

'No,' he said, looking into her blue eyes, and shifted over her welcoming body.

* * *

After Sadie left, Carruthers got up and sat on the edge of his bed with his mobile. He would like to savour the memory of what, for him, had been perfect sex but he didn't have time now. *Later.* He called Fletcher. He could still smell Sadie's perfume on his body.

'How's Cuthbert?' he asked, feeling sleepy, trying to force the image of Sadie naked out of his mind. He had slipped on his underpants and jeans. He didn't feel right talking to Fletcher naked.

'It's good news. He's been brought out of his medically-induced coma. As you know, it's a slow process, but he may be out of hospital within a week. How's Tallinn this afternoon? Found out anything useful?'

'I have some more information on Hanna Mets. According to Aare, Voller wasn't just running her as a prostitute. Aare thinks they were sleeping together.' Again, images of Sadie's slim body slipped into his mind. He forced them out. 'He's confirmed she was an undercover police officer.'

Fletcher whistled. 'So was the dead girl on the beach definitely Hanna Mets?'

'We've exchanged photographs and I'm more positive about it being Mets. Aare told me Voller killed Hanna Mets' sister so for Mets this was personal. It all fits.'

'I'm meeting Aare later,' continued Carruthers, thinking about how that bit of unexpected exercise would be sure to increase his appetite. 'I hope to find out more information about Hanna Mets then. Did you get the safe house sorted?' he asked.

'Yes, Cuthbert's going to stay with one of our contacts. We've used them before.'

'Good,' he said. 'Well, keep me posted.'

Carruthers finished the call and threw the mobile down on his bed. But before it had even hit the bed sheets it started to ring. Carruthers leant across and grabbed it. Aare.

'I've made a reservation. It's called the Restaurant Leib and it's on a street called Uus close to the Old Town. I thought you might enjoy it as the Scottish Club has a room inside the restaurant. It's also excellent food.'

Carruthers was touched. Grabbed a pen and took a note of the name. Promised to meet Aare at the restaurant at seven.

He sat at the small desk by the window in his room and made notes of his conversation with the man. He was still only half-dressed, even his feet were bare. It was warm in the room so it felt liberating to be without his shirt. Any thoughts or impressions he had about the man or Tallinn he wrote down, too. There was something bothering him but he couldn't work out what it was. It was a niggle, a doubt, but it wasn't a fully-formed thought and every time he tried to think about it, it evaporated back into being nothing more than a vague concern. He still couldn't understand what concrete help he could give Aare aside from an exchange of information and brainstorming with his Estonian counterpart. He was starting to feel anxious at being away from Scotland for too long. And he'd already had almost one full day in Tallinn. What had he actually learnt in that time? He went over his conversation with Aare once more, referring to his notes as he did.

That the Russians had their grip on neighbouring little Estonia. That cheap drugs had flooded in from Russia. That corruption at the highest level was a worry, as witnessed by the concerns Aare had over the allegiances of some of his fellow police officers. He knew a sizeable number of people living in Estonia were Russian or of Russian descent. Had the Estonian police been infiltrated by members of the Russian Mafia who in turn used to be part of the KGB?

Barry Cuthbert used his connections to target acquaintances for their works of art. Especially if the artwork was British. Cuthbert's point of contact was Aleks Voller. Somehow the art was being smuggled out of the country, back to Estonia then on to Russia, most likely to be sold on the black market. But why wasn't it just smuggled direct from Britain to Russia? Surely it would be much simpler. There had to be contacts in Estonia. So who were they, apart from Voller's brother, Marek? Aare had been vague. Did he really not know or was it just that he was not saying? And if so, was that for Carruthers' benefit or for his own? Carruthers stroked his chin, feeling the spiky bristles. He needed to have a think about how to make the meeting that evening most profitable for himself.

His thoughts turned to what Aare had got out of the earlier meeting with him. Had he given the man too much information? He ran through the information now at Aare's disposal. Aare knew Cuthbert was in hospital, days from being transferred to a safe house. He also now knew Cuthbert was being offered police protection for turning informant.

Carruthers thought ahead to his meeting with Aare over supper. Carruthers could start by finding out what had happened to Marika Paju. If she was a prostitute it was possible she was also a junkie. Was it just another sad junkie's death? Or was her death more sinister?

He glanced at his watch. Standing up, he put his hands behind his head and stretched. Striding over to his bed he stripped off what he was wearing. Leaving his jeans and pants in a heap on the floor he walked into the bathroom naked. He jumped into the shower examining his arm under the hot jets. Was pleased to notice it was less painful when he prodded it, the bruises fading to green. The swelling and bruising around his knee had gone down too.

By six o'clock he was fully dressed and ready for supper, so decided to have a drink in the hotel bar before the fifteen-minute walk to the restaurant. As he went down the stairs he glanced into the dining room. It was now a Tex-Mex restaurant. Ashtrays were long gone, of course, but Carruthers looked suspiciously at the salt and pepper pots on each table. Since his visit to the KGB Museum he knew he wouldn't view the hotel in the same light. He walked into the bar. There were a few guests at various tables talking softly over quiet music. Noticing there was no dark beer he ordered a lager and sat on a bar stool drinking it. He wondered if he would run into Sadie and was disappointed that she didn't make an appearance. He hadn't asked her how long she was staying. Hoped he'd get a chance to see her again.

At 6.40pm he stood up, grabbed his jacket off the bar stool, paid his bill and set out into the evening. He knew, looking at a map he'd picked up from reception, that there was a quicker way to the restaurant, but being a creature of habit, he decided to go the way he knew.

The oppressive heat hit him as soon as he stepped outside. He strolled down the Vana Viru and after a few minutes' walk took a right onto Uus. He paused to admire a brick church behind high railings. Sadie had been right. The centre of Tallinn was pretty compact, everything within easy reach. He enjoyed walking down this new street seeing different sights. The street appeared to be quieter than others, more residential. Music filled the air and he passed a Moldovan restaurant then an embassy on the right. Tried to make out the red, yellow and green flag but failed. The signage said Lietuvos Republikos Ambasada. He supposed it was the embassy of Latvia. He heard a distant roll of thunder. He looked up at the sky. Thunderclouds like lead weights were rolling in. The wind had picked up since he'd last been out, buffeting him as he walked. The first fat drops of warm rain hit. He cursed at not bringing an umbrella. The drops became heavier and, before long, rain was bouncing off the concrete pavements.

Swearing, Carruthers slipped into the doorway of a smart block of flats to sit out what he hoped was the worst of the storm. A couple of umbrella-carrying Estonians hurried past, their faces cast down, but otherwise the street was empty. Carruthers looked up and down the street. He was suddenly aware that another man had stopped in another doorway thirty metres behind him. The man was wearing black trousers and a beige jacket. He watched the man shake out his umbrella and turn to look at something that had caught his eye through a window.

Suddenly Carruthers felt anxious, tension pulling at every fibre. He didn't know why. Once again he experienced a sharp twinge in his chest. He glanced down the street once more. The man in the doorway was still there, this time lighting a cigarette. There was something about the man that made him uneasy. Some sixth sense made all the hairs on the back of Carruthers' neck rise. The man was still studiously looking at something in the window. The first impression he had of him was that he too was trying to get out of the rain. But then why would he need to since he had an umbrella?

Carruthers put his jacket on, turning up the collar and made a dash for it. He ran almost three hundred yards then took shelter in the doorway of another residence. He turned round sharply to look over his shoulder and saw a flash of movement behind him.

The man in the beige jacket was also on the move. Carruthers felt fear prickling his scalp. He looked at the weather-beaten face of an old woman as she hurried past, then at a couple of young men with their hands shoved in their pockets. Suddenly everywhere he saw potential enemies. He glanced to his left. The man in the beige jacket had stopped again, too. This couldn't be coincidence. He was being followed. Probably since he'd left the hotel. Was the man former KGB?

Adrenaline flooded his body, his breathing harsher. His mind was going into overdrive trying to decide what to do. Should he stay put and see if the man moved first or should he make another run for it? His hands felt cold and clammy. He smoothed his forehead and found he was sweating. He put his hand into his trouser pocket and felt for his mobile. It wasn't there. He cursed. He'd left it lying on the bed. Now he was truly on his own. On his own in a strange country where he knew nobody but a single policeman. And how well did he even know the policeman?

The rain eased off, leaving pools of water glistening on the pavements. The flash flood had caused rivulets of water to run down the street. Carruthers made a decision. He came out of his doorway and walked quickly towards his destination. He wasn't sure if the man behind him was still following or not and didn't want to draw attention to the fact he knew he was being followed by turning round. After walking five minutes he came to a fork in the road. He took the left fork that took him away from his restaurant. Wondered if there was somewhere he could hide. He was in luck. There was a large white delivery van parked by an unlocked black gate that gave access through an arch to a courtyard. Carruthers slipped inside the gate and hid in the shadows. A few moments later he saw the man hurrying past.

There was another rumble of thunder. Carruthers came out of his hiding place, glancing ominously up at the sky. He retraced his steps to the end of the street and then took a left, back onto the main street. The restaurant couldn't be too far away now, could it? He glanced back over his shoulder but there was no sign of the man. He must have shaken him off. Finally and with relief he came across the red-fronted weather boarding of the restaurant. He opened the door.

Carruthers spotted Aare sitting at a table towards the back of the restaurant. He got to his feet when Carruthers entered the room.

'It's terrible weather out there,' Aare said. 'We get bad summer storms here, I'm afraid. Sometimes flash floods.' Frowning, he looked Carruthers over. 'Are you OK?'

Carruthers shook his head. He wiped his wet face. 'I think I've been followed from the hotel. I managed to shake them off. This is why I'm late.'

'Followed?' said Aare, eyes widening in shock. 'But nobody knows you're here. We've been so careful. But this is terrible.' He glanced around the restaurant with suspicious eyes. He grasped Carruthers' arm. 'Perhaps we should leave.'

'No, I've shaken them off. Did you tell anyone we were eating here tonight?'

'Only my wife, and I trust her with my life.'

'Then we're safe. Maybe it's in my head.' Carruthers laughed but it sounded hollow even to his ears. 'Perhaps, given everything, an outing to the KGB Museum was a mistake.'

The waitress arrived at the table and gave Carruthers a menu. 'What would you like to drink?' she asked.

'A glass of red wine,' he said, without giving it much thought. He opened the menu but found he couldn't concentrate on it.

Aare leant in closer and spoke in a whisper. 'How sure are you that you were followed?'

Carruthers mirrored the man's movements and leant forward. At some point he must have picked up his napkin. Found he'd shredded it before he knew what he was doing. His hands felt damp. He was still perspiring. 'I'm certain. Are you sure the rooms aren't still bugged in the Viru?'

'We're not back in the bad old days yet, my friend, although I'm sure Putin would love to get his hands on little Estonia.'

Carruthers watched Aare as he lifted his glass and took a sip of his beer. With Russia walking into Ukraine, he wouldn't blame former Eastern Bloc countries for being a little nervous.

At the end of the meal, Aare said, 'Do you feel safe going back to your hotel? Would you rather come stay with me and my wife?'

Carruthers thought this over for a few seconds. 'Thank you, but I don't think that will be necessary.'

'Well, let me escort you back, if nothing else,' said Aare. 'In fact, we'll get a taxi and I'll drop you off at the hotel. I live on the edge of town so I'd have to take one anyway.'

After saying goodbye to Aare, Carruthers walked through the deserted and dimly lit foyer of the Viru. He thought back to his conversation with Aare. He was now convinced that the body on the beach had been that of Hanna Mets. The way Aare had described her she had sounded a maverick, a loner. And, sadly, a woman out for revenge which had ultimately cost her her life. He had also discovered how porous the border was between Estonia and Russia, which had answered his question of why the smuggling wasn't done directly between the UK and Russia.

Sighing, he pressed the button to take the lift up to his floor. As he waited, he glanced around nervously. His senses were in overdrive. He squinted at the shadows, imagining enemies at every turn. Wondered how many people over the years had been followed in and out of this former KGB hotel. How many conversations had been heard by the men on the twenty-third floor? And, more to the point, what had the KGB done about them? No doubt there would be a basement somewhere where some had been tortured, their screams unheard by passers-by thanks to soundproofing and windows of concrete.

Getting out of the lift, he walked quickly down the corridor. He jumped when he heard a door slam some way away. As soon as the key card opened the door he walked into his room and stopped dead in his tracks. Stopped as if he was about to tread on a mine. Somebody had been in before him. He could sense it.

He stood absolutely still, not moving a muscle. He could feel his heart hammering in his chest.

He felt so tense his neck muscles were sore. He looked round him, trying to remember where he'd put the few personal possessions he'd brought with him. His shaver, which had been sitting on the dresser, was still there, but Carruthers had the feeling it had been moved, as had his book. He picked up the book. The bookmark was in the wrong place. Could it have been the maid? The sheet wasn't turned down so had she even been in? He let out a sigh of relief. His mobile was still lying on his bed.

Switching the bedroom light off, he navigated his way in the dark over to the window. Hiding in the shadows he peeked out to the road below. Cars made their way up and down the street, sloshing through the rivulets of rain. The lighting cast its sickly yellow glow over the wet pavements. Carruthers didn't know what he was looking for. Someone, his Eastern counterpart, also lurking in the shadows? When he thought of spies watching a hotel he imagined a tall gaunt man wearing a long coat and dark trilby standing with his back leaning against a car, smoking a cigarette. He didn't see anyone lurking on a street corner or standing against a car but knew they wouldn't look like they'd stepped out of a 1930s noir film.

The window rattled as the wind picked up again. He moved away from it, closing the curtains as he went. He heard another door slam and then voices in the corridor. Switching the light back on, he walked over to the door and locked it from the inside. Debated moving the bedside table up against the door but decided against it.

Just as he was taking his shirt off there was a knock on his door. He buttoned the shirt back up and unlocking the door, called out, 'Who is it?'

'Reception.'

Carruthers hesitated then opened the door a fraction. Seeing the young man who was behind reception earlier he opened the door wider. The man thrust his hand out.

'I have a letter for you.'

Carruthers took the sealed envelope. Looked over the man's shoulder. 'Did you see the person who left this?'

'No. It wasn't given to me. It was given to my colleague. But apparently it had to be delivered to you tonight.'

'Man or woman?'

'Man.'

'Has anyone been into the room while I've been out? A maid perhaps?'

The man from reception looked confused. 'No, sir.'

Carruthers quickly ripped open the envelope, read the letter. It was short. It read, 'Don't trust Kert Ilves. We think he works for the Russians.'

Sixteen

C arruthers sat on the edge of the bed holding the note in his hand. Who the hell was Kert Ilves? And who had written the note? Who were the 'we' to which it referred? Carruthers picked up his mobile. Started punching in Fletcher's number then stopped. Broke the connection. Should he leave the hotel and ring her, or sit it out until first light? Who was to say the room wasn't bugged? Or that his phone hadn't been tampered with? Or was he being ridiculous? He no longer knew.

He decided he couldn't trust his mobile. Made the decision to buy a pay-as-you-go the next morning. Tried to get some sleep but it wasn't easy to come by. He tossed and turned. Lay wide-awake, eyes open, arms behind his head. At 3am he was still listening to the sounds of the hotel. The occasional voice from the street below, slosh of a car driving by on wet streets. At 3.15 he got up. Padded naked to the curtain and pulled it back to look out onto the street below. He couldn't see anything other than the silhouettes of the city so got back into bed. Fell into an uneasy sleep at around 4am.

* * *

At 8am he awoke with a start at the sound of a car backfiring. He felt exhausted and anxious. Had a hasty shower and a cup of coffee in his room. Leaving the hotel he went in search of a mobile phone shop. Didn't have far to go before he found one. Amongst other surprises he had found out that Estonia was a leader in technology. Bought a cheap mobile and called Fletcher from a street corner.

'Listen, Andie, I don't have much time to talk. Do me a favour? I need you to find out about someone for me. Anything you can find out about a man called Kert Ilves.' He thought for a moment. 'And while you're at it…' He hesitated. 'Gunnar Aare.'

'Sure. What's up?'

'Don't ring me on my mobile. Can you call me on this number?' He gave her his new number. 'And, Andie? Quick as you can.'

He severed the connection. Walked into a coffee shop. Ordered another coffee and a croissant. Drank the black liquid and ate the croissant, although for all he tasted, it he could have been eating cardboard. Waited for Fletcher to call back.

He leapt as his new mobile rang. Snatched at it and cradled it under his chin as he grabbed the pen from his shirt pocket.

'I've got that information you wanted,' Fletcher said. 'Who shall I start with? Gunnar Aare or Kert Ilves?'

'Either. Just give me what you've got. What have you got on Gunnar Aare?'

'Gunnar Aare was one of the three men killed in the shoot-out. He died alongside Mikael Tamm and Olev Lepp.' Whatever Carruthers was expecting, it wasn't this. His throat suddenly felt constricted, as if someone was trying to squeeze the very life out of him. He couldn't breathe. He felt his heart pounding somewhere in his throat. 'You sure about that?'

'Yes I am. What's going on, Jim?'

Jesus, thought Carruthers. If it hadn't been Gunnar Aare he'd been meeting with, who the hell had it been? He felt himself going hot then cold. Of course there was only one person. Kert Ilves. He couldn't believe he could have been duped like that. He felt a sharp stab of anger. And fear.

Ignoring her question he said, 'What about Kert Ilves?' He felt another momentary prickle of fear.

'He used to be attached to the Tallinn Police. He left three years ago under a cloud. How much detail do you want?'

'As much as you've got,' said Carruthers.

'That information was harder to find, but I did discover he's got an Estonian father and a Russian mother.'

'His mother's Russian?'

'That's right. Now, are you going to tell me what's going on?' said Fletcher.

'Why did he leave the police?' Even as he asked the question Carruthers wasn't sure he wanted to hear the answer.

'I have no idea.'

As he spoke, Carruthers' eyes flicked over the other customers. Decided none of them was a threat. 'Don't worry about me,' he said. 'Just look after Barry Cuthbert. How's he doing, by the way?'

'Much better. Reckon he's ready to talk. Knows what side his bread's buttered on.'

'Has he said anything?'

'Not yet.'

'Make sure he's never left alone. I'll be back soon.'

'OK. Jim? I should tell you that Bingham's appointed a new DCI. She's starting next month.'

Carruthers swore.

'It was a shock to all of us,' said Fletcher.

It hadn't been a shock to him, but to appoint her so soon? 'Have you met her?'

'All I know is her name's Sandra McTavish. Comes from CID Lothian and Borders.'

Carruthers finished the call, paid for his coffee and walked briskly back to his hotel. He could feel his skin prickling with anger. Anger over McTavish's appointment. And fear. Kert Ilves kicked out of the police. No wonder Ilves didn't want Carruthers to meet him at the station. He didn't work there anymore. Carruthers raked his hands through his grey hair. Picked up his pace. His mind was working nineteen to the dozen. His breathing was fast and shallow so he deliberately slowed it to calm himself.

The situation was bad, however, what it also showed was that someone – the man who had written the note – was a friend; and he needed friends. He was also in a far better position than he had been twenty-four hours before. Now he had the heads-up on the situation, when he met 'Gunnar Aare' again he would know he was actually most probably speaking to Kert Ilves. He wondered if his acting skills were up to it.

Once back in his room he sat drumming his fingers on the bed for ten minutes then made a decision. He was going to go to the Tallinn Police Station. Brave or stupid? He didn't know. What was he going to do when he was there? He didn't know the answer to that question either. All he knew was that doing nothing was not an option.

He grabbed his jacket. Took the stairs. Got to the foyer and approached the front desk of reception. They were busy checking a couple out. Carruthers didn't recognise either of the reception staff. Both were young women. Carruthers stood in line until they were ready for him. He glanced around. Noticed a man reading a newspaper on the sofa. When it was his turn to speak he told the receptionist his name and asked if there were any messages for him. Having been told there were none he turned to leave and the man who had been reading his newspaper stood up.

'Jim Carruthers?' he asked.

'Who's asking?'

The man walked up to him. 'Can we go somewhere to talk?' he said.

Without smiling, Carruthers said, 'Not until you tell me who you are.'

'I left you that note last night. My name's Janek Kuul.'

Under his breath Carruthers said, 'Even if you are who you say who you are, why should I trust you?'

'I sent you the information on Aleks Voller. Inspector Carruthers, you are a foreign police officer in a strange country. No doubt you feel you are in over your head. You need to trust someone. You feel very alone at the moment, I should think. And I am one of the good guys. Come, let's walk. But first I want to show you this.' He put his hand in his trouser pocket and pulled something out.

Carruthers jumped, wondering just what he was concealing in his pocket. Then he relaxed. It was a police ID badge.

'No doubt Kert Ilves showed you his badge?'

Carruthers nodded.

'It isn't genuine,' continued Kuul.

'How did you know who I was? That I was coming over to Tallinn?'

'I was with Mikael Tamm when he took your call. He told my colleague and myself he'd set up a phone meeting. Before he was killed.'

'Who is your colleague?'

'A man called Andres Jakobson. You can trust him.'

'I got told you'd transferred,' said Carruthers.

'I haven't transferred and I do not know who told you I had. But it confirms to me that there is at least one person who is a spy at the Tallinn Police Station. Let me ask you something if you don't want to believe me. Why do you think Ilves brought you out here?'

'For information.'

'Exactly. And how much information have you given him?'

Carruthers remained quiet. Once again, he was going over in his own head all the information Ilves had got out of him. He wasn't about to tell this man, though.

'Too much, then. And how much did you get from him? Precisely nothing, I'll bet. Nothing useful, anyway.'

'That's not completely true,' said Carruthers, feeling defensive.

'He will have given you as much or as little information as he wants you to know. No more. No less.'

'So he brought me out here because he wants information?' said Carruthers.

'Exactly.'

Carruthers wasn't liking the way the conversation was going. 'And now?'

'If Ilves thinks you've given him all the information you have to give, then,' he paused, shrugged, 'he won't hesitate to kill you. Have you? Given him all the information?'

Carruthers felt his heart turn cold. There was a quick stab of pain in the left side of his chest. He wondered, with hereditary heart disease running in his family, unless he could get his stress under control, what would kill him first? Ilves or a heart attack? He momentarily wondered how his mother would react to the news of a second heart attack in the family.

The sound of the man's voice brought Carruthers out of the hole his dark thoughts were digging.

'Just out of interest, what sort of questions was he asking you?'

Carruthers thought for a moment. 'He was asking about Aleks Voller. About his whereabouts.'

'This is interesting. I wonder... we heard that the group had been double-crossed by someone. Perhaps Aleks Voller is one of the middle men.'

'He would need allies in both Scotland and Estonia, surely?' said Carruthers. 'After all, they still have to get the paintings out.' *How many middle men are there?* thought Carruthers. *Barry Cuthbert? Aleks Voller?*

'It's just curious Ilves is asking about Voller. Why would he do that? I wonder if Voller and the middleman got greedy. Perhaps Voller is trying to double-cross Ilves. Or even his brother, Marek.'

'What do I do?' asked Carruthers.

'What you have to do is make Ilves believe you still have information he wants.'

Carruthers said nothing once again but thought about this. It made sense. It was about the only thing that did. 'I was followed, yesterday,' he volunteered, taking a punt on trusting this man. The man was right. He did have to trust someone. He felt his options were running out and fast.

'I know. I was watching.'

'You were the man watching me? Following me?'

'No. I was watching the man who was following you.'

'Do you know who he was?'

'One of Ilves's men. Tell me, if you are still undecided, did Ilves tell you not to go to the police station?'

'That's right.'

'And now you know why, don't you? Because of course if you did, you'd realise he's impersonating Gunnar Aare, who is now dead.'

Carruthers thought quickly about this. If Kert Ilves had been kicked out of the force some years back and he'd been impersonating Gunnar Aare, who had he, Carruthers, been talking to on the phone? It certainly hadn't been Ilves or Aare. Somebody, though, who was on Kert Ilves's side. It could only be a bent copper.

Carruthers' eyes narrowed. 'Was it you who went through my things in my room?'

'Yes, sorry about the invasion of privacy. I needed to be sure of you.'

Carruthers felt angry even asking this question but he had to know. 'Did you manage to intercept my phone and text messages?'

'Yes, I did. I needed to know whether you were the type of police officer who might be bribed.'

Carruthers' mouth felt set like a steel trap. 'And what did you conclude?'

'I concluded that being the type of police officer who could be bought off or bribed,' he paused, 'might be the only way you're going to get out of this alive. Unless you follow my instruction.'

Never having been particularly good at chess Carruthers was now starting to feel like a pawn. The only problem was that he wasn't sure whose side he was playing for and who he was playing against. Idly he wondered if the man also knew he had slept with Sadie Andrews. Would she now be in danger?

'Tell me what I need to do,' said Carruthers.

'You need to get in touch with Ilves. Set up another meeting. Make it sound as if your station's been back in touch with you. That they're going to give you some big piece of important news. Maybe about the art thefts. You're an intelligent man. I'm sure you'll think of something.'

Carruthers didn't feel very intelligent. In fact, he was feeling pretty stupid at coming all the way to Estonia to do nothing but put his life at risk. After all, what had he really discovered? Very little.

However, he also thought he should do his best to help the Tallinn Police flush out the spy.

'Tell me one thing about Hanna Mets,' said Carruthers.

'Ah yes, poor Hanna.'

'Did you know she was pregnant when she was killed?'

'No. I didn't.'

'Did she know about Ilves? About what was going on at the station? That it had been infiltrated?'

'She knew we had a spy. She just didn't know who he or she was. None of us did then. Just before she went missing we managed to contact her. She was told to get out. Being undercover had become too dangerous. We were pretty sure her cover was about to be blown.'

'And that's when she turns up in Scotland.'

'So it would appear. You know her sister was killed by the Voller brothers?'

Carruthers nodded.

'She had recently found out it was by Aleks Voller.'

'Who was now operating in Scotland.'

'He's back and forth but, yes, his main operation is setting the business up in Scotland. There's not much we can do for Hanna. You should focus on saving yourself. Ilves will want to know what your piece of news is. He's not going to kill you until he gets it. You'll have to think fast, though. I'm afraid time isn't on your side. And once you've thought of something, you're going to have to keep stalling him. That's going to be an art form in itself.'

'Why haven't you arrested Ilves?' asked Carruthers.

Kuul grasped Carruthers' arm. Exerted pressure to the point of pain. 'There's something else.'

Carruthers looked up in alarm.

'You're getting close to Ilves and we need your help. We know Ilves is passing information to someone. Information that's coming out of the police station. We want that bent cop. We don't know who this person is. That's why we haven't arrested Ilves yet. Perhaps we should. Mikael Tamm and Gunnar Aare might still be alive.

Nobody's managed to get close to him. Before we close Ilves down we need to find out who this other man is. We need you to feed Ilves false information. The stakes are high. This is not just about art theft anymore. The integrity of the Estonian security services is at risk. But it is also dangerous.'

'This other person is involved in the art world?' asked Carruthers.

'We don't know if they are directly involved in the art world. But we think Ilves is involved to some degree in the art thefts. And this gang is getting its money from somewhere. It's a little unusual, though,' said Kuul. 'Criminal gangs in Eastern Europe are not usually involved in art heists. It is usually drugs and prostitution.'

'What do they normally do with the money they make?' asked Carruthers. As he asked the question he thought about what he'd been told about how art thieves, particularly in the UK, were becoming more violent. And how there was now a closer link between art theft, drugs and prostitution.

'They normally invest it in real estate. There was a case recently involving a family who were attacked by criminals over disputes involving real estate. Investing the money in art is unusual. More unusual still is stealing works of art, especially abroad. It shows they are getting more and more daring.'

Carruthers frowned. He was deep in thought. 'These gangs here in Estonia that run prostitutes – do most of the prostitutes stay in Estonia or are they taken overseas?'

Kuul shook his head. 'Estonia is a source country for the trafficking of women to countries like Norway, Finland and the United Kingdom.'

Norway and Finland Carruthers could understand. Especially Finland. After all he'd seen where the big cruise ships from Helsinki had docked. The passage between the two countries was only a short distance.

'Most of the women trafficked are poor members of the Russian-speaking community in the north east part of the country,' said Kuul.

Carruthers thought of the anonymous call he had taken from the dead girl's friend. Could she have been a Russian speaker? He then thought about Marika Paju and her parents. They didn't fit that description.

'Often they answer ads offering jobs abroad. They think they are going to be maids or child minders. Once they leave Estonia they find things are unfortunately very different. I need you to go through every detail of every conversation you've had with Kert Ilves,' said Kuul.

As best he could, Carruthers detailed the conversations he had had over the previous couple of days. It felt strange being the one interrogated. Usually he was the one doing the questioning. He didn't like being on the receiving end one little bit.

Kuul listened thoughtfully to what Carruthers said. When Carruthers had finished, Kuul nodded. 'Well, at least Kert Ilves was right about one thing. The Russians are dangerous. They are a threat. Definitely not to be underestimated.' He glanced at Carruthers. 'Look, I don't want you to think all Russians are bad. They are not. There are some really good people. But some Russians, especially the former KGB… well. And it might sound farfetched to you to say that even one bent cop in the Estonian police might threaten the very fabric of Estonian society and culture but it's not an exaggeration.'

Carruthers noticed Kuul staring at him intently.

'I can see that you are not convinced. Of course, you will know what is happening in the Ukraine. We are all very worried about this escalating situation. But did you know that a few months ago an Estonian intelligence officer was kidnapped at gunpoint at the Luhamaa border checkpoint? Like I said, on the border but still within Estonia.'

'What was he doing when he got kidnapped?' asked Carruthers, feeling uncomfortable.

'The man was simply investigating an incident of cross-border crime. Gun smuggling.'

'What will happen to him?' asked Carruthers.

'Thank God he's been released. However, he'd been charged with espionage and was facing twenty years in prison.'

'Why?'

'Because they can. The Russians are flexing their muscles. His arrest came just days after Barack Obama visited Estonia to give us Washington's support over the Ukraine crisis. It was a warning.'

Carruthers said nothing but was inclined to agree. It was most definitely a warning.

'Have you given any thought to what I said?' asked Kuul. 'About the big piece of news that you have for Ilves?'

Carruthers couldn't think. His mind had gone blank. *What big piece of news could he give Ilves?* And then he thought of something. A seed of an idea was starting to take hold in his mind. Something to do with a diary and Hanna Mets. 'I've thought of something,' said Carruthers.

'Set up a meeting with Kert Ilves,' said Kuul, giving Carruthers his business card. 'Ring me when you've spoken to him.'

Seventeen

Carruthers left the hotel in the afternoon. He was now in the habit of taking the stairs rather than the lift. He didn't much like confined spaces at the best of times. And these were hardly the best of times. He'd seen too many spy films where the victim was dispensed with in the lift by a man carrying a silencer. The body dragged away by the assailant, heels scraping, only to be bundled into the boot of car.

'You wanted to see me? What's this news you have?' Ilves drew a long drag on his cigarette. He exhaled the smoke through his nostrils.

Carruthers stared into the man's narrow blue eyes, aware Ilves was watching him intently while trying to perfect the casual look. He was finding it hard to digest the news that it wasn't Gunnar Aare he was having a conversation with, but Kert Ilves, the double-crossing former police officer.

'It's Hanna Mets.'

Ilves looked up sharply at Carruthers. 'What about her?'

'Apparently she kept a diary.'

Ilves drew a sharp drag on his cigarette and flicked it onto the ground. Carruthers could see he had Ilves' full attention. Lifting his head up slowly he asked, 'Has it been found?'

'Yes,' said Carruthers cautiously. 'We're hoping it'll be a great help in furthering the investigation, but we have nobody who reads Estonian.'

'Get them to send it over here,' said Ilves, quickly.

'To you?' said Carruthers.

'Yes, that's an excellent idea. To me.'

I bet you think it's an excellent idea, you little piece of shit, thought Carruthers. 'I'm not sure I'll be able to do that.' He needed to stall and this would work as well as any device. 'In cases like this, we rarely let potential evidence go out of police control. But I'll speak to my superintendent. Since I'm here and you're willing to translate for us, he might agree and send the diary over.' *And what would you do with it, if it existed?* Bitter thoughts ran through his mind. *Read and destroy it. Like you destroyed all those good men at Tallinn Police Station. And let's not forget Hanna Mets. You would have been responsible for her death, too.* Carruthers looked at the man he now considered to be a despicable piece of filth, and wanted to punch him.

'Do you know when Barry Cuthbert's being moved to the safe house?' said Ilves suddenly.

Carruthers felt a sucker blow to his gut. 'I'm not sure,' he said slowly.

'But he's still in hospital?' asked Ilves.

Carruthers thought about lying but realised that Ilves would have his spies in Scotland. *Maybe he's testing me,* he thought. *Perhaps he knows I'm onto him. I can't let my guard down. Not even for a minute.*

'Yes, I believe, he's still in hospital.'

'With an armed guard?'

Christ, thought Carruthers. *He's not going to try anything while Cuthbert's in hospital, is he? He must think Cuthbert's got information he could pass on that could blow his operation or cover sky-high. But what information? And how do we get it out of Cuthbert?*

Carruthers thought quickly. 'I need to phone the station and get the latest on Cuthbert. I was under the impression he was being moved for his own safety.'

'While you do that I need to go to the toilet,' said Ilves. Carruthers watched Ilves walk away. Carruthers grabbed his mobile out of his pocket and made a call to Fletcher. While he did indeed ask for the latest on Cuthbert, the real purpose of the call was to find out if the station had managed to secure a search warrant for Cuthbert's place.

* * *

'We had to let him go.'

'What?' said Ilves.

'Barry Cuthbert. We had to let him go,' said Carruthers.

'I thought you said he was going to help you, you were going to grant him immunity from prosecution?'

'Not anymore.' Carruthers was thinking quickly on his feet. He had no choice. He realised Barry Cuthbert's life was in mortal danger. Frankly he didn't give a stuff about Cuthbert but Fletcher was on her way over to interview him again on Bingham's instructions. What if she got caught up with an attempt on Cuthbert's life? This man would have phoned his contacts in Scotland by now. If anything happened to Fletcher how would he forgive himself? Carruthers thought quickly. Already a plan was forming in his mind. He just hoped it would work.

'Cuthbert's being released. I didn't want to say anything earlier. I knew you'd be disappointed. He's refusing to talk and we have nothing on him. No hard evidence anyway.'

'I thought you said–'

'He's got a good lawyer, who no doubt would get him off on a technicality.' Well, that wasn't a word of lie. Barry Cuthbert would have a good lawyer. His sort always did.

'So he's not going to help the police? Turn informant?'

'No.' *No, he's not going to turn informant,* thought Carruthers. He had a far bigger role lined up for Mr Barry Cuthbert. But first he needed to enlist the help of Fletcher. Fletcher's role, in his absence, was pivotal. And Cuthbert, who was at the centre of Carruthers' plan, was needed to lure Aleks Voller in the open.

* * *

'I want you back on Scottish soil, Carruthers, ASAP. It's too dangerous out there.' This was just the reaction Carruthers had been expecting from Bingham. He'd finally bitten the bullet and rang his boss on his new mobile. Explained his plan. Bingham was none too happy about it.

'We need to draw Voller out,' said Carruthers. 'I believe he's directly responsible for the death of at least two people in Fife. I can't do that if I'm back in Scotland.' He could hear Bingham remonstrating with him on the phone but rather than listen he decided to talk over him. Time was short and he didn't have the luxury of a drawn-out conversation. Lives depended on swift action. His, mostly. 'Our best bet is to go through Ilves,' continued Carruthers. 'Look, while Ilves still thinks I believe he's Gunnar Aare—'

'I want you on the next flight back, Jim, and that's an order.'

'We can draw Voller out by going through Cuthbert. Ilves is already asking questions about Cuthbert's whereabouts. I don't think he'd try anything while he's in the hospital but if we set up a safe house and leak it to Ilves, I think he'll send Voller to kill him. Cuthbert knows too much. We can set a trap. Kuul agrees with me. Thinks this is the best plan.'

'How the hell do you know whether you can trust Kuul?' said Bingham. 'After all, you've been taken in once, already.'

Carruthers was smarting. 'I can trust him,' he said, determinedly. He refused to think about the consequences if he was proved wrong.

'And who's going to talk to Cuthbert? Get him on side with you in Estonia?' said Bingham.

'Andie's agreed to do it.'

'Jesus Christ, Jim. You've already spoken to Fletcher about this? Before you spoke to me?'

'I'm sorry. I was just sounding her out.'

'The search warrant's come through for Cuthbert's place,' said Bingham. 'I'll have to get Fletcher and Watson to go after all. I don't feel we can sit on this.'

'There's a trail that leads from Cuthbert to Aleks Voller in Scotland to Ilves and Marek Voller in Estonia to… God knows who. Kuul thinks there's a spy at the Tallinn Police Station.'

'A bent copper? Wouldn't be the first. Look, Jim, we're not Interpol. Leave the Estonians to deal with their own affairs.'

'I can't do that. I wish I could. Five people are dead because of this gang. Five people we know of, anyway.' As he said this, the image of the dead woman on the beach, Hanna Mets, came into his head. It was an image he knew he'd have to live with for a very long time. He also heard the voice of Mikael Tamm in his head and the crying of the female police officer. 'I won't have the blood of anybody else on my hands,' he said. 'We have a chance to bring down one of the most ruthless criminal gangs in Estonia, a gang who's already starting to operate in Scotland. Art thefts are just the tip of the iceberg. They're using the thefts to fund their cross-border operation. God only knows what else they're doing with the money. Gangs like these who have spies in the Estonian police and government are helping to destabilise the whole Baltic region.'

Carruthers finished the call and lay down on the bed. It was deathly silent in his room. He imagined he could hear the ticking of his watch. He could certainly feel the hammering of his heart. Once more he wondered if the room was being bugged. Should he try to move hotel? No, of course not. That would look really bad. He stared at the white ceiling while trying to put his thoughts in order.

He suddenly felt very alone. More alone than perhaps he had ever felt before. Now he understood the difference between feeling alone and feeling lonely. When his wife had first left him, and for a long time after, if he was honest, he had felt lonely. Now he just felt alone. Even with Kuul on his side. But after what Bingham had said, whom could he trust? He felt a fear that he had never felt before. Perhaps all the people he could have trusted, at least in Estonia, were now dead. Perhaps his enemies were just waiting until he was able to lead them to Cuthbert and then he, too, would be killed. Cuthbert would be slain in Scotland and he would be murdered in Estonia. No doubt his death would be made to look like an accident.

Thinking of Aare, he sat upright and drew out the card he'd been given with Kuul's phone number on it. Reached over and grabbed his mobile. Punched in the number and waited. And waited.

There was no answer. He heard it going to voicemail and hung up. He waited a few minutes then dialled again. Still no answer. Carruthers sat on the end of the bed tapping the end of the mobile against his chin thoughtfully.

He reached across the bed, grabbed his jacket, wallet and keys and left his room. He took the stairs rather than the lift but just as he reached ground floor his pulse quickened. Walking into the lift was Sadie Andrews.

Carruthers was just about to call out when he realised she wasn't alone. Closely behind her was Kert Ilves. As he hid behind the wall, Carruthers' heart lurched. Their heads bowed close together; they were murmuring. As the lift doors shut Carruthers watched, nauseated, as they kissed.

Eighteen

Fletcher and Watson stood on the top of the stone steps of Barry Cuthbert's house. Fletcher rang the doorbell and it was answered by a young woman, polished and poised from the top of her blonde chignon to the hem of her business suit. When Fletcher asked, she gave her name as Pip McGuire.

So this is the elusive estate manager, thought Fletcher getting out her ID and flashing it in front of the superior-looking woman.

'DS Fletcher and DS Watson,' Fletcher said. 'We have a warrant to search the premises.'

'It would be better if you came back when Barry's out of hospital,' Pip McGuire said, frowning, as she looked behind them to see Dougie Harris and three DCs disembarking from the second car. 'I don't feel comfortable letting you in when he's not here.'

''Fraid that's not possible,' said Watson, barging past the estate manager. Fletcher followed Gayle into the interior. She was aware that Harris and the other DCs were taking up the rear.

'Where do we start?' said Harris behind her.

'Back outside and take the outbuildings. Break the doors down if you need to.'

'If you break the doors down you'll have me to deal with. Anyway, no need for that,' said Pip McGuire, changing her countenance and suddenly looking alarmed. 'I have keys to every building and room.'

Fletcher watched the woman anxiously sprinting off, presumably to get the keys. 'On second thoughts, go with her, Dougie. Make sure she doesn't call anyone.'

Harris followed the young woman's retreating back.

'Reckon a good place to start is Barry's drawing room,' said Fletcher, leading the way down the corridor. They entered the large high-ceilinged room in the centre of which was a crystal glass chandelier. Fletcher looked around her. Her eyes narrowed when she took in the ostentatious velvet chaise longue, mahogany table and paintings on the wall. She walked over to the empty area of wall where the stolen Stubbs had hung. Watson joined her.

'Do you think he staged his own robbery?' asked Watson, looking at the now empty wall.

Fletcher bit her lip. 'I honestly don't know. I wouldn't put it past him, but he took quite a hammering from the assault.'

'It's unlikely whoever did it meant for him to hit his head as he fell. That sort of thing can't really be planned.'

'Maybe,' said Fletcher. She turned to Watson. 'Just say the robbery was staged and the Stubbs was still in the house. Where would you hide it?'

'I dunno, but do you really think he'd keep any of the paintings here? He doesn't strike me as someone who's naïve.'

'No, "naïve" isn't a word I'd apply to Cuthbert.' Fletcher looked at Watson. 'But "cocky" and "arrogant" are.'

'I take your point. So if he's cocky enough to keep the paintings in his home I'd say in a locked room nobody else would have access to? Somewhere out of the way. In an attic, perhaps? Not sure of a basement or cellar, though. Might be too damp. Does he have a safe?'

'Would have to be a bloody big safe,' said Fletcher. 'How big was the Stubbs? Three by three feet would you say?'

They both looked at the blank part of the wall where the painting had hung. Fletcher turned to Watson. 'Do we have the dimensions of the other stolen paintings?'

Watson shook her head. 'Not here, but back at the station.'

'Well, we know he's got a locked gun cabinet room. But I doubt he'd hide the paintings in there.'

They left the room and continued walking down the corridor. Fletcher put her head round another door. 'Bloody hell,' she said.

'He has his own billiards room.' Watson eagerly edged forwards, keen to get a look. Fletcher walked into the room, putting the light on as she went. Overhead lighting illuminated several tables. 'Grief.' She walked over to the nearest table and stroked the green felt.

'Where would you hide a work of art?' asked Fletcher.

'Beats me. I'm not an art connoisseur.'

Fletcher entered the room, looked underneath a couple of billiard tables and then felt her way along the walls, banging on them.

'He must have a study somewhere. Usually they're totally private. I'm wondering if there could be a hidden room.'

'You might be onto something, but I don't think we'll find it here.'

Footsteps sounded and Harris and the two DCs approached. 'Found anything?' asked Fletcher.

Harris shook his head. He started checking his mobile for messages.

Fletcher frowned. Wondered if it was police business. Knowing Harris, he could be setting up a drinking night with the boys. 'Where's the estate manager now?' she asked.

Harris shrugged.

'Go and see if Cuthbert has a study he keeps locked. And keep Pip McGuire in your sight at all times.' Harris disappeared.

The two women left the billiards room and tried the door to the right. It was a bathroom with an enormous sunken bath. 'Don't think they'd be kept in here. Too much condensation.' As they were leaving there was lighter footfall in the corridor.

'There is a study Barry keeps locked, but only he has the key,' said the estate manager. 'Thought I might as well tell you. You'll find it anyway.'

'Show us,' said Watson.

They took a flight of stairs and second left she stopped outside a closed door.

'This the room?' asked Fletcher.

'Yes, but like I said, Barry is the only one with the key and I don't know where it is.'

Fletcher looked at Harris who sighed, took a step back and then shoulder-charged the door. It splintered and Harris nearly fell into the room. He stood aside as Fletcher edged past feeling for a light on the wall. Her hand came into contact with the switch and she pressed it, illuminating the room and all its contents. She gazed around her at the wide pine desk, black leather chair, two bookshelves and drinks cabinet that held nothing but a bottle of whisky and two glasses. 'Shit. I was so sure…' She walked over to the desk and opened the drawers. Empty except for a manila folder and a couple of cheap pens. She brought out the folder and leafed through it. 'A print-out of Cuthbert's accounts for this tax year.' After flicking through she put it back in the drawer which she shut. 'Looks legit. This doesn't make sense. Why would you keep a room locked when there's nothing in it but books?'

'Unless there's another room behind this one,' said Watson, walking over to one of the book cupboards. 'Secret rooms or hidey holes are often hidden behind book cupboards.' She took a few books out. Most of them were on accounting and business practice. Put them back. She walked over to the other bookcase. 'This one isn't just a bookcase,' she said.

'Looks like a bookcase to me,' said Harris.

'No, it's more than a bookcase. It's a door frame. And I reckon there's something behind it. We just have to find how to open it.' She turned to Fletcher and grinned. 'I have a wee thing about secret rooms. I've done loads of research on them.' She walked up to one end of the bookcase and pushed at it. Nothing. She walked to the other side and did the same. It didn't budge. 'I wonder,' she said. Fletcher watched fascinated as Watson selected a heavy leather tome at the end of the middle shelf. Carefully she pulled it. Fletcher heard a click. 'Got it.' Watson pushed the door open.

'Oldest trick in the book. No pun intended.'

Hardly listening to Watson, Fletcher took a deep breath. She peered over Watson's shoulder. There in front of them propped

against the wall in a space smaller than her tiny bathroom was the
Stubbs. But not only the Stubbs, there were two other paintings,
both of which were unmistakable if you knew what you were
looking for.

'The missing Vettriano and Constable. I don't see the Sisley
though. So he hasn't managed to sell them all on, yet,' said Fletcher,
staring at a small safe which was attached to the wall. 'I'd really like
to know what's in the safe.'

'I'll get that organised,' said Watson. With an expression of
quiet satisfaction Fletcher said to Watson, who was still staring
at the paintings, 'We've got him. I'm going to get over to the
hospital.'

'I'll meet you there,' said Watson. 'I've got a couple of things
to do first, not least organise for someone to get into that safe.'

* * *

The rain that had been threatening all day started to fall. The sky
was a heavy leaden grey, fast-moving clouds scudding across it.
A chink of blue light pierced the horizon, promising a return to
summer. Fletcher ran to her car and yanked open the door, sure
Harris would give Watson a lift back to the station.

As she sat down she smoothed her skirt with her hands. Under
no illusions as to the importance of the task ahead, she only hoped
that she'd be able to convince Cuthbert to cooperate with the
police. She hadn't predicted the turn the investigation had taken.
She, like everyone else, had been caught out.

As soon as she'd parked up and entered the hospital Fletcher
bought herself a coffee from the canteen. She took the lift to the
second floor where Cuthbert was in his private room. As soon
as she got out and turned down his corridor she stopped in her
tracks. The place was in uproar. White-coated doctors running
everywhere. She saw PC Murray's overturned chair. There was a
pool of blood outside Cuthbert's room. The door to the room was
wide open. She saw a flash of white inside as a medic leant over
the bed. Fletcher's mouth went dry.

Fletcher dropped her coffee into a waste bin and sprinted towards the room. She could hear alarms beeping as she drew closer. She grasped the arm of a young doctor who was beginning to close the curtains on the patient in the bed.

'What's happened?'

She was just in time to see three medics leaning over an unconscious man, one giving CPR.

'Are you family?'

She tried to lean over his shoulder as she answered. 'No, I'm a police officer.'

'I'm sorry, I can't talk to you right now.' The medic jerked his head towards the man's unconscious form. 'He's in a bad way.'

'What's happened?' asked Fletcher, with a growing feeling of dread.

'He's been shot.'

Shit, thought Fletcher. *Shit, shit, shit.*

'You'll have to wait outside.' As she said this, one of the medics drew the curtain firmly round the bed, preventing Fletcher from any further view.

'Did you see who did it?' asked Fletcher but the woman had disappeared behind the curtain.

Fletcher threw her arms up. Wildly she turned round to look for someone to ask.

She stopped a young doctor who was half running down the corridor towards Cuthbert's room. 'Where's PC Murray?'

'He's being operated on.'

Fletcher's blood ran cold. Whoever was doing this was always one step ahead. And if Barry Cuthbert didn't pull through, where would that leave the investigation? And where would that leave Jim? Wide open and vulnerable in a foreign country. Cuthbert had to pull through. He was the only link to the crimes and Aleks Voller. First Tamm. Now Cuthbert. With a heavy heart she turned away and fished out her mobile. Called Carruthers. No answer. Just as she was about to ring Bingham she was aware of movement within the room. The voice of a doctor said, 'Time of death is 4.36pm. I'm afraid Mr Barnes' next of kin need to be notified.'

Fletcher snapped her mobile shut. Three serious white-coated men walked out of the room. As the last of the three passed her Fletcher whipped out her police ID and said, 'Mr Barnes? I thought this was the room of Mr Barry Cuthbert?'

The man stopped. Unsmiling, he said, 'Barry Cuthbert got moved twenty minutes ago. I'm assuming he was the intended target?'

'Looks likely,' said Fletcher. 'But what about…?'

'Then he's a lucky man. Luckier than Mr Barnes.'

'How did this Mr Barnes end up in Barry Cuthbert's room?' said Fletcher, frowning.

'As you know, Barry Cuthbert has been brought out of his coma.' To answer Fletcher's confused look he said, 'He's been transferred to another ward under another consultant. The James Mitchell Ward, next floor up.'

'But why was PC Murray still down here?' asked Fletcher.

The medic, clearly in a hurry, told her as he walked off, 'He would have been waiting until Mr Cuthbert was properly settled in his new room, I suppose.' Fletcher mumbled her thanks. She knew Murray wouldn't leave his charge like that. She stared at his overturned chair, noticing his jacket on the back. More likely he'd returned to collect his jacket.

She ran down the corridor, out of the ward and took the lift to the new ward Cuthbert had been so recently moved to. Breathless, she stopped by the nurses' station and, after showing her police ID, got directed to the new room Cuthbert was now in.

The door was shut. She peered in through the glass panel. She could see his chest rise and fall. He was sleeping. *He must have been given some pretty strong drugs to knock him out in all this mayhem,* she thought. *Barry Cuthbert definitely dodged a bullet.* Sighing with relief she phoned Bingham, who was as shocked as she at this turn of events.

'Stay where you are,' ordered Bingham, recovering quickly and taking charge. 'I'll get armed response over right away. Interview everyone who was in the vicinity. Staff and patients alike.'

Watson came running down the corridor. 'Fuck, Andie. What's going on?'

'A man called Barnes has been shot,' gasped Fletcher. 'He's dead. PC Murray's in theatre. Undergoing an op to remove a bullet. Cuthbert's one lucky bastard. If he hadn't been moved...'

She watched as a nurse wheeled a patient down the corridor towards them. Fletcher grabbed Watson's arm. 'We need to treat the hospital like a crime scene.'

'We need the armed response team,' said Watson.

'Bingham's already on it. We need to be careful. The intruder might still be on the premises.' Once again she reached for the mobile in her pocket. 'Need to contact Jim. He's not answering his phone.' She punched in his number, his new number. Motioned for Watson to draw closer. 'See what you can find out about Murray.' Watson nodded and walked towards the nurses' station.

No answer. Carruthers' mobile went to voicemail. Fletcher snapped her phone shut. Just as she put it back in her pocket a male cleaner carrying a bucket of disinfectant and a mop walked through the exit door towards Cuthbert's room. Frowning, Fletcher put her hand out. 'I'm sorry. You can't go in.'

The man remained silent. She watched him, noting his hooded eyes and dark hair swept into a ponytail. What was he? About six foot? He glanced at his wristwatch. A Rolex. Since when could cleaners afford Rolexes?

'No problem,' he said. His voice was heavily accented. Eastern European.

Fear flashed through Fletcher. She looked into his eyes. They were hard and emotionless. Aleks Voller. Had to be. He took a step towards her. She glanced behind him to the open door. She took a deep breath and tried to make a run for it but as she ran past him he caught her arm, bringing her closer in to him. In a flash he had produced a gun, had it to her head.

'If you scream, I'll pull the trigger,' he said.

She could smell his bad breath on her face.

She could feel the cold weapon against her head as she closed her eyes. It was a gun that had already shot two men. Her breath caught in her chest. She was too frightened even to swallow. She heard a scream down the corridor. She opened her eyes. A nurse must have seen Voller holding the gun to her and had taken flight.

Voller dragged Fletcher down the corridor with him. Kicking open the fire exit he half dragged, half pushed her down a flight of concrete stairs.

'You won't get out of here alive. I've called for armed backup. There'll be police everywhere.'

'That's why I've got you with me, you stupid bitch. You're my ticket out of here.'

They descended another flight of stairs. Voller had his huge hand wrapped round her wrist in a vice-like grip. It hurt. His Rolex dug into her skin. At least he no longer had the gun to her temple. As they approached another flight of concrete stairs a door on the next landing opened and two female medics came out. It caught Voller off guard. He hesitated. There was a scream. Fletcher took her chance. She stamped on Voller's foot then kneed him in the balls. The gun he had been holding clattered down several stairs.

'Get back!' screamed Fletcher to the medics, who seemed to be rooted to the spot. They disappeared through the door and it shut with a bang. Fletcher ran down the stairs as did Voller. She lunged for the gun but Voller managed to grab it first. Fletcher's heart seemed to stop in that moment. In the distance she could hear footsteps running towards them.

God, I hope it's armed backup, she thought.

Voller, keeping a tight grip on the gun, pointed it at Fletcher's head. Showing discoloured teeth he smiled menacingly at her. As he cocked the gun, the door to the stairway opened to eject two uniformed officers. Voller sprang round and aimed the gun at one of the two officers. Fletcher, seeing what Voller was about to do, threw herself at him. The gun went off, the bullet hitting the wall. Voller cursed before bounding down the steps and away.

'Stand down! We need an armed response here,' shouted Fletcher getting up from the ground.

One officer followed her command, but the other sprinted after Voller.

'Are you OK?' The second police officer who stayed for Fletcher was young and dark-haired. Before she was even able to answer him the shakes took over and if he hadn't helped her to sit, she would have fallen.

Nineteen

Carruthers was sipping a coffee in an office in the Tallinn City Municipal Police Department. He was still feeling sick to his stomach that he had been duped by Sadie Andrews. If that was indeed her name. He had spent the time since he'd seen her get into the lift with Kert Ilves wracking his brain trying to think what he'd said to her in their quiet moments together. Well, what was done was done. He pushed the thought of her out of his mind as he nervously awaited the arrival of Andres Jakobson, Janek Kuul's colleague.

The door opened and a tall, dark-haired man in his thirties entered. 'I believe you wanted to speak with me? I'm Andres Jakobson.'

Carruthers assessed the man as they shook hands. Jakobson's hand was dry and the handshake was firm. Carruthers approved of the first impression. *He's either got nothing to fear or he's a cool customer.*

'I'm trying to get hold of Janek Kuul. I can't raise him. It's a police matter. He mentioned your name. That's why I'm here.'

'Why do you wish to speak with him?' Jakobson asked. 'And what brings you out to Tallinn? I take it that this is not a vacation?'

Carruthers leant forward. 'How well do you know Janek?' he asked.

'I've known him for fifteen years. We're friends as well as colleagues. Why do you ask?'

'I need to find him. Is he due back in the station today?' asked Carruthers.

Jakobson rolled up his shirt sleeves. 'I haven't seen him today. I believe he had some holiday owing.'

Carruthers played with his coffee cup. 'Have you got a home address for him?'

'You know I can't give that out. Look.' Jakobson took his phone from his pocket. 'I'll give him a call.' He tapped in some numbers and waited. Giving nothing away with his eyes, he spoke a sharp torrent of Estonian. Carruthers could feel his hope soar. But when Jakobson cut the call and placed the mobile on the table he felt the hope die away again.

'Voicemail. I asked him to ring me immediately he gets the message. Sometimes he goes fishing.'

Carruthers could feel the man assessing him.

'He won't be fishing,' said Carruthers. 'Like I said, he's waiting for my call. He would answer it if he could.'

'Do you want another coffee? And to tell me why you need to speak with him so urgently? You think something's happened to him, don't you?'

At that moment the door to the office opened and a thin man in his forties with a receding blond hairline entered the room with a sheaf of papers.

They exchanged a few words and Jakobson waved him impatiently away. Carruthers could feel the man's curious eyes on him.

'Look, I need to speak to you in strictest confidence. I've only been in Estonia a couple of days and it's been a very…' Carruthers chose his next word carefully, 'eventful time.'

'We will not be overheard if we speak in this office.'

'OK.' Carruthers leant forward. He looked into the eyes of the man opposite him. He saw both curiosity and concern. *He's OK,* Carruthers thought. *He's one of us. One of the good guys.* He decided to trust his instinct and put his cards on the table. 'I know about the deaths of Olev Lepp, Mikael Tamm and Gunnar Aare.'

As Jakobson went white, Carruthers continued quickly. 'I flew to Estonia because a couple of cases I'm working on in Scotland, murder cases, involve one of your high-profile criminals.'

Jakobson raised his eyebrows.

'A man known as Kurat, the devil,' continued Carruthers. 'Marek Voller.'

Carruthers' mobile started to ring. He brought it out of his pocket and looked at it. It was Fletcher. The call would have to wait. He looked back at Jakobson. Was annoyed to see that he had missed the man's initial reaction to the name of the gangster.

'What do you know of the Voller brothers?' asked Jakobson.

'I take it that name's familiar to you?'

Jakobson nodded. 'Local pimps, drug dealers. Connection to Mafia. They're nasty pieces of work.'

'He marks his prostitutes with a tattoo of an eye on the ankle,' said Carruthers. It was more a statement than a question.

'That's Kurat's trademark.'

Carruthers could see that Jakobson was sizing him up, deciding whether he could be trusted. *It works both ways,* thought Carruthers. *Have I done right to trust Jakobson?*

'I see you are well informed,' said Jakobson. 'How do you know this?'

'I spoke with Mikael Tamm on the phone hours before he was killed. And Kuul filled me in. I've also met Kert Ilves.'

'Kert Ilves?' Jakobson frowned. 'He left the police force. Must be three years ago.'

'He didn't tell me his name was Kert Ilves,' said Carruthers. 'He introduced himself to me as Gunnar Aare.'

'But Gunnar Aare is dead.'

'Exactly.'

'Kert Ilves knows we're getting close to Aleks Voller. Voller is currently operating in Scotland. Apart from supplying prostitutes for parties of influential people, we also believe he may be behind a spate of art heists. He has connections to a local estate owner called Barry Cuthbert.'

Jakobson shook his head. 'I don't know this name.'

'Aleks Voller is supplying prostitutes to Cuthbert. For a large cut we believe Cuthbert is helping Voller target local bigwigs–'

'Bigwigs?'

'Important people. People with money. And art. What we don't know is how this art is being smuggled out the country. And up until recently we didn't know who Voller's contact is here in Estonia.'

'It's Kert Ilves.' It was a statement rather than a question.

'Yes. But Janek Kuul also thinks Ilves has a contact who works for the police here in Tallinn. In this very station.'

'Who sent Mikael Tamm and Gunnar Aare to their deaths.'

'Not just them. Hanna Mets, too. She was working undercover, wasn't she?

'She's dead?'

'Discovered on a beach in Fife. She'd fallen to her death.'

Jakobson swore in Estonian. 'And you think it was the work of Aleks Voller?'

'She had his tattoo on her ankle. She was pregnant when she died. It's possible she'd been raped just before her death.'

Suddenly Carruthers' mobile started its shrill noise. Fletcher again. He cursed.

'Perhaps you should take that call,' said Jakobson. 'It might be important.'

Carruthers nodded and took the call.

'Jim, I'm at the hospital.' Fletcher's words came out in gasps. 'There's been an attempt made on Barry Cuthbert's life. He's fine. They'd switched him to another ward. Some other poor sod copped it instead. I'm afraid PC Murray got shot. He's been operated on. I've been told he should make a full recovery.'

Carruthers didn't want to say too much. 'Are you OK?'

'Yes, yes, I'm fine. Can you talk now?'

'No, not really. I'm at the Tallinn Police Station. Let me give you a call later when I'm on my own.'

He cut the call, wishing he'd been able to talk further.

Twenty

Fletcher and Watson travelled back to the station together. They had spent several hours at the hospital with an armed response team trying to locate Aleks Voller. He was nowhere to be found. They'd both concluded he must have escaped the hospital grounds. Watson had insisted on driving. She looked across at Fletcher. 'Are you OK?'

'I'm fine,' said Fletcher, although she could still feel her teeth chattering. Guessed it must be the adrenaline.

'You're not, though, are you?' said Watson. 'Fine, I mean. I wouldn't be. You could have been killed.'

'I wasn't, though.' But Watson was right. She could have been killed. She imagined how it would have been for Lara, had her baby lived, growing up without a mother. She couldn't imagine it. She wondered what her daughter would have looked like. She tried to put the image of Lara out of her mind. It was funny. Most of the time she was alright. And she was being honest when she told Carruthers the counselling had helped. But every so often painful memories or feelings intruded when she least expected them. She turned to Watson, chasing the ghosts of the memories away.

'I got the impression Jim couldn't speak freely,' said Fletcher. 'He was at the police station. He sounded nervous. He's going to ring me later.'

'You didn't tell him about your run-in with Voller?'

Fletcher shrugged. 'What good would it have done? You know he would have just worried. He's got enough on his mind just now.'

'Why would Aleks Voller try to kill Barry Cuthbert?' said Watson.

Fletcher pulled a face. 'It happens. Criminals turn on each other. We've said all along. Perhaps Cuthbert got greedy.

Wanted a bigger cut. Or Voller thinks Cuthbert's going to rat on him. We're going to have to try to move Cuthbert to the safe house a bit sooner.'

'Not sure the hospital will like that.'

'Cuthbert seems to be making a pretty rapid improvement. They wouldn't have moved him to another ward so soon.'

'S'pose. Well, at least we've increased the security in the hospital for the time being.' They had organised for two armed police officers to be positioned outside his hospital room.

'How's PC Murray?'

'He'll live, but it will be a while before he goes back to active duty. He'll be offered rehab and counselling.'

Fletcher remained silent. She stared at the road ahead as Watson drove the pool car.

A shrill noise interrupted her thoughts. It was her mobile. She answered, listening to the person on the other end. 'Right, we'll come straight back.' Watson threw Fletcher a worried glance. Fletcher turned to her colleague. 'That was despatch. There's been another shooting. In the car park of the hospital.' As she said it, Fletcher could feel the hair on the back of her neck stand up.

'Shit. Who's the victim?'

'All I know is he's male.'

'Christ, at least he's already at the hospital.'

Fletcher shook her head. 'Won't help him. Apparently he's dead.'

Watson drove on until she found a gate leading to a farm and did a speedy U-turn. Fletcher felt herself pushed back in her seat by the extra speed Watson was now pulling. Mercifully the country roads were quiet. 'Good thing we were on the back roads. Any holiday traffic is on the other road,' Fletcher said. They sped past fields of wheat and barley. They turned into the hospital car park to be greeted by a uniformed police officer who peered into their car.

'No further, ladies. This is a crime scene.'

Watson flashed her badge at the man. 'Oh, sorry, ma'am. On you go.'

'Have the SOCOs been called?' asked Fletcher.

'They're on their way.'

'You haven't touched him?'

'No, no. It was obvious he was dead. My colleague is with him.'

Fletcher thanked the officer, as Watson swept in the car park and pulled in to the first available parking place. Both jumped out of the car. A knot of onlookers had formed a semi-circle. Fletcher looked around her and took in the scene. A noise made her look over her shoulder. Another two cars were being stopped at the entrance to the car park. 'Dr Mackie's arrived.' The second car held the scene of crime officers.

'Keep back, please,' shouted Watson as the two of them made their way through the crowd.

The victim was lying on his back with his eyes wide open and staring. His head was at an angle, displaying the greasy black ponytail. He hadn't stood a chance. He'd been shot right between the eyes.

Watson peered at the victim. 'Isn't that—'

'Aleks Voller.'

'Looks like a professional hit.' Watson took out her mobile.

'Who are you calling?'

'My partner. Looks like I won't be in for supper tonight.'

'Who found him?'

'I did,' said a red-haired police officer walking towards them. Fletcher didn't know him, but she was sure she had seen him about the station. His uniform was neat and crisp, and unlike a lot of them, he hadn't seemed to be affected by the recent heatwave. Another time she might ask him how he managed that. She looked up the two necessary inches as he stopped in front of her. 'I even saw the man who killed him. He took off when he saw me. He was stooping over the body as if checking he was dead.'

'Is there a gun on him?'

'Don't think so. He didn't have it in his hand, anyway.'

Most likely taken by the killer, unless it was still on him somewhere. Fletcher looked into the dead, staring eyes of the man who could have killed her. A flood of unexpected hatred nearly drowned her, for the fear he had made her feel. She felt like kicking his lifeless body. It was likely the killer had checked to see if Voller was carrying anything that could incriminate the rest of the gang. Unlikely the assailant was checking to see if Voller was dead.

'You know the drill,' said Fletcher. 'I'll need to see your statement.'

'You're keen,' said the officer. 'I haven't had a chance to write it yet.'

'What did the assailant look like?'

'Male, five foot eight, stocky, blond haired.'

'Did you hear him speak?'

The police officer shook his head.

Dr Mackie came striding up from behind the two women wearing his coverall, latex gloves and paper footwear and holding his black medical bag.

'You're certainly keeping me busy, lassie,' he said to Fletcher.

The SOCOs were also busy getting into their coveralls. A police officer was shooing onlookers away. Another starting to tape the exclusion zone. Soon enough a tent would be erected and the painstaking task of gathering evidence would start.

'Dr Mackie, do me a favour, will you?' said Fletcher.

'Don't tell me. You want me to have a feel in his pockets to see if he's got any means of ID?'

'Already know who he is,' said Fletcher. 'What I want to know is if he has a gun or mobile on him.'

With a groan, Mackie knelt down by Aleks Voller. 'Bugger, this is a job for a much younger man.'

'Or woman,' said Watson.

'Indeed,' said Mackie. He patted Voller's trouser pockets, bringing out a small mobile.

'Think this is what you are looking for,' Mackie said, producing an evidence bag. He dropped the mobile into it and then passed it to Fletcher. 'No sign of a gun.'

Fletcher looked down at the evidence bag holding the cheap Nokia mobile. 'This little beauty goes straight to the techie guys.

With a bit of luck within a few hours, we'll have Voller's entire contact list.'

'Jim'll be pleased,' said Watson. 'This might be the break he's been waiting for.'

'So, where does that leave things?' asked Watson.

'Aleks Voller tries to murder Barry Cuthbert. Within an hour Aleks Voller is killed. Well, we only know one thing,' said Fletcher, 'the perpetrator wasn't Barry Cuthbert.'

Watson touched Fletcher's arm. 'I still think we need to interview Cuthbert.'

They left the SOCOs and entered the hospital, showing their ID to security as they walked in. They took the lift to the second floor and approached the room Barry Cuthbert was in. There were two armed police officers on the door. Fletcher opened the door and walked in, followed by Watson. Barry Cuthbert was awake.

'What's going on?' he said.

'You were very lucky you moved rooms,' said Watson. 'There's been a couple of shootings.'

'I know about the attempt on my life. Aleks Voller tried to shoot me. Is he in police custody?'

'No,' said Fletcher. 'A man's been shot dead in the hospital car park. We believe it's Aleks Voller.'

Cuthbert tried to sit up. His eyes were full of pain and something else. Fear. He grimaced. 'Oh, Jesus Christ. I need to be given more security.'

Fletcher pulled up a visitor chair and angled it close to Cuthbert's hospital bed. 'You better tell us what's going on, Barry.'

'We know you and Aleks Voller were working together,' said Watson, also pulling up a chair and sitting. 'We suspect you were using prostitutes at parties for a start. These girls were being supplied from Eastern Europe by Aleks Voller. We also know you were behind the art thefts.'

Barry Cuthbert didn't answer.

'We've had a search warrant for your house, Barry,' said Watson. 'Game's up. We found the stolen paintings. And it's only a matter of time before we get into your safe. I wonder what the McMullans and Warristons are going to say when they know you were behind the thefts. You're finished. You do realise that. You'll be looking at a prison sentence.'

'Reckon that'll be the least of his problems when the Estonians find out he's still alive,' said Watson.

The silence in the room was punctured by the noise of Fletcher's mobile phone again. She fished it out of her handbag. It was Carruthers. She left the room and turned her back on the two guards.

'Jim. Are you OK?'

'I'm fine. Where are you just now?'

'The hospital. I've been with Barry Cuthbert. I came straight from his place to the hospital. Jim, we've found all the stolen art. At Cuthbert's. We can start by charging him with theft.' Fletcher looked through the glass door. She could see Watson was speaking to Cuthbert. She turned her back on the glass door and lowered her voice. 'There's been another shooting. The man's dead. Shot in the hospital car park. We believe it's Aleks Voller. The good news is that we've got his mobile. The man who killed him was interrupted before he had chance to snatch it. Who would try to murder Aleks Voller? Unless… unless Voller and Cuthbert both got greedy. Decided to go into business for themselves.'

'How is Cuthbert now?'

'As nervous as hell. Now Voller's out the picture I guess he's just waiting to be bumped off by whoever killed Voller. Guess he feels like a sitting duck. He's demanding even more protection now. We might be able to exploit his vulnerability. What's going on with you, Jim?'

'I can't talk freely. Lean on Cuthbert, Andie. Get him to talk. Keep an eye on the head gamekeeper, Sturrock too, will you? He definitely knows more than he's saying. If you need to bring Sturrock in and question him you have my full backing. I'll try to call you later.'

The line went dead. Fletcher put her mobile in her black handbag and went back into Cuthbert's room.

'You need to move me. I'm not safe here.'

Fletcher scrutinised Cuthbert; taking in his pale lined face, his shallow breathing and the sheen of perspiration on his forehead. *He is scared, really scared,* she thought.

She pulled the chair even closer to the bed and sat. Leaned in. 'We'll move you as soon as you give us the information we need, and not before, Barry.' She looked across at Watson.

'What information?' he asked.

'You know what information,' Fletcher said. 'What is your connection with Aleks Voller?'

'You don't have anything on me except that the stolen artworks were found in my house. I have a vast number of staff. Anyone of them could have thieved them.'

'I don't think so, Barry,' said Watson. 'And we have a lot more than just finding stolen art at your house. One of your gamekeepers is dead, Barry. We have information that you've used prostitutes at parties, almost definitely Eastern European and more than likely trafficked into the country. The man we believe supplied them is now dead. You are up to your neck, Barry, in shit. A charge of theft is the least of your problems. You're going down for multiple murder.'

'You can't be serious? You have no evidence.'

Fletcher had had enough. She stood up. 'Come on, Gayle. Let's head back to the station.'

Watson stood up.

Cuthbert looked alarmed. 'You're leaving me?'

'We are, Barry.'

'The officers outside my door will stay though, won't they?'

'No. We need them back at the station.'

'But I'm a sitting duck!'

'Not our problem, Barry,' said Fletcher, enjoying seeing the once over-confident Cuthbert grovelling. The two officers headed towards the door. Watson opened it.

'OK. OK. Look, I'm willing to cut a deal.'

Fletcher turned round to face Cuthbert. She wasn't surprised. After all, Carruthers had already said that men like Barry Cuthbert would do anything to save their own skin.

'I'm listening.' She kept her voice calm and face neutral but inside she was bubbling with excitement. While Carruthers was out of the country she was the senior investigating officer on this case. If she was the one to crack the investigation from the Scotland end – well, it wouldn't do her career any harm at all.

'If you promise to waive all charges and keep my name out of the press I'll tell you what I know,' said Cuthbert.

Fletcher hesitated. She knew waiving all charges would be impossible and she should run cutting any sort of deal by Carruthers first but given that he was not easy to get hold of…

'What do you know?'

'Get me out of here, first.'

'Give me a reason to.'

Fletcher could see Cuthbert weighing up, assessing how much or how little he needed to tell the two officers in order to get what he wanted. 'Alright, yeah, so I had girls at my parties. They was young, they was foreign, but they didn't object and I swear I didn't pick 'em underage. They was for, well, you know. Some of my guests, they… they had… certain tastes. Had to keep 'em sweet.'

'So you admit to being involved in a prostitution ring. Were these women sex slaves, Barry?'

Cuthbert attempted to look horrified. He put his hand on his heart. 'On me mother's grave, I know nuffin' about sex slaves. Those girls were willing.'

'Run by Aleks Voller?'

'If you say so.'

Fletcher turned away from Cuthbert and started walking towards the door. She gestured for Watson to do the same.

'OK, OK. Yes. Supplied by Aleks Voller. Happy now?'

Fletcher hesitated, turned round, grabbed the chair and sat down again.

'Did you kill Hanna Mets?' said Watson.

'Who?'

'The young woman who fell to her death from the cliffs at the beach at Pinetum Park Forest,' said Fletcher.

'Do you know the penalty for killing a police officer?' said Watson.

'A police officer? I thought your gaffer told me she was a prostitute.'

'We originally thought she was a prostitute,' said Fletcher. 'Turns out she was an undercover cop.'

Cuthbert shook his head. 'I had nuffin' to do with her death. Or anybody else's.'

'Could she have been killed by Aleks Voller?' Fletcher looked in the man's eyes as she asked the question. He was certainly a lot of things. Would clearly sell his own grandmother if the price was right. But murder? Fletcher didn't think so.

'We believe your young gamekeeper, Joe McGuigan, was murdered because he knew something. Or had seen something. One of the two. Most likely seen. And he wanted to talk. He wanted to talk about what he'd seen while he was out on the cliffs laying poison to kill birds of prey on your orders.'

'Could that girl's death not have been an accident?' Cuthbert asked.

Fletcher thought quickly. If it had been an accident why would Joe McGuigan have been murdered? Not for just wanting to talk about poisoned birds of prey, that's for sure. However, they still had no proof Hanna Mets had been murdered. It *could* have been an accident or suicide. Unlikely, though. Perhaps they would never find out.

'You're right. We don't know yet how Hanna Mets died. We suspect murder. But what we do know is that she'd been drugged before she'd been killed, Barry. It's also possible she'd been raped.'

Cuthbert's face drained of colour. 'Oh no. You're not pinning that on me. Look, maybe she crossed the line with Voller and he killed her. He was a bit of a psycho. I was scared of him.'

The two police officers exchanged looks once more. Watson snorted. 'I can't imagine you being scared of anyone.'

'Did you ever meet her? Hanna Mets?' said Fletcher.

'No. That photograph you showed me wasn't familiar. But if she was an undercover police officer and Voller found out…' His voice trailed away. 'But she could have been pregnant by him. He was sleeping with several of his girls.' Cuthbert cleared his throat. 'Look, if you must know, I was being blackmailed by Voller. He insisted I use his prostitutes at my parties.'

'What did he have on you?' asked Fletcher.

'Do I get my protection from you guys or what?'

'You have it,' said Fletcher.

'Not that it's worth much,' he said. No doubt he was thinking of the earlier shootings.

'You're under armed guard.' Fletcher watched the potential of that implication sink in.

'What about the protection for the information I'm giving you? I want immunity.'

'We'll do what we can, Barry. But do you really think the police are your biggest problem right now?'

'Oh, Jesus, look. Yes, I had girls at my parties. I used to get them from Glasgow then Aleks Voller appeared on the scene. He started putting pressure on me to use his girls. He's not a man you can easily say no to.'

'Keep talking,' said Watson. 'What did he have on you?'

Cuthbert licked his lips. 'I might have… sold a few paintings on. He found out. Said if I didn't go in with him, he'd make sure my business went down.'

'Sold a few paintings on?' Fletcher snorted. 'That's an interesting euphemism for fencing, but you were doing a bit more than that, weren't you, Barry? You were stealing the paintings, too.' She looked at this man who clearly thought nothing of stealing from his friends and business associates. 'You're behind all the art thefts in the area.' It wasn't a question.

'Nothing more than a middleman.'

'Oh, I think a lot more than just middleman, Barry. Don't you? You found out through your golf club connections which members had valuable works of art and passed on that information. I imagine you still had contacts from your time in prison. You probably thought you had a nice little number going until you met Aleks Voller.' As she said this, Fletcher felt the bile rise up in her throat for a man who could sell out his friends and colleagues the way Cuthbert had. 'We know Aleks Voller has a brother. Who do they work for?'

Cuthbert shook his head. 'He never gave me a name. Said I was better off not knowing. Just said something strange about my doing the devil's work.'

Fletcher weighed up whether she believed him or not. She did. After all, what would Cuthbert care where the artworks went as long as he got his money. *Blood money,* thought Fletcher, remembering the growing number of dead.

She stood up. Decided they had enough to be going on with. 'OK, Barry, we'll continue this later when we make it more formal. In the meantime we need to get back to the station but we'll get you moved somewhere safe.'

Barry Cuthbert nodded. 'How soon?'

'Soon as we can,' said Fletcher, picking up her handbag and putting it over her shoulder.

She and Watson left the room. 'We need to get back to Dr Mackie,' said Fletcher. 'See what he's got for us. We also need to get Voller's mobile to forensics. See if there's anything on it that can help Jim.' They walked out of the hospital and to the car. As Fletcher was climbing into the passenger seat, Watson's mobile rang. The older woman answered it as she sat down. Somehow she managed to put her seatbelt on as she held the phone glued to her ear.

'They've managed to get into Cuthbert's safe,' she hissed.

Fletcher found she was holding her breath. And her heart skipped a beat at what Watson said next.

'They found passports. British passports. Eight of them. All for women aged between sixteen and twenty-five.'

'Forged?' asked Fletcher.

'I'd put my money on it. Wouldn't you?'

Twenty-One

Carruthers sat in the Estonian sunshine sipping a coffee. He looked at the phone numbers in front of him that Fletcher had sent. Thank God for iPhones that had access to email. With the help of John Forrest, the station's resident IT geek, Fletcher had managed to access Aleks Voller's phone. The contacts from the man's mobile were laid out in front of Carruthers. He sipped the bitter aromatic coffee as he scanned the numbers. There was one that was already familiar. That of Kert Ilves. Proof positive of the connection between the ex-Estonian policeman and the ruthless Tallinn criminal gang. He wondered if Kert Ilves had been the man responsible for the deaths of his former colleagues. Now what he needed to do was pass on this information to Jakobson.

The net was closing in.

* * *

Aleks Voller's mobile had certainly turned up trumps. As well as the list of numbers, they had intercepted a voicemail. Now they knew where Voller's flat was. A nondescript street in the centre of the former mining town of Kirkcaldy.

Fletcher and Watson stood at the door of Voller's rented accommodation. Both were wearing stab vests. Fletcher hadn't spent much time here socially. Mostly she came here on police business, however she had been to the famous Kirkcaldy Links Market, held in April, reputedly the longest fair in Europe. She couldn't remember who she'd been with but she did remember that she'd gone on a fairground ride that had left her feeling sick for hours after.

Fletcher steeled herself then gave the sign and two male officers, wearing both stab vests and riot helmets, used the battering ram on the front door. The wood splintered on the third attempt and finally the lock was broken and the door swung in. The officers ran into the premises with Fletcher, Watson and several other officers taking up the rear. Fletcher took out her truncheon. She wrinkled her nose. There was a mixture of smells – urine, sex and sweat. A sense of foreboding gripped her. The two officers who had used the battering ram disappeared into the back of the flat.

Fletcher walked into the first room on the left with her truncheon raised. It was a small bedroom dominated by a double bed in the middle of the room. What little furniture there was in the room was cheap. The bed was unmade. Dirty sheets rumpled. The stale smell of cigarettes, sweat and sex. A used condom lay on the bed. An open packet of cigarettes on the cheap bedside table. She opened the wardrobe. A couple of expensive white shirts and a pair of black trousers hung in the wardrobe at odds with the grimy, uncared for appearance of the flat. She shut the door.

'Nothing in here,' said Watson. And she was right. Aside from the clothes there was no sign of personal effects anywhere. No photographs, no books, nothing.

Fletcher followed Watson out of the room and shut the door. They entered another room. A bathroom. There was an old discoloured towel hanging from the towel rack. Fletcher opened the cabinet. Mouthwash, toothpaste, a travel toothbrush and some cotton wool. Fletcher shut the door behind them. This time they entered the living room. No personal effects, just a sofa and small table.

'He must have another flat somewhere,' said Fletcher. On the table lay a diary next to a packet of cigarettes. Fletcher picked it up and flicked through it. 'Strange this diary being here.'

'Maybe it was left by accident?' This from Watson who was checking down the back and sides of the sofa. She unearthed nothing more than a dirty hanky and a cheap black ballpoint pen.

Fletcher, still flicking through the diary, opened the page on that day's date. 'There's a time written here – 6pm, and a word, "Muuga". Another word I can't pronounce and then the number 9. A meeting of some sort?' She looked up, hearing footsteps on the scratched wooden floor. One of the uniform officers now walked towards her. He was young looking as if he was straight out of police college, his face awash with acne.

'We've found something. You'd better come see, ma'am,' he said.

'What have you got?' Fletcher shut the diary, placed it in an evidence bag she took out of her pocket, quickly unzipped her shoulder bag and dropped the diary in before zipping it back up. She'd have to read it later.

They walked down the corridor. He opened wide the door to the back room. The interior was dark. She could see it was larger than the previous room but all she could see were shapes. There was no natural light.

'See for yourself,' he said. 'Oh, by the way, the light doesn't work. Already tried it.'

Before Fletcher walked into the room she heard a sob. She took a tentative step forward as her eyes adjusted to the gloom. And another. But it was the unassailable smells that made her nose wrinkle. Sweat, sex and urine. As it was still too dark to see properly she brought out her mobile and used the light from that to show her the way. She narrowed her eyes as she tried to focus on what was in the room. Twelve pairs of frightened eyes stared back at her. All the girls were crouching on the floor at the back of the room. They wore tiny little tops and skirts exposing skinny arms and legs. Some of the girls had needle tracks in their arms, all of them looked young and malnourished. Fletcher was drawn to a pretty blonde girl wearing a pink mini skirt, with a tattoo on her ankle, older than the rest, who had her arm round a girl who looked no more than fifteen. Fletcher recognised the tattoo immediately as the same tattoo that had been on the ankle of the dead girl, Hanna Mets, and on the prostitute photographed with Barry Cuthbert. Here was the mark of the Haravere gang, and the mark of the devil.

'Is he dead?' asked the girl with the pink miniskirt. Her voice was thickly accented.

'Who?' asked Fletcher.

The girl nodded. 'The man with the ponytail.'

'Yes. He's dead.'

The girl said something in a foreign language to the others before turning back to Fletcher. 'Good,' was all she said.

The girls stayed quiet, withdrawn. All the fight gone from them, their spirits broken. Fletcher knew these young women would take a long time to recover. Some never would. She wondered how their parents would recover from their daughters' trauma. After all, it would affect the whole family. She swallowed hard. How would she have... no, she wouldn't go there.

Her gaze was drawn to a girl a little older than the rest. Still looked a teenager though. She also had blonde hair. There was a familiarity about her. Fletcher felt she had seen her recently. Or an older version of her. The resemblance to Marika Paju's mother, Karen Paju, was so striking her heart jumped in her mouth.

'Marika Paju?' Fletcher asked. The girl looked at her and nodded. She couldn't believe it. What were the chances? Fletcher made her way over to her and knelt down beside her.

'Your parents are looking for you,' said Fletcher. 'You are safe now.' Fletcher took the girl's hands in hers and rubbed them but the girl wordlessly took her hands away and let them fall into her lap. 'We will take you back to your mother? Do you understand?'

The girl nodded again.

Fletcher looked into the dead eyes of the girl. She didn't want to imagine what a horrifying ordeal Marika had been through. Fletcher felt a lump the size of a golf ball in her throat. For a brief moment she wondered how the girl would adjust when she got back home. If the parents had been overprotective before, they probably wouldn't let their daughter out of the house now. Knowing this wasn't her problem, she steeled herself to be professional.

'Can you all stand up?' Fletcher addressed her question to the blonde girl who in turn said something to the other girls. One by one they got to their feet. All except the girl who looked about fifteen.

'Why can't she stand up?' asked Watson.

'We think her leg is broken. He did it this morning. She tried to run away.' Fletcher now saw the unnatural position the leg was in. Fletcher's eyes welled up and momentarily she turned away, tears obscuring her vision. Some of these girls looked so young. Hardly into, let alone out of, puberty. There was another small stifled sob from the youngest girl.

Fletcher composed herself, and thinking of the girl with the broken leg, turned to the officer at the door and said, 'Call the ambulance service, will you? And try to find some blankets or coats for them.' She turned round and, directing her next question to the blonde haired girl, said, 'Where are you from?'

'Most are from Estonia, one from Latvia and she,' she said pointing at another girl, who stood with her back against the wall, 'is from Moldova.'

Fletcher fished out Aleks Voller's diary. 'Do you know what this means?' She showed the girl the entry in the diary by the light of her mobile.

The girl squinted although she was probably more used to the poor light than Fletcher. Fletcher wondered how long the light had been broken and how long the girls had endured being kept in the dark.

"Shipment. Muuga. It's a harbour. Quay Nine. Household goods. 6pm."

'Household goods?' echoed Fletcher. 'I wonder what sort of household goods.'

'I hear him talking on the mobile. The man with the ponytail. I pretend to be asleep. I do not know about this particular entry but they have regular shipments leaving Tallinn harbour.'

'What's in these shipments?' asked Fletcher. 'People?'

The girl shrugged. 'People. Sometimes. Also other stuff.'

'Art? Pictures?'

The blonde girl shook her head. 'I do not know.'

'Where do these shipments go?' asked Watson.

'Finland. After Finland? Who knows?'

Fletcher placed a hand on the girl's bony shoulder. 'How did you get here, to Fife?'

'Is that where I am?'

Poor girl, thought Fletcher, *she doesn't even know where she is.*

'Aleks Voller, he has a passport for me.'

Forged, thought Fletcher.

'And the other girls. Three of us come over together. We are told we have good jobs to be nannies.'

Fletcher thought about Barry Cuthbert's safe and the passports that had so recently been found. Marika started crying quietly. She'd been promised a well-paid job working in her dream country. Instead she had ended up working as a sex slave after being moved like livestock. All her dreams would be in tatters now.

Fletcher kept her phone in her hand as she knelt down beside Marika. She chided herself. Now wasn't the time to be asking these questions. An in-depth interview would have to wait. She had to get the girls checked out in hospital, especially the youngster with the possible break. She glanced at her watch. And if there was a shipment coming in at 6pm there wasn't much time to alert Carruthers. She called him. Prayed he'd answer.

* * *

Carruthers was down by the harbour watching a huge white cruise ship set sail for Helsinki when his mobile rang. The wind had picked up and the waves were choppy. As he watched the ship slip out of the harbour he held the pay-as-you-go mobile closer to his ear. As Fletcher was talking he glanced at his watch. He didn't know where Muuga Harbour was but if there was a shipment leaving the harbour at 6pm they had two hours before it was due to leave. He started to walk away, conscious that he didn't want to be seen down by the harbour. He wound up the conversation with Fletcher then called Jakobson. He'd walked fast and was standing on the edge of the Old Town within ten minutes. He tasted the salt of the sea and his perspiration on his top lip.

Jakobson had some news of his own. 'We've located Janek Kuul.'

'Where? Is he OK?' Carruthers looked around him to see if anyone was listening. Despite it being the summer there was a chill to the wind that cooled his perspiring forehead. One thing he hadn't been ready for had been the weather. He'd never been in such a heatwave. Much worse than anything he'd been through down south. The Scots generally didn't do well in hot weather. He looked down at his pale Scottish arms. The Estonian sun was bringing out his freckles. He was wearing a short-sleeved white shirt. His arms were already starting to burn. He wondered vaguely if the weather had broken in Scotland yet.

'He's fine. He apologises for not being in touch. He had to lie low for a while. I've passed on the mobile phone numbers you've given me. He says to say thanks. That list has been hugely helpful. What with that and the information you've just given us we've got enough to bring down the Haravere gang. Most crucially, we now also know who their contact is inside the police station here. We're setting a trap for the man. We think you should get out of Estonia soon. An earlier flight than the one you booked has been organised for you. The Estonian police will pay all expenses.' The man sounded jubilant. 'There is, however, one last thing you can do for us.'

'Which is what?'

'Come to the police station in thirty minutes. We want you to be in on this. Now, I need to go. I need to get organised for our trip to the docks.'

Carruthers looked at his watch. He wondered what Jakobson had planned.

* * *

'Is this really necessary?' said Carruthers as he took his bulletproof vest from Jakobson.

'Yes. This is very necessary. We're not taking any chances.' They were in an office at the station. Jakobson had locked the door from the inside and had put the blinds down so they could dress without being disturbed by prying eyes.

'What do you expect to happen?' Carruthers asked anxiously.

'We're going to arrest the man or men responsible for the deaths of my colleagues. We've already got someone about to pick up Kert Ilves. And, as I said, we now know who the informant inside the station is. Since you helped bring the gang down I thought it was only fitting you get to sit in on the arrests, as it were.' Jakobson looked at his watch. 'We're having a station meeting in fifteen minutes. I've asked everyone to be there. Don't worry. If all goes to plan, you'll have enough time to get to the airport for tonight's flight. I'll drive you myself.'

* * *

Carruthers sat and waited expectantly for the meeting to start. Thirty people were assembled. There was an air of anticipation.

Jakobson stood up to speak. 'As we have a special guest with us who is here helping our investigations from Scotland, DI Jim Carruthers, I am going to conduct this station meeting in English. Is everyone OK with this?'

There were low murmurs and nods of approval.

Jakobson continued speaking. 'We have all experienced a terrible personal loss with the deaths on active duty of three of our friends and colleagues this week.'

Carruthers looked around the room. One or two people were visibly upset. A young woman brought a large handkerchief out of her pocket and dabbed at her eyes.

'We've known for a long time that we have in our midst a spy who has been passing on information,' said Jakobson. 'The information he passed on recently led directly to the ambush and murder of three good people.'

'You said, "he," does that mean you know who it is?' said a slim-built man in his fifties from the back of the room.

Jakobson hesitated. Carruthers could see that he was choosing his words carefully.

'Not yet but we are close.'

Carruthers frowned. That's not what he had been told. Perhaps this was their strategy. They were going to draw the man out rather than just name him. Carruthers had to assume Jakobson knew what he was doing; however, he wouldn't have wanted to name the man responsible for the death of three of their colleagues in a room full of grieving and angry police. Surely they would rip him to shreds?

'In the meantime we have some excellent news,' continued Jakobson. 'Aleks Voller has been located in Scotland. Unfortunately he is dead.' Jakobson couldn't suppress a smile and a murmur that sounded suspiciously like a restrained cheer circled the room. 'As far as we can tell, this information hasn't yet got to his brother or the rest of the Haravere gang and I would like to keep it like that. The Scottish police have also raided one of Voller's flats and have discovered and released twelve trafficked girls.' There was applause from around the room. 'We also now know that there will be a shipment leaving Muuga Harbour tonight which we plan to intercept. Once and for all we will finally bring this gang down.'

He paused. 'Now I would like to thank DI Carruthers for flying over from Scotland to assist us. He had forged a close bond with Mikael Tamm before his death.'

There was a ripple of applause. *Well, that's not strictly true,* thought Carruthers. *I only spoke to him a couple of times.*

'Now, let's get down to other business. I'm going to assign some jobs.' As Jakobson said this, Carruthers was aware that a youngish man from the centre of the room stood up and made his way towards the door, clutching his mobile.

'Martin, can you keep your bathroom break for later unless it's absolutely urgent?' said Jakobson. 'I'm going to start with your assigned jobs.'

'I'll just be a minute.'

'Well, can you keep your phone in the meeting room?'

Martin looked confused. 'My mobile?'

'You won't be needing that in the bathroom, will you?'

It all happened in a second. The penny dropped for Martin and he suddenly sprinted towards the door. However, Jakobson was too quick for him and blocked the door with his body. Carruthers saw Martin slip his right hand into the band of his jeans.

Carruthers found himself shouting, 'He's got a gun.' He heard a woman screaming from inside the room.

Carruthers saw the glint of the gun as Martin managed to withdraw it from his trouser band but Jakobson felled Martin with one punch. The gun skittered across the floor. Martin got heavily back to his feet but he was no match for Jakobson who grabbed him in a neck lock, and Carruthers watched in fascinated horror as a heavy-set, middle-aged man with a red face picked up the gun and strode over to Martin pointing it at the younger man's head. *There can't be a single person in this room,* thought Carruthers, *who doesn't want to kill Martin.* He wondered how Jakobson was going to get him out alive.

Martin faced his colleague, daring the older man to shoot him. *He'd rather be dead than face his paymasters after a failure,* thought Carruthers. Now Martin was unarmed, Jakobson released him from the neck lock. Jakobson shouted something in Estonian. *He's probably telling the other man to stand down.* The older man reluctantly lowered Martin's gun. It all happened so quickly. Martin suddenly made a lunge for the gun but the older man was on the ball and too quick for him. The older man stepped out of the way, aimed the gun level with Martin's knee. A deafening noise and an ear-piercing scream as the bullet shattered the man's kneecap and he fell to the ground.

'It was reasonable force, sir, he would have killed one of us, I had to do something.'

Carruthers knew that was way beyond reasonable force but in all likelihood that would never appear on any official record.

* * *

'Where are we going?' asked Carruthers, fifteen minutes later.

'Muuga Harbour,' said Jakobson. 'Largest cargo port in Estonia. We have to be quick so grab your jacket. It will hide your Kevlar.'

Carruthers didn't need to be told twice. He swept the jacket off the back of the seat and put it on in one move. The bulletproof vest felt bulky under his jacket. They left the building and made their way to a convoy of cars. Carruthers, with his long, lean strides, easily kept up with the Estonian men. He had only been in Estonia a couple of days but he already knew so much more about the country, about the crimes, than when he first arrived. Little Estonia, Europe's fastest growing economy, and Europe's largest drug problem.

'You come in my car,' said Jakobson. Carruthers didn't need to be told twice. He hopped in the passenger seat of Jakobson's car, struggling to buckle up over the cumbersome bulletproof vest and jacket. Jakobson started the engine. 'It's not far. Only thirteen km north east of Tallinn.'

They drove out of the city to the vast flat area of Muuga Harbour.

'It's huge,' said Carruthers, in awe.

'Twenty-nine quays. We're going to park up in the car park of a nearby quay where there's a big shipment arriving. That way we won't arouse suspicion. From there we'll set off on foot.' Jakobson parked up in the car park of Quay Seven. Carruthers watched as Jakobson 1took out a pair of binoculars and scanned a couple of quays down. 'I've got them in my sights.' Carruthers followed the Estonian man's line of vision. Even without binoculars Carruthers could see a freight ship in a nearby quay being loaded with lorries. He wondered if these lorries contained the 'household goods'. *The phrase 'household goods' covers a multitude of sins but does it also cover stolen works of art, drugs, women and God knows what else?*

His stomach twisted. He knew that trafficked men, women and children were transported by lorry. Jakobson handed Carruthers the binoculars. Carruthers trained them on the freight ship. He watched as three men jumped out of the lorries. They stood in a knot, laughing and smoking. They seemed relaxed, joking with each other. *As well they might,* thought Carruthers. They didn't know they were being watched. He passed the binoculars back to Jakobson and tried to settle his nerves. Their not knowing was a good thing. He wondered if they were members of the gang or just cheap labour.

'What are we waiting for?' asked Carruthers.

'We're waiting for Kurat, for Marek Voller to arrive,' said Jakobson.

Carruthers raised his eyebrows. He hadn't expected Kurat himself to show.

They didn't have long to wait. In his peripheral vision Carruthers could make out three men walking down the harbour. The man in the middle was of particular interest to Carruthers. Even if he hadn't recognised him, or rather a likeness of him, Carruthers would have understood the importance of the tall, lean man who was flanked by two shorter, muscular men.

Bodyguards, thought Carruthers.

The man in the centre had his dark hair tied in a ponytail. Carruthers gestured for the binoculars. He was given them and trained them on the man. Carruthers found he was holding his breath. The man was the spitting image of Aleks Voller.

Carruthers once again handed the binoculars back to Jakobson. 'Aleks Voller's brother,' was all he said.

'Marek Voller. The mastermind behind the gang. And the man they call "Kurat",' Jakobson confirmed.

'They'll be armed.' It was more an observation than a question from Carruthers.

'Don't worry. We have the border guard with us. They have semi-automatic machine guns,' said Jakobson as he opened the door. 'Although we want to try to take them alive. Now we get out of the car and start walking.'

Both men alighted from the car. Carruthers hoped there wouldn't be a bloodbath. But he couldn't see, if both parties were armed, how bloodshed would be avoided. He thought back to the ambush that had killed three of the Estonian police. He hoped this outcome would be very different.

'The problem has always been that we need to catch them red-handed.' Jakobson walked briskly. 'Up until now they've always been one step ahead, too clever for us.'

Carruthers' breathing was becoming shallow, his hands were sweating. Not so much from the exertion, more from the adrenaline that was coursing through him. He wondered if this was how Mikael Tamm had felt before his ill-fated ambush. What if this gang were still one step ahead of them and staging another trap?

A shout in Estonian down by the quay distracted him. He looked up to see a thin young woman wearing a skimpy blouse and skirt running out of the freight area.

'Jesus, he has women as part of the freight cargo, after all,' Carruthers said.

'Then this is the real thing and we've got him,' said Jakobson, brandishing his weapon.

Carruthers swallowed a hard lump in his throat.

'Get ready, but I want you to stay here,' said Jakobson. He had hidden himself behind a parked car. 'No heroics.' Jakobson drew out a walkie-talkie from his jacket pocket and fired off a blast of Estonian into it.

Carruthers shivered. How could this not be a bloodbath? These were the ruthless criminals who had murdered three of these men's colleagues in cold blood. How would he feel if he were one of these police officers? Would he be able to maintain his professionalism? The truth was that not only did he not know any of the men well enough to know how they would react, he didn't even know how he would react if he were one of them. Would they not want revenge? Could they be entirely professional?

As Jakobson was speaking, one of the two men walking with Voller broke into a run after the girl. She veered away and Carruthers was appalled to see her, after hesitating a brief moment, jump straight into the water. *Jesus Christ. I hope she can swim.*

Carruthers also realised that this was an excellent time to hit this gang while Voller and his men were distracted by the girl.

Jakobson fired a single word into the walkie-talkie and Carruthers held his breath as he watched a firearms team descend on the three men. Voller and the second bodyguard were staring into the murky depths of the water. The man who had been pursuing the girl stopped running towards the harbour edge, turned round. Carruthers could see him start as he saw a police officer running towards him. In an instant the man withdrew a gun from his waistband and pointed it at the nearest officer. Before he had a chance to fire, a shot rang out and Voller's bodyguard went down, clutching his leg.

Want to disable, not kill, thought Carruthers with some relief.

The men who had been loading the freight dropped the cargo they were carrying and ran. *Hired help. That is good.*

The Estonian police broke cover, Carruthers with them, and also started running, guns drawn. Carruthers had a kaleidoscope of thoughts whirling through his head but the overriding thought was that he hoped the girl in the water was still alive. Everything seemed to happen in slow motion.

He watched aghast as Marek Voller pointed his weapon at one of the approaching police officers. Marek fired straight into the man's chest. The man went down. Carruthers felt physically sick. Another shot rang out, this time from a marksman, and Marek's weapon was shot out of his hand and skittered along the tarmac.

Great shot.

As Voller made for his weapon another marksman shot Voller in the shoulder. Holding his shoulder with his opposite hand, Marek carried on running until a second shot rang out and Carruthers saw Voller collapsed on the ground. A shot to the leg had knocked him from his feet, but the man wasn't stopping. He was dragging himself towards his weapon. Carruthers found himself crouching, wondering when he could make a bolt for it and try to help the poor girl in the water. Making a decision and ignoring what the Estonians had told him, he rose from his crouched position and ran towards the tarmac of the harbour. Carruthers arrived at the edge of the quay and looked over into the murky depths. What he saw made his blood run cold. The girl was floating face down in the water.

Ignoring the metal ladder he jumped into the water. The cold made him gasp out loud as he struggled over to the girl, his bulletproof vest making movement difficult. As he drew level he turned her on her back, and putting his hand under her chin he swam her to the side of the quay. He dragged her lifeless body back up the metal rungs with difficulty and finally laid her out on her back on the tarmac. He kneeled beside her and proceeded to give her two emergency breaths mouth-to-mouth and chest compressions. He heard another couple of shots ring out around him but he ignored them. He knew Marek Voller had now been disabled and was confident that the Estonian police were on top of the situation.

After what seemed like an age he felt a warm hand touch his arm.

'She's gone. There's nothing more you can do for her.'

It was Jakobson's voice. Still Carruthers refused to accept that the girl was actually dead. He gave two more rescue breaths and was about to start the chest compressions again but he felt himself being physically pulled up by Jakobson. Carruthers stood up shakily to see the Estonian had taken his jacket off and was covering the girl's body. Carruthers looked away. *Should have moved sooner.*

Jakobson was gesturing at Carruthers to follow him. Clearly he wanted to examine the cargo. Carruthers stood up. It was only then that he realised he was dripping wet. Great puddles of water were pooling at his feet and despite the heat of the day he shivered. He followed Jakobson who walked into the dark of the container. Carruthers saw Jakobson open the heavy looking bolt that had locked the first lorry.

'What is the shipment meant to contain?' asked Carruthers.

'Household effects.'

Of course. *Household effects.* Carruthers felt his heart in his mouth. This was the moment they had been waiting for. He couldn't go home with nothing. He just couldn't. He could just imagine what Bingham would tell the new DCI about him. *Yeah, he went all the way to Estonia and came back empty-handed.* He imagined this new DCI being offered a glass of whisky in Bingham's office the way he had. He wondered idly if she drank whisky. He was the rightful DCI, damn it!

Jakobson managed to open the stiff bolt and pulled it back, opening the back of the lorry. The sound of weeping, and the stench was unmistakable. He shouted something in Estonian and one of his men came over with a torchlight. He switched it on and pointed it into the back of the lorry. About twenty women and girls were crammed into the lorry.

'Jesus Christ,' Carruthers said. How long, he wondered, had they been in there?

Jakobson took in a deep breath and held on to it before motioning for two of his men to come forward and they boarded the lorry to help bring the trafficked women out safely. Shaking his head, he turned to Carruthers. 'I have a daughter the same age as some of these girls.'

Twenty-Two

Aweary Carruthers walked into Castletown Police Station the next morning. He'd not slept properly and every muscle ached. He felt tired yet wired, as if his body was still flooded with adrenaline and cortisol, even though it was now ten hours since his flight back from Estonia. He stroked his short, grey bristles. He needed a shave. And a decent night's sleep.

Fletcher put her head round his office door. 'Welcome back.'

He beckoned her in.

'How have things been here?' he asked, once she was in front of him.

She had a cup of coffee in her hand. He could smell the coffee beans. She looked down at the cup.

'Sorry, didn't think. Should have got you one.'

He shook his hand. 'It's OK. I'll get my own later.' He had done nothing but drink coffee the last few days. 'So, how have things been?'

She grinned. 'We got by without you, if that's what you mean, although–' She suddenly looked serious.

'Although what?'

Fletcher bit her lip. 'Pip McGuire's done a flit. Looks like she was in on it. I'm sorry we didn't keep a close enough eye on her.'

Carruthers pursed his lips. He *knew* there'd been something that had disturbed him about Pip McGuire.

'We've got people looking for her. I'm really sorry, Jim.'

It rankled that they had let McGuire – if that was her real name – slip through their fingers. He had a sudden longing for wild spaces and the mountains of Skye. He could take the annual leave that was owed him. Pack his tent, a good book, a bottle of

Talisker and wild camp. He wondered how bad the midges were this summer. He also wondered if there was a start date for the new DCI.

'It was a pretty big feat to rescue those poor girls. Thank God you got to them in time.' Fletcher's words broke into his thoughts and brought them back onto the case.

'Yes, but will they ever be able to go back to a normal life after what they've been through?' said Carruthers, trying hard to push all thoughts of his new DCI out of his mind. *Time to think about her later.*

Fletcher took a sip of her coffee. 'Who knows? But if they have a loving family behind them they'll have a better chance than some.'

Carruthers nodded.

'Were they all Estonian?'

'Mostly Estonian but of Russian descent.'

'Who was the girl who ran out of the container?' said Fletcher.

'Apparently she was Lithuanian.' That much he had found out. He thought of the Lithuanian girl and Hanna Mets, the two women they hadn't been able to rescue.

There was a moment or two of silence.

'What will happen to the girls trafficked to Scotland?' asked Fletcher.

Carruthers thought of the baby-faced photo of one of the girls he'd seen. She'd only looked about fifteen. He knew he'd remember those empty eyes for a long time to come. He thought again of the girl who had jumped into the sea in Tallinn. The fact she risked death to get away from the Haravere gang only to end up drowning sickened him.

He looked at Fletcher. 'Three of those girls were under sixteen,' he said. 'They're covered by the Scottish Child Protection Services. Once they've been processed and their families located they'll be returned to their home countries.' Carruthers sighed. 'Scotland's prostitution problem is definitely getting worse and since most of those trafficked will be working behind closed doors we have no idea how many women are working against their will, despite the statistics we're given.'

'Being involved in this case makes me somehow feel personally affected,' said Fletcher. 'Bugger professionalism. At the end of the day we're only human. Is there anything we can do to highlight these people's plight?'

'I've found out the NCA are launching a campaign to increase public awareness. The campaign is also going to encourage people to report suspicions. It's sad to say but most members of the public will have come across a victim who has been exploited without even knowing it.'

'I think a public campaign will be a really good idea,' said Fletcher, sipping her coffee. 'Can we do something locally? Is this something I can get involved in personally? I'd like to. We could put some information together to let the public know what to look out for. You know the sort of thing. When the rented flat at the end of the road is being visited by different men all through the day and night or when their neighbour's nanny never seems to leave the house and is too scared to talk to them…'

Carruthers watched Fletcher's face light up. 'I think having a local campaign would be a really good idea,' he said. 'I'll have a word with Bingham. See what we can do.'

'So what's the story with Barry Cuthbert and Aleks Voller?' asked Fletcher.

'Cuthbert had a nice little thing going with stolen art, as we know. Apparently he had kept in touch with his old prison mates. He was a member of an exclusive golf club that happened to bring him into contact with some wealthy art lovers. It was all too irresistible. Cuthbert obviously cultivated a whole network of thieves including those in Estonia.'

'Aleks and Marek Voller,' said Fletcher.

'Yes, but Cuthbert got in over his head. Cuthbert may or may not have known that, apart from running high-class prostitutes, Voller also had a people-smuggling business. On a visit to Scotland to meet up with Cuthbert to talk about the art smuggling, Aleks

Voller clearly saw a business opportunity for expanding his empire. Perhaps the Commonwealth Games in Glasgow was the reason. I assume Cuthbert was made an offer he couldn't refuse.'

'Or wouldn't be allowed to refuse.'

'That too,' admitted Carruthers. 'Of course, Aleks Voller had a paymaster back in Estonia. His brother. And then there were the links with the Russian Mafia. But both men, Voller and Cuthbert, were greedy. Thought they could do away with the third party and handle the stolen art themselves. More money in it for them, of course. But Aleks Voller made one huge mistake.'

'Crossing the Mafia?'

Carruthers shook his head. 'Crossing his brother. Marek was always the brains behind the operation. And of course when the police started to visit Cuthbert in hospital Aleks Voller must have panicked. Thought Cuthbert was starting to turn informant. That's why he tried to kill him.'

'So will we ever find out who killed Voller and the undercover Estonian cop?'

'Hanna Mets? If she'd been one of the trafficked girls who'd managed to run away I would have said suicide was much more likely, but from what I found out about Hanna Mets I doubt she would have taken her own life. Most likely both Joe McGuigan and Hanna Mets were killed by Aleks Voller. I reckon her cover was blown as soon as the real Marika Paju got trafficked to Scotland. My theory is that Mets was taken up to the cliffs and pushed to her death. And whoever killed Voller is long gone. No doubt someone sent by his brother.' There was a moment or two of silence.

'I wonder why Hanna Mets took the name of a real person?'

'That ended up being a big mistake. I guess at the point Hanna Mets took the name of Marika Paju, Marika was just another missing girl. Possibly a runaway. There was a suggestion she'd turned to prostitution but the Estonian police had no evidence she'd been trafficked by the Vollers, least of all to Scotland.'

'I'm just grateful we can return Marika Paju to her parents,' said Fletcher. 'Hopefully with the right support and counselling she can recover from this awful ordeal. God, you should have seen the look of pure relief on their faces when they first realised the dead girl wasn't their daughter. But then I spoke to them afterwards and they admitted that the not knowing was the worst part. Makes me realise how many other parents are out there worrying about their missing girls.'

Carruthers could see Fletcher was lost in thought. 'Are you OK, Andie?'

'Yes, but I'm just thinking how terrible the sex slave trade is. All those vulnerable people.'

'We can't save everyone.'

'Makes you think, doesn't it?' said Fletcher. 'We never know what goes on behind closed doors.'

'Police Scotland have succeeded in freeing numerous sex workers they believe to have been trafficked, but they have found it very difficult to convince the victims in such cases to make formal complaints.'

'Well, it would help if these girls weren't made to feel as if they are criminals,' said Fletcher. 'They're the victims.'

'The law is changing, Andie, but attitudes are always slower to change, aren't they?'

Fletcher turned to Carruthers. 'What will happen to Barry Cuthbert?'

'He'll go to prison,' said Carruthers. 'We've got him with handling stolen artworks and with supplying forged passports.' Cuthbert was still maintaining he was forced to keep the passports for Voller but whether that was true or not didn't interest Carruthers. He was in it up to his neck and Carruthers had him by the short and curlies. He had no time for the Barry Cuthberts of this world. 'He's fully cooperating in the hope of a shorter sentence. Personally, I'd like to throw the book at him.'

'What about Derek Sturrock? How much did he know?'

Carruthers thought about this. 'I don't think he had a hand in young McGuigan's death.' He remembered the man vomiting into the bushes. Nobody could have faked that. 'But he definitely knew more than he was saying. I think he decided to turn a blind eye to a lot of Cuthbert's activities. We've got enough to bring him in for questioning.'

'Just out of interest, do we know what would have happened to the stolen artworks, had they been smuggled out the country?'

'With the links the Haravere gang had to the Mafia, my guess is they would have gone into Russia. Perhaps into the hands of private collectors.'

'Even though they couldn't sell the paintings on?'

'Sometimes owning a beautiful painting is enough, isn't it?' said Carruthers, thinking about the amount of wealth now in the hands of certain oligarchs in the former Soviet Union. Remembering what John Stevenson had said, he added, 'Or perhaps they would be used as currency or collateral for those dealing in drugs and God knows what.'

'Still we got some of them back though *and* helped crack a gang of sex slavers,' said Fletcher. 'I think that calls for a little celebration.'

'How many more gangs are out there, though?' said Carruthers.

'Hey, what have you just said to me? You can't take on the world. What are you doing after work tonight? Have you got plans? Fancy a quick drink, you know, to celebrate?'

What Carruthers really fancied was a long hot soak in the bath, a home-cooked meal and an early night but he didn't say so. Instead he nodded and when he thought about being back in a Scottish pub, drinking a nip or three of his favourite single malt in good company, a slow smile spread across his face.

THE END

Acknowledgements

As with any book a great many people helped make this publication possible.

Thank you to Gail Williams for the initial edit and manuscript critique. Thanks also to Clare Law at Bloodhound Books.

My thanks go to Piret Dahl in Tallinn for her close supervision of the story to make it as authentic as possible. And to Gunilla Rosengren for her stories of what it was like as a Finn to stay at the Hotel Viru in Tallinn in the 1980s.

A big thank you to first readers Sarah Torr, Alison Baillie, Ian Brown and Jackie McLean for their painstaking work in whipping the manuscript in to shape. It is much appreciated.

Thank you to Bloodhound Books for giving me a three book publishing deal, especially Betsy, Fred, Sarah, Sumaira and Alexina who are so supportive and helpful. And the rest of the pups in the kennels for their ongoing support.

All the bloggers, readers, writers and friends. I've had terrific support particularly from Jacky Collins, Kelly Lacey, Vic Watson, Louise Ross, Lynsey Adams, Amanda Gillies, Ian and Lynn Reid, Malcolm Fraser, Caroline Young, Kim Haworth, Ian Skewis, Louise Morrall, Jackie McLean, Allison Brady, Leigh Russell, Gill McLaren (who becomes a character in the book!) and Miranda Jacques-Turner. I've likely forgotten some folk. Apologies.

I would like to say a very personal thank you to my next door neighbours, Dougie and Margaret Hunter for their support and friendship over the last fifteen years. I don't honestly know what we would do without Margaret to look after our cat, Smudge, when we are away and Dougie for all his DIY expertise! I also can't forget Lynsey Duncanson and family across the road for stepping in to help with cat feeding duties when Margaret is away. Finally, thank you to Dougie's brother George for his firefighting advice.

This is a work of fiction but some of the storyline is based loosely on certain real events. Those who know the East Neuk of Fife will recognise the fictional town of Castletown as being closely modelled on St Andrews. After much debate I decided to grow the town and change the name. With three books now behind me there is every possibility this might grow in to a long running series. Who knows? I'm not sure St Andrews would be able to cope with so many murders. Although this is a police procedural I hope I can be forgiven if I have stretched things a wee bit to suit the storyline. Any mistakes are my own.

Lightning Source UK Ltd.
Milton Keynes UK
UKHW012341050419
340551UK00001B/115/P

9 781912 604180